BERNARD LILE;

AN

Historical Romance,

EMBRACING THE PERIODS OF

THE TEXAS REVOLUTION.

AND THE

MEXICAN WAR.

BY

THE HON. JEREMIAH CLEMENS.

PHILADELPHIA:
J. B. LIPPINCOTT & CO.
1856.

DEDICATION,

TO

GEORGE W. NEAL, HUNTSVILLE, ALABAMA.

MY DEAR GEORGE,—

I have taken the liberty, without consulting you, of inscribing your name on this page. The play-mate and class-mate of my childhood and boyhood—the zealous and unwavering friend of a manhood which the shadow has darkened as often as the sunshine has gladdened, I should have been untrue to myself if I had failed to mark my appreciation of a friendship so warm and so unselfish.

Between you and me professions of kindness are not needed. We can afford to take each other's good will on trust, unless the experience of more than half a lifetime is valueless; but it may not be ungrateful to your children to know, that others have appreciated the upright manliness, the stainless integrity, the clear judgment, and the untiring energy of a father's character. It is a far higher legacy than any other you may have to bestow, and I would have them cherish it with increasing pride and satisfaction.

JERE. CLEMENS.

PREFACE.

THIS book owes its existence to an accident, which for months prevented me from participating in the more active duties of life. Although a romance in name, imagination has had little to do with its preparation. It records events the most of which will be familiar to many who read it. Most of the characters are drawn from real life. Not a place is described I have not visited. Scarcely a scene is depicted which is not based upon an actual occurrence. It is a book of life—of life not as I wished it, or thought it ought to be, but as I have found it. It has no plan, for human life has none. A thousand unforeseen circumstances are for ever swaying our purposes, and making a mockery of our firmest resolves. It makes no attempt to paint the author's ideal of a perfect man. In all "the busy, bitter scenes" through which I have passed, I have met no such character, and believe not in its existence. There are none of us so free from errors that we can afford, without self-condemnation, to be uncharitable to the sins of others; and I know of no good that can be accomplished by freeing the hero of a romance from the faults incident to humanity.

The reader will find in this volume no approach to the extravagancies of language attributed to the South-West by almanac makers and scribblers, whose knowledge of the country and the people is bounded by a steam-boat excursion down the Mississippi. The South-West *has* a language of its own; but it in no degree resembles the miserable caricatures with which the country has been flooded. Sometimes whole sentences are uttered not only in the purest English, but in the loftiest strain of eloquence. Then again every line is filled with inaccuracies, but the figures are always striking, and the words chosen best calculated to convey most forcibly the speaker's meaning. Born upon the frontier myself, and passing the most of my life among its rudest scenes, I know the people well, and have sought to preserve their language *exactly as it is.*

Every man who writes a book, I suppose has a motive; but very few tell it honestly in the *preface.* Perhaps I shall best escape the suspicion of like disingenuousness by keeping mine a secret; remarking only, that if the American, when he lays it down, feels in his bosom a warmer throb for his country, a higher appreciation of its excellencies, and a more devoted attachment to its institutions, he need not look further for the *motive* which induced the author to undergo the labor it has cost, or the *hope* which sustains him in submitting his production to the criticism of the press.

THE AUTHOR.

LIFE.

How little do we know the secret source,
  From which life's fountain bubbles into day?
How little can we guide its wandering course,
  As on it flows upon its turbid way?

We watch it as it rises from the spring,
  And follow for a little way the tide;
Then doubt and gloom their heavy shadows fling,
  On all that we would wish to know beside.

Of one thing only can we certain be;
  That care and sorrow never leave the bed,
That little stream must journey to the sea—
  Still constant when all brighter things have fled.

BERNARD LILE.

CHAPTER I.

> "I can bear—
> However wretchedly, 'tis still to bear—
> In life what others could not brook to dream,
> But perish in their slumber."

It was a gloomy night, towards the close of October, 1835. The wind whistled along the broad avenue that leads from the Capitol to the mansion of the president, and the blinding sleet was driving fiercely in the face of a pedestrian, who, closely muffled in a heavy boat-coat, was moving rapidly over the broken and uneven pavements of the Federal City. Turning into a cross street, he was lost amid the deep darkness every where reigning, save upon the lamp-lit avenue. Let us follow as he pursues his solitary way through night and tempest. What is it that drives him forth at such an hour? In that wide city all the hopes and fears, the cares, the sorrows, and the joys which make up the sum of human life, have found an abiding place. Ambition, avarice, venality, corruption—the petty vice, the daring crime, are strangely mingled with all that is elevating in patriotism, generous in feeling, or manly in action. But it is not at the bidding of passion, or of duty—of vice or of virtue, that our wanderer braves the elements. Gold he does not seek, and the schemes of political managers are strangers to his bosom. It may be that such things have occupied his thoughts in other days, but they have long since palled upon the taste. He is a slave to that wild, fierce, never-ceasing *want*, which assumes a mastery over the soul, when the heart has been burned to ashes by the fires of former passions. Upon all the past one word was written in lurid characters—AGONY;—on all the future—DESPAIR. He knew his doom—had walked with it hand in hand for many a year, until grown so familiar no shudder followed its contemplation. Still it drove him on, and on, and on, he knew not where, and cared not, so the pathway was stormy and dangerous. It is hard enough to walk through the world with no object but forgetfulness; no hope but to chase way the dark thoughts and bitter memories that hang around us. Yet this is peaceful tranquility compared with the restless wretchedness of a strong human mind, too proud to bend, too inflexible to break, too haughty to shun reflection, or seek for sympathy to soothe the miseries of existence.

"War with all things,
And death to all things, and disease to most things,
And pangs and bitterness; these were the fruits
Of the forbidden tree."

But there is a higher curse; a sterner condemnation, which fell upon the rebellious angels, and falls now, at intervals of centuries, upon some son of earth, whose nature, like theirs, scorns the obedience Omnipotence demands, or the submission or repentance necessary to forgiveness. That curse is never written on the brow. It steals not away the symmetry of form, and leaves untouched the beauty of feature. Petty vices, such as debauchery, avarice, licentiousness, all these leave their traces behind them. But the victim of a loftier curse hugs the fatal secret to his bosom, and lives on without love, without hope, without fear; guarding with sleepless vigilance against every outward manifestation of suffering or of grief. Of such a nature was the solitary night-wanderer whose footsteps we propose to trace. Above human pity, he would have spurned human sympathy as an insult. Whatever his lot might be, he sought no support, but wrapped in the settled firmness of his own soul awaited, without a tremor, all he could be called on to endure.

Steadily, without turning or pausing, he passed along the gloomy street, until he reached a plain brick dwelling of no outward pretensions. The door was opened at his knock, and, depositing his hat and over-coat in the entry, he moved without question to an inner apartment. It was evident that he was no unfamiliar guest. Within that room, decked with the splendor of an Eastern queen, half sat, half reclined, a female of startling loveliness. Her costume was that of another land, and the vivid light flashing from her dark eyes, told of passions which had their birth beneath a fiercer sun than ours. Twenty summers might have passed over her head, but of this the gazer was in doubt, for while her form denoted maturity, there was in every motion that elastic freedom and buoyancy so seldom surviving early girlhood. She wore a robe of crimson velvet over a dress of satin, richly worked, and sparkling with jewels. Below the short skirt, wide trowsers of the finest lace extended to the ankles, where they were gathered with diamond clasps. The costly band that had confined her hair was loosened, and it now hung in jetty masses about a neck and shoulders whose whiteness might have shamed the snows of Ararat. A little foot, of perfect symmetry, was resting on a cushioned stool, and at the moment her attention seemed to be occupied by the precious stone which supplied the place of a buckle to her satin slipper. She looked up with a glad smile when the door opened, and, though she did not rise, there was joy and music in her silvery voice.

"You are welcome, Bernard. Oh! so welcome, for it is a wild night, and I feared you would be late."

"I thought not of the night, Zerah, and in truth it is not so very bad. I should have liked it better, if it had been more stormy. The war of the elements is far more grateful than the petty struggles of my kind."

He threw himself upon the sofa, and added, as he gently took her hand in his own. "Order some refreshments. Brandy if you please, for I have a story to tell, and a little of that fiery poison Satan sent into the world for his own purposes, will not be amiss."

The bell was touched, glasses and brandy placed on a stand before him, and his lovely companion, leaning her head on her hand, prepared to listen without a word of comment to all he saw fit to relate. He did not keep her in suspense. With a low but firm and steady voice his narrative was begun.

"This is my native land. Many years ago it witnessed a terrible tragedy. I will not shock you by relating the horrid tale. It is enough that it made me what I am. To-night I have gone through it all again. To-night it has risen up before me, clear, vivid, distinct, as in that hour when my hand was first dyed with human blood, and I became a curse to earth, an outcast from heaven. Before the sun of Asia had first pressed its fiery kiss upon that heavenly brow of thine, my Zerah, I loved with a wilder fervor than the angels who deserted heaven and its joys, for the sweeter embraces of the virgins of earth. It is needless now to go over all I felt, enjoyed and suffered. Still more needless to describe one who was everything to me—who has been nothing to you heretofore, and whom I have no wish should hereafter be a sad and sorrowing memory. We were wedded according to the forms of that religion you despise and hate. Her after story must remain a sealed book to you; but from that time I became a wanderer. Peace, rest, forgetfulness were gone forever. The first taste of blood had created a never-ending thirst for more; and in many a land the pathway of Bernard Lile has been marked by havoc, and bedewed with tears. I met you and there came a calm. With that came, also, a yearning desire to visit once more the home of my youth, and tread among the graves of those I had known and loved, long, long ago. The rest you know. To-night in one of those halls, so common in crowded cities, where fortune is first lost, then honor, character, the sense of shame, and often life itself, I watched a young man at play, whose golden locks, bright blue eyes, and speaking face too vividly placed before me the image of one I had last seen wrapped in a purple shroud. He lost until his last farthing was gone, when he rose from the table, passed into another room, and drank deeply. I followed—placed my hand on his shoulder, and inquired, 'Is your name Wilson?'

"'Yes, sir,' was the hoarse and almost inarticulate reply.

"'The son of Robert Wilson of——?'

"'The same, sir, did you know him?'

"'Well, very well. He is dead I infer from your question; but James, Sarah, and Willie, where are they?'

"'Gone, all gone; I am the last of my race.'

"You have seen me, Zerah, when the cobra capella had wound its folds about my limbs, and not a muscle quivered beneath its slimy touch. You have seen me when the lightning shivered the rock on which I leaned, and not a movement betrayed consciousness of the terrible danger. But that boy's brief, sad story—that history of woe condensed into a single line, so shook me for a moment, that I could not trust my voice in reply. He was the first to break silence.

"'You seem, sir, to have known my family well. May I ask you your name?'

"'It would not enlighten you, if you heard it. I was an exile before your birth, and the name I now bear was assumed in a foreign land. But pardon the seeming rudeness, and allow me to ask you a few other questions. Your father, when I knew him, was far from rich. You have lost heavily to-night; can you afford it?'

"'I am ruined, penniless,' was the reply, in a tone that showed despair had already folded its wings on his young heart, and begun to fit it for a life of crime, a death of shame.

"'How much have you lost?'

"'Every cent I had in the world. Fifteen hundred dollars.'

"Taking out a card, and writing on it, Bernard Lile, care of Monsieur Evadne, Banker, New York, I handed it to him, with a roll of notes, about twice the amount of his losses; adding, 'You will do me a favor, my young friend, by accepting this money as a loan, and a still greater favor, if at any time you should need a friend, by dropping a note to this address.'

"He trembled, stammered, and then burst into tears.

"'I thank you, sir. I thank you. From my soul I do. I will keep your card, but I cannot take this money from a stranger. I can never repay it. I am a Lieutenant in the army, and can live upon my pay, but I cannot live under the sense of such an obligation.'

"'I am no stranger to any of your blood. The money I must insist upon your taking. The devil never had so efficient an agent as Poverty. When you see your comrades indulging in a style of living you cannot afford, you will be contriving means to indulge in it also. When you lie down at night, you will be dreaming of your losses. At first you will curse the folly that sent you to the gaming-table. Then you will begin to think that "luck may change." You will be induced to try it again. The tempter will be always whispering in your ear, and if you do not seek the cowardly grave of the suicide, you will end by becoming bankrupt in character, as well as in fortune. Take the money you must; unless you would have me think that the son of an old friend, the last scion of a gallant race, is utterly lost to himself, and his country.'

"'But you, sir, you,' he faltered, 'can you spare so large an amount? for it will be long before I can pay you, if ever.'

"'Spare it! Aye, and five hundred times the sum if it were needed to save you. Once I was young and unstained as you are—the future bright with promise, and glorious with hope. Then I became an outcast, poor, much poorer than you are: friendless and penniless—half naked, and half dead with hunger. Now I am rich; richer than your wildest calculation would equal. But I went through that to obtain it, which would have withered a thousand frames like yours, and frozen the life-blood in a thousand hearts. To-morrow I shall see you again—for the present good-bye. I do not tell you to avoid the gaming-table, for this is a lesson I think you will not readily forget. It is only men whose hearts are cased in ice, or worse, like mine in fire, who can be gainers here.'

"And so, without waiting for a reply, I left him, and have come to tell you I shall soon be a wanderer again. That boy is the brother of her whose grave I dug."

Calmly, coldly, without a sign of emotion, without a shade upon his brow, his story had been told. Even the fair listener, who knew so well the strange being with whom her fate was linked, wondered at the mighty power of that unconquerable will, which, to all outward seeming, could silence remorse at pleasure, and bind down agony with fetters of adamant. Whatever emotions may have agitated her while listening to this dark recital, they found no voice, and called forth no questioning.

Rising slowly, when it was ended, she threw one lovely arm around his neck, smoothed back the hair from his pallid brow with the other hand, and imprinting a kiss upon it, inquired seriously, but not sadly, or complainingly,

"Well, Bernard, when shall we go?"

"Ah! there is the worst of it, for it will give you pain. I go alone."

"Alone!" she exclaimed, starting to her feet, with sudden and passionate energy. "Alone! and wherefore?"

"Sit down and listen. When I left this continent it was a wilderness, except a narrow belt of land on its eastern coast. Since that time, wave after wave of bold, hardy and adventurous spirits have poured across the mountains, and penetrated the pathless forests of the west. To these were added the desperate and the lawless for whom civil society had become an insecure abiding place. Splendid cities now stand where the panther and the savage then held divided dominion, and palaces are floating on the bosom of streams nothing had ever rippled save the light canoe of the Indian. As arts and civilization advanced, the first adventurers, and others of like character, were driven farther west, until they reached, and crossed that mighty river not unaptly named 'the great father of waters.' Our own territory, vast as that was, seemed too contracted for those restless wanderers. They reached the confines of a neighboring nation, and plunged without hesitation into the wide prairies stretching for miles and miles along the northern frontier of Mexico. Nor were they at first unwelcome visitors. Practiced, from early infancy, in the daily use of the rifle—fearless as the lion of the desert; and ready at any moment to engage in the most dangerous undertakings; it was fondly hoped they would prove an efficient protection, to the timid inhabitants, from the merciless inroads of the savages. And so they did; but as time wore on they began to think that the land defended by their valor, ought of right to belong to them: and that the government from which they derived no protection was entitled to no allegiance. Difficulties, discontent, quarrels with the central government, were the necessary result. These disputes have reached their climax, and the world is about to witness the most extraordinary spectacle in its history.—A little community of not more than five thousand inhabitants, boldly defying a nation of eight millions of people, and appealing to the decision of the god of battles. In that struggle, when it does come, I must have a part. The wild chivalry which gives it birth, the desperate odds, the iron men who have raised the tempest, and defy its power, all possess attractions I would find it difficult to resist. Above and beyond this, for the first time in many years, a ray of hope has dawned on me. There is a low, sweet voice forever whispering in my bosom, *go*, such a work may be accepted in some part as an atonement for the past. In a war begun and carried on to secure the right of self-government, and the higher right of interpreting the word of God according to the light of our own reason, rather than the corrupt and interested relations of Romish priests, the powers of good cannot be indifferent. Every drop of blood shed in such a cause is hallowed—every good blow struck, lightens the burden of former sins, and infuses new life and energy into the weary and heavy laden.

"I pretend not to question, Bernard, that whatever you do is for the best. I only ask to go with you, no matter what sky may look down upon the land you visit. I have slept upon your bosom among the Caucasian mountains—

together we have traversed the desert of Zahara, and together we inhaled the deadly malaria of the Africa gold cost. There can be nothing new to me in the sights and sounds of battle: or do you fear that this life of sloth has subdued the strength and courage of the Georgian girl?"

"No, Zerah, no. I know all that you can do, and all that you can endure. Place a keen sabre in this little hand, and I would rather trust it in the hour of danger than a dozen of the silken things of cities who are misnamed men. It is the faith, the religion, and above all the customs of those among whom I must sojourn, that makes our separation for a time needful. In that land, and among that people, it would be impossible to avoid things at which you would shudder more than at the carnage of a battle-field. There, no such thing as seclusion exists. Every one, men, women, children, and even strange visitors sleep in the same cabin, without so much as a canvass screen between them. Their meals are all in common. The women cook the game the men bring in, wash and mend the coarse garments soiled or torn in the chase. Of Mahomet they have never heard, and would very likely laugh at you whenever you attempted to go through your devotions. They would intrude upon your privacy at all hours, and without the slightest ceremony. They would expect you to go through the same drudgery to which their own wives and daughters are accustomed. All this too would be done without any wanton purpose to wound your feelings, without a suspicion that it was repugnant or distasteful. Yet the least one of these things would be worse to you than a dagger's wound. I have seen," he continued, lifting her jewelled hand from the arm on which it fondly rested, "I have seen these diamonds flashing around the hilt of a Turkish yatagan, and it seemed to me not inappropriate, but they would be sadly out of place if employed in scrubbing the iron frying pan of a western settler.

"Why go, then, Bernard; why mingle at all with these ill-mannered savages?"

"Because I cannot help it. It is written in the book of fate, and I have no power to avoid my destiny. A great work is to be done. The instruments are rude and untutored, but they have been fitted for the task before them by danger and privation. They have been taught in a stern school the needful lessons of daring and endurance. They are now about to begin the dismemberment of an empire, whose doom has been pronounced by that All-wise Being, whom you and I worship alike, though we have accepted different prophets. It is my fate to carry there that superhuman strength, and that wonderful skill in arms, which was given for higher ends than those I have heretofore pursued."

He ceased. There was no reply. Like all of her faith, and race, she was an undoubting believer in destiny, and to such an argument, her mind was prepared with no answer. She sighed heavily—cast her eyes upon the floor, silently and sadly for a time, then threw herself upon his bosom, and spoke long and earnestly in some far foreign tongue. Her theme was not the trials and troubles they had endured together. She spoke not of their early separation, of the fears that agitated, or the hopes that softened the parting hour. It was of *love*, burning, passionate, present love. Her eyes were sparkling with a light not of earth—in every radiant feature there was a loveliness beyond that of Eve before sin had visited the garden of Eden—her voice fell upon the ear of him to whom she clung, in tones so soft, so low, so sweet, that it seemed the breathings of an angel choir, and his strong arm pressed her to a breast from which beauty and music had for a time chased the demon away.

CHAPTER II.

"And then her step, as light
Along the unconscious earth she went,
Seemed that of one born with a right
To walk some heavenlier element;
And tread in places were her feet
A star at every step should meet."

Two days had passed away, and on the third morning, a young man, clothed in the uniform of a Lieutenant of Infantry, was seated at a writing-desk in one of the large hotels of Washington. He had evidently been long engaged in some occupation not altogether pleasing, for it had cast a deep shade of thought over features otherwise femininely beautiful. It was not anger, nor impatience, nor sorrow; but rather doubt, perplexity, anxiety. It was a strange expression for one so young—for one who ought to be so free from care—for one whose proverbially light-hearted profession, rarely encourages the indulgence of any grief, except that of manly sorrow over a comrade's bier. There is an open letter before him, perhaps its pages may reveal what it is that has flung the shadow on his brow.

"A strange, wild adventure has happened to me, even here, in the Federal City, Charles, where no man in his senses ever imagined that anything could befal a young officer on leave, of sufficient importance to fill up a page in a letter of kind remembrance to a distant friend. While I write, I almost doubt whether I am awake or dreaming.

"More than once I have laid aside the pen, walked to the window, and looked out upon the busy street, to assure myself that no troubled slumber had raised up unreal visions to annoy and perplex me. The broad sun is looking down as usual upon this human ant-hill, and a restless throng of insects are hurrying to and fro, urged on by motives and impulses as various as the bodies they inhabit. I am awake. No spirit from the land of dreams has been playing delusive pranks with imagination. It is real, all real. When you read my story, you will say that I ought to rejoice; that its promises are all tinted with the rose; and so my reason tells me, but somehow I cannot drive away an unaccountable depression, a warning of approaching woe and danger.

"Three days ago a mere accident drew me to a gaming table. I lost more than I could well afford, and in my anxiety to recover it staked the last dollar I possessed. 'All done?' asked the cool and passionless banker. 'Turn on,' was the response of the betters. He did turn on, and I was penniless. I left the table utterly ruined, and then, must needs make a still greater fool of myself, by swallowing large draughts of brandy, while the blood was already running like molten lava in my veins. I had noticed a gentleman at the Faro Bank staking immense sums upon the most desperate odds, yet always winning, although you would have judged from his manner that he was scarcely thinking of the game, and was utterly indifferent whether he won or lost. When I left the table, feeling very much like digging for myself an unhonored grave, he followed, and commenced a series of questions it is wonderful I did not resent as impertinent. There was about him an air and manner which impressed, awed, and fascinated me beyond expression. I cannot explain to you the feeling, but it seemed as if he had the power, and the right, to control and govern me as he willed. He spoke of my father, and other relatives—said he had known them well in his youth, and finally forced me to accept, as a loan, a sum more than double what I had lost. When I inquired his name, he handed me a card, on which was written Bernard Lile, care of Mons. Evadne, banker, New York. At the same time giving me to understand that was not his real name, but one he had assumed in a foreign land. You will not be surprised to learn that this singular gentlemen absorbed every thought for the remainder of the night. Morning found me resting on a pillow slumber had not visited. He appeared to have known my family so well; to take so deep an interest in my welfare; was undeniably so gifted, as well as so rich. Above all, there was about him that nameless spell, seldom met with more than once in a lifetime, but when met it clings to the memory, defying forgetfulness, as it conquers disobedience. It is not genius, nor strength, nor courage, but the three combined, drilled and disciplined by experience, and governed by an adamantine WILL no power can shake, no difficulty embarrass. Every word he uttered; every tone of his voice was remembered. Every time I closed my eyes, in vain attempts to sleep, the tall form, and the firm martial step were painted on my vision. He has been a soldier, I know; and I shall esteem it an instance of good fortune if, at any time, it falls to my lot to follow such a leader to the embattled plain.

"While still occupied with the reflections his presence and conduct had excited, he called as he had promised. After a few unimportant inquiries, altogether personal to myself, he spoke of his early departure from the city, said, that he had much to do in the meantime, but he could afford to trespass for an hour upon other engagements for the purpose of introducing me to one whose acquaintance, he trusted, would prove both agreeable and profitable. I signified my readiness to accompany him of course, for in truth I had no excuse for declining, and no power to refuse if a thousand excuses had been at hand. Haughty, imperious, self-willed, as I am represented to be, I believe if that man had told me to stab the first person I met on the street, I would have obeyed him on the instant. On the way he inquired the number of my regiment, and where it was stationed. He looked surprised when I told him that it was scattered in various directions, with scarcely more than a single company at a point. Addressing me again, after a brief pause he said—

"'I am afraid you will think me very ignorant, when I inquire the strength of your army; but you must remember that I have been long a stranger here, aud know less of my own country than almost any other.'

"When I told him that the whole infantry force of the Union consisted of eight regiments, he exclaimed, 'Ah! is that all?' then added, musingly, 'eight skeleton regiments to guard a mighty empire! Why, that force would scarcely suffice to drive the robbers from the mountains to the northward of Jerusalem. Yet even there, among that rude banditti, I have never heard the name of America mentioned without respect. Strange land; strange people. In the old world the means employed must be proportioned to the effect sought to be produced; but here the mightiest results not unfrequently flow from the most insignificant causes. A dozen men with axes and rifles crossed the Alleghanies, and an empire sprung into existence as if by magic. A dozen more, with the same implements, crossed the Mississippi, and another empire is about to be added to the Union. The snows of the Rocky Mountains will next be passed, and the Atlantic joined to the Pacific by a living Anglo-Saxon tide. Every day reveals some new miracle, and the tales of the Arabian Nights are surpassed by the reality. Providence has appointed a great work to be done, and it may be, my young friend, that you and I will meet hereafter, in a field, where both shall be employed as laborers. "But who is worthy to open the book, and loosen the seals thereof?"'

"He spoke no more, but walked on, absorbed with his own reflections, and apparently unconscious of my presence. We soon reached a house in one of the upper wards of the city. Upon the door he gave a single rap, and opening it without further ceremony, invited me to enter. We were met by a servant in the entry, to whom he addressed a question in a language I did not understand. Her reply was given in the same tongue: when it was received he opened another door with as little ceremony as the first. I followed him to the threshold, but there stopped, spell-bound, and absolutely incapable of motion. Rising from a work stand, where she had been engaged in some feminine employment, and advancing to meet us, was a female of such surpassing grace and beauty that, at the moment, I fancied she had descended from another sphere. Coming forward with the light springy steps of the antelope she extended her hand to her husband, and said, in a voice clearer and sweeter than the music of a German flute.'

"'And this is your young friend, Bernard?'

"'Even so, Zerah, and, as you have saved me half the trouble of an introduction, I have only to say to Mr. Wilson, that this,' laying his hand upon her glossy head, 'is my young bride. The only thing of much value that half a lifetime of wandering and danger has brought me.'

"She extended her hand with a frank welcome. I took it with the expression of a hope that an acquaintance promising to be so agreeable might not soon terminate.

"'Never fear, young sir, I rarely lose sight of those whom Bernard loves. You are much more likely to get tired of me than I of you.'

"I said something, I know not rightly what. I tried to

be gallant; very possibly I was only foolish. She motioned me to a seat, and in a little while we were engaged in a conversation upon the ordinary topics of the day. But every sound of that voice thrilled through me like an electric flash, and every glance of that dark eye wakened emotions wild and new. It was not admiration; that word expresses not one tenth part of what I felt. It was not love; that I knew would be madness. The woman who had once given her heart to him she called husband, would shudder at the far off footsteps of another passion. It was not adoration; for there was much about her to remind you of earth. I know not what it was, and can only describe it as a fascination that won and enchained me until I lost all feeling, all desire, but that of rendering myself pleasing to the enchantress whose spell was upon me.

"It was not very long before Mr. Lile rose, and remarking that he had something to show me that might be of interest to a soldier, led the way out of the apartment. 'This,' he said, as he opened the door of another room, 'is my small armory.' It was hung round with guns of every description, and style of workmanship. Swords, daggers and pistols. The collection was a rich and curious one. I did not fail to express the surprise I felt, adding that it must have been gathered at great cost, as well as trouble.

"'No,' he replied 'they are the weapons of the countries in which I have been a sojourner, and were collected one by one without much cost or trouble. This,' he continued, taking down a richly mounted cimeter, 'belonged to a Mameluke officer who tried the experiment of shortening my stature by a head, and lost his weapon in the effort. It is a pretty blade, and a dangerous one, but it requires a skilful hand to wield it. Strength avails nothing; it is all skill and practice.'

"'So saying, he drew the bright and glittering steel from

the scabbard, and turning to where a large nail was driven in the planking of the room, severed it at a blow. So admirably was the blade tempered that the iron made no impression upon it, and I found it, along its whole length, smooth and keen as before.

"Before returning the cimeter, I made several inquiries as to the manner of tempering steel in the East. Spoke of the fact, that our mechanics had never been able to attain such high perfection in the art, and incidentially alluded to the feats of Saladin, as described by Sir Walter Scott.

"'I doubt,' he replied, 'if that story was altogether an invention. In all its essential parts it was probably true. Sir Walter only transferred to the Sultan a dexterity possessed by hundreds of his subjects. Still I like not the weapon; for a downright blow on the battle field it is useless. Here is something that suits me better.'

"The sword thus indicated, was shaped very much after the fashion of the British artillery sabre, but longer, and more than twice the weight of any I had ever seen. It occurred to me, that no human arm could wield that ponderous blade for any length of time. He must have divined my thoughts, for he said, as he took it from my hand,

"'I had it made to suit myself. It is too heavy for most men, but I find no difficulty in using it. Besides its weight, the temper is just as admirable as yon Damascus cimeter, and with ordinary force will easily cleave through greater obstacles than a rusty nail.'

"We now passed on to a rack where his pistols were suspended. He made some remarks upon each, indicative of the place of its manufacture, or the manner it was obtained. Near the end of the rack he took down one of Colt's revolvers.

" 'This,' he said, 'is of native growth, and for service is worth all the others together.'

" 'Do you value it so highly ?'

" 'It is impossible to value it too highly. Revolving guns have been known for a hundred years, but they were so clumsily constructed as to be worthless. This is a different affair. It is capable of great improvement, and no doubt will be greatly improved by its inventor, if he be the man of genius his past achievements indicate; but even now, without further alteration, I have seen nothing to equal or approach it.'

" My attention was now directed to a full length portrait of my host, hanging against the wall, at the extremity of the room. He was dressed in a rich foreign garb; the long heavy sabre I had just been examining was in his hand, the point resting on the earth, while at his feet was the figure of a man, evidently a vanquished and pardoned enemy, who was apparently rising slowly and painfully from the ground, where he had been hurled. Underneath were the words:

"That mercy I to others show,
That mercy show to me."

"Both of us stopped and regarded the painting in silence. What was passing through his mind I know not. Mine was filled with many thoughts. I wandered away, in imagination, to the distant clime where the words of forgiveness had followed the deadly struggle. A new phase had exhibited itself in the character of my new acquaintance. Mercy clothed him with her downy mantle and my heart yearned towards the strong man, as to a gentle and loving brother. His voice broke a reverie, pleasing enough to make me wish it longer.

" 'That is Zerah's work. It records an incident which

affected her greatly, and that picture was painted to perpetuate its memory. You see, also, that she is not unacquainted with our English classics; though she little dreams from whence Pope borrowed the sentiment.'

"I ventured to say, 'I was not aware it had been borrowed.'

"'Because you have never taken the trouble to think about the matter at all. You have repeated the original, I dare say, hundreds of times, *Forgive us our trespasses, as we forgive those who trespass against us.* In my opinion, the alteration has marred its beauty. But come, Zerah brooks no neglect, and we must return to her now, if we would find that angel-face as radiant as we left it.'

"'She is indeed an angel.'

"'Yes! and the more lovable for the strong human passions which inhabit that exquisite form.'

"We found the lovely mistress of the mansion looking over the pages of a richly bound volume. It was laid aside immediately on our entrance. The conversation that ensued was far from gay, but it was cheerful, and left none but pleasant impressions behind. When I rose to depart, he took my hand, and, speaking warmly, and kindly, bade me remember 'that he had left an address in my possession, and that he expected me to apply to Monsieur Evadne in case any of the trials incident to youth should overtake me.'

"'I did not bring you here,' he continued, 'for the trifling purpose of an hour's conversation, or the still more trifling one of exhibiting the toys you have just been examining. I am going on a long journey, and shall not be here to assist you, if you should need assistance, but a letter addressed to Monsieur Evadne will reach Zerah, and you must be in a sore strait if she does not find the means of relieving you.'

"I thanked him earnestly for his kindness, and in my turn proffered any assistance I could render his wife during his absence.

"'My dear sir,' was the reply, 'Zerah is a genuine Moslem. She goes to no plays—no parties—no places of public amusement. She never leaves her own door without being closely veiled. She does not understand, and would not accept the courtesies so common among us, and so grateful to a lady mingling in American society. In all else she is provided for. She can command those who are both shrewd and worldly, and whose interest it is to be faithful, obedient, and honest. Leave her your address, and keep Evadne advised of your whereabouts. She will send for you if she needs you, and fail not on your part to apply to her.'

"He dropped my hand. His wife advanced, and gave me hers. I heard the tones of that silvery voice, and knew it was a blessing she invoked, but the words were lost in the music that gave them utterance. I raised the little hand respectfully to my lips, and turned away. In another moment the door had closed between me and the friends I had found so strangely, and parted from so suddenly.

"You cannot conceive the strength of the impression they have made upon me. One or the other is incessantly rising up before me. Sometimes it is the man; mysterious, incomprehensible. With his wonderful powers of mind and body; his marble face, calm, unruffled, cold, still and passionless. Speaking always in a voice of unconscious command, and hiding every emotion without seeming effort. Once only did I detect any change in his impassable features. When he raised that heavy sabre, and let his eye glance along the polished blade, there was a flash that told of the volcano slumbering within. Then again, the vision changes, and his wife appears in her supernatural beauty; looking as if she had just descended from above, and had not remained on earth long enough to soil her satin slipper. The melody of her last adieu is even now floating around me, and never did Cherub, or Cherubim, utter notes more enchanting. Who are they? What can they be? Ask among the old men in the neighborhood if they remember any one to whom my description will apply. I dared not asked *him* more than he chose to tell; but a curiosity has been awakened which must be satisfied. Write at once and let me know what you can find out.

"ROBERT WILSON."

Poor boy! how little he knew his own heart! How ignorant he was of the dreadful precipice on whose outmost verge he was standing. Not love the woman who had so captivated his fancy! Not love her! and because he was hopeless of a return. Oh! what a low and earthy thing would love be, if it could be cramped by such boundaries. If hearts were put up in the market, bargained and bartered for, like silk or sandal wood, in the marts of Arabia. If the young are to go out, with triple armor round their bosoms, saying to the beautiful and the good, I have a heart hidden somewhere within me that I am willing to dispose of, but I must first know what I am to receive in return. If you will give me an assurance that yours is to be trafficked for, I will take off this outward covering, exhibit mine, and begin to arrange the terms of an exchange. This is not the passion whose celestial birth has been sung in every land where the letters of Cadmus have penetrated; not the passion that exalts, informs, and purifies our nature till we become in truth, but a "little lower than the angels." Love, genuine love, comes unbidden, and remains, uninvited. No matter what difficulties may surround it — no matter if Hope never put forth its leaves, or putting them forth, they had early sickened and died, still it lives on, changeless among the changeful — immortal amid the dying. Who that has looked from a high balcony upon a garden of roses, ever stopped to inquire if he could pluck the flower before admiring its beauty. Shall a higher sentiment, the highest that has winged its way from its natal home beyond the stars, be driven shuddering back by the cold calculations of a peddling trader. No, oh, no! We are bad enough; the fruits of the forbidden tree have not all been gathered, but neither has the atonement been in vain; and Robert Wilson penned a libel on himself when he wrote that he could not love Zerah Lile, *because* he knew she loved another. He did more; he lulled himself into security when the outposts of the citadel were taken, and its inner defences fearfully weakened. He who continues to read these pages will have occasion to remember his self-deception, and to note its consequences. What answer was returned to his inquiries in relation to the husband, is unknown. It is very improbable that he obtained the information he sought. Time, war, toil, and suffering, are no gentle playmates. In all things they work changes inward and outward. The boy of twenty is often no more like the man of forty, than the lamb of the hill-side resembles the tiger of the jungles. Whatever had been the Bernard Lile of yesterday, it was not the Bernard Lile of to-day. That very calmness, no fear, no love, no hate, no astonishment ever chased away, only betrayed the ordeal he had passed. He had conquered, and was master of himself, but the victory had cost him dear, and the traces of the struggle would remain forever.

CHAPTER III.

> "This should have been a noble creature: he
> Hath all the energy which would have made
> A goodly frame of glorious elements,
> Had they been wisely managed."

In the year 1835, there stood upon the bank of the Mississippi, near the mouth of the Arkansas river, a rude collection of log cabins, intended for the accommodation of the hunters of that wild region, and of the gamblers who congregated there, for the purpose of cheating these sons of the forest out of the hard earnings of the chase. At that period there were floating on every boat, and infesting every landing place along the entire length of the "Great Father of Waters," a class of men, now happily passing away, whose sole business it was to cheat the inexperienced and the unsuspecting of whatever money or produce they might possess. Generally of good manners and insinuating address, with an extensive knowledge of human nature; liberal to profusion when their ever-varying fortunes permitted liberality; equally ready for a fray or a feast; it was difficult to avoid their companionship, and to become a companion was almost certainly to become a victim. Among their most favored resorts was the *landing* to which allusion has been made. Here came the hunter when the chase was done; and here came the trader to barter for his furs and peltries. The gambler looked upon both as pigeons to be plucked, and it mattered little to him who was subjected to the operation. His object was to obtain money to squander in the sensual indulgences of the cities on the great river and its tributaries. To do him justice, he never thought of the wide misery he sometimes inflicted. He took no account of agents defrauding their employers to obtain "a stake," or of families deprived of the common necessaries of life by his skilful manipulations. Place immediately before his eyes a case of poverty or of suffering, and he was much more ready to relieve it with his purse, than many of those whose charities not unfrequently find a place in the newspapers. Often blackened by other vices, careless of public opinion, lost to the sense of shame, there was still one green spot in his heart, and the needy never applied to him in vain if he had the means to relieve them. Nor were other virtues wanting; springing among thorns and branches—choked and cramped it is true, but virtues nevertheless. If we could read the private history of one gambler's life; if we could trace each step of his downward progress; realize the allurements that enticed, the temptations that beset him, we should doubtless find much in the record to demand both pity and forgiveness. They do not spring into the world full-fledged and ready to prey upon their kind. Nine times in ten they are victims before they become plunderers. All are not thoroughly bad, but it is well for the young to remember, that all who indulge in such practices, are liable to become so—all *are certain* to give great pain where they little dream of inflicting it, and all *are certain* to be sufferers themselves.

It was night. A clear, star-light night, with just enough frost in the air to make the large wood-fire blazing in the front cabin pleasant and comfortable. Around the fire were grouped six or seven stalwart hunters, watching with eager interest a game of "seven up," going on between one of their number and a man whose profusion of ruffles and ornaments, indicated his profession as plainly as if it had been written on his brow. In a corner sat an individual who was paying but little attention to the game, casting only an occasional glance at the players, and then turning his eyes again to the blazing logs on the hearth stone. He wore the air and manner of a stranger whose stay in the place had probably been caused by one of those accidents common to travellers. To complete the picture, the landlord was leaning with his elbows upon a rude counter, dignified with the name of a bar; dividing his time pretty equally between marking the points of the game, and puffing at the corn-cob pipe he held between his lips.

"How is the game, Williams?" said the gambler, turning to his host.

"You are five to his four."

"Then I beg."

"I give," said the hunter, who had dealt the cards.

"That makes six, and here's the low spot, showing the lowest trump, which puts me out."

"The game is closed," was the commentary of the hunter, as he rose from his seat. *"I'm busted!"*

The gambler rose also, and carelessly putting the stakes in his waistcoat pocket, remarked to those around,—

"Well boys, as I'm in luck to-night, I'll stand treat. Williams, give us some of that real old Bourbon—none of your Tennessee bald-face. Stranger," turning to the traveller in the corner, "won't you join us."

The invitation was coldly, but politely declined.

"Well, no harm done. You lost that last game, Tom Simpson," addressing his late adversary, "by begging on the first hand. I had *narry* trump, and if you had stood on the Jack, I was bound to be beaten."

"No matter how it was lost," replied Simpson, with a knit brow and a clenched hand, it's lost; and the money has gone into your pocket, like all the rest I have made for the last five years. But," he continued, striking the counter with a force that made the bottles and glasses jingle, "look out, Jim Black, I know you are none too good to cheat. I believe you have been cheating me all along, and if ever I catch you at that game, I'll drive my knife through your heart in less than half a minute afterwards."

"There is no use in talking that way, Tom. I know it as well as you do; and you needn't be telling a fellow of it every time you see him. Just wait 'til you catch me."

"I will; but, by God, when I do catch you, you won't have many seconds to say your prayers."

Black was a man of dauntless courage, which the enervating effects of a life of debauchery and licentiousness had failed to subdue. Looking calmly into the face of the fierce and powerful man who confronted him, he replied,—

"Well, Tom, I hope to have the pleasure of drinking your health very frequently before that time comes. Here's to you, old fellow, better luck the next time, if it is to my cost," and he drained his glass to the bottom.

The stranger, who had listened to the foregoing conversation, with far more attention than he had bestowed upon anything going on around him, now rose from his seat, and approaching Black, inquired,

"Is it true that you have been playing cards with this man for years, with the full knowledge that your life was, every moment, in imminent peril from his suspicions?"

"Why, yes! Everybody knows Tom Simpson is much more likely to cut a throat than to talk about it. But I trust a good deal to my luck, and a good deal more to skill and coolness."

"Now, this is something I call worth living for," said the stranger, earnestly. "I never expected to envy a human being, but I do envy you, sir. I would give fifty thousand dollars for one week of such excitement."

Simpson's brow grew darker, and his eye flashed with a deadlier light. Stung by his losses—almost maddened by the conviction that he had been cheated, and was unable to detect it: he was exactly in the condition to quarrel with any body, or on any pretext. Laying his hand firmly on the shoulder of the last speaker, he growled rather than said.

"So you think there would be something funny in having Tom Simpson's knife pointed at your heart. By the Lord God you had better try it."

There was a dead silence in the room. The giant strength and desperate character of the backwoodsman were known to all; and each one held his breath with the conviction that very soon the floor would be stained with murder. The stranger alone was unmoved. Not a shade passed over his marble face. For an instant the dull, sleepy look vanished from his dark hazel eye, and a flash as vivid as the lightning took its place. But it was for an instant only. Calmly lifting the strong man's hand from his shoulder, he said, slowly and sternly.

"I should indeed like to make the experiment, if I did not know it would be useless. You are no match for me—have no power to harm me, and there could be little excitement in a struggle, when I know before hand how it must result."

"You think so, do you?" howled Simpson, aiming a blow at the head of his antagonist that would have prostrated an ox.

Quick as thought, the arm of the infuriated hunter was knocked up, and the next instant he was hurled, as if driven from a catapult, into the extreme corner of the room. A yell of rage and pain escaped him as he rose from the floor, and drawing his knife, he sprang with the bound of a tiger towards his foe. With the right foot thrown back, the left knee slightly bent, and the left hand raised to the height of the elbow, that foe awaited his coming, watching every motion with a lynx's eye. The broad, bright blade rose on high, glittering in the light of the fire with a sickly bluish glare—it descended, but not on the bosom at which it was aimed. The arm that held it was enclosed in an iron grasp, and Simpson dragged froward with a sudden jerk, lay upon the floor, stunned and senseless. Instantly springing upon his prostrate enemy, and drawing his arms forcibly behind him, the stranger bound them fast with his silken handkerchief. Then taking a leathern thong from the wall where it was hanging, he proceeded deliberately to fasten his feet in the same manner. When this was accomplished he rose from the body and quietly remarked,

"There, sir, I do not think it will take long for you to get cool in that fix."

All this had happened so suddenly, that not one of the spectators had time to utter a word or raise a hand to interfere. Now, that it was over, they turned their eyes from the prostrate hunter, with wonder and awe to the seemingly passionless victor. He had resumed his seat with as much composure as if the terrible conflict he had provoked was the mere pastime of children; and was again gazing into the fire with the same half-sleepy, half-abstracted look he had worn during the earlier part of the evening. Simpson, who had now recovered partially from the stunning effects of his fall, was regarding his late antagonist with a look of mingled astonishment and curiosity.

"Stranger," said he in a tone no longer indicative of passion or defiance, "will you tell me what is your name, and where you hail from?"

"My name is Bernard Lile. No matter where I came from. It is enough that I am an American."

"Thank you for the information. I rather think," he continued, "I have come out second best in this skrimmage, and may as well *own up*. I'm licked bodyaciously, out and out, and since I've acknowledged the corn, you might as well untie these knots. This is not exactly a feather bed I'm lying on, and my shoulder is burning as if a hundred red hot spindles were stuck in it."

Without a word Lile rose, and removed the shackles from the prostrate huntsman. Then placing one hand above, and the other below the shoulder joint, he pressed it with considerable force. The examination satisfied him that no great harm was done, for he turned away, saying,

"It is not out of joint, it is only sprained. Rub it well with camphor—I suppose that is the best thing you can get here—and it will be well in a day or two."

The landlord had no camphor. "Then give me some whiskey," exclaimed Simpson, "and rub it in hard. Jim Black will pay for the sperits out of the money he has won from me."

"Certainly," assented the gambler. "Not only that, I will make you a poultice to-night, and insure it to take the soreness out by breakfast to-morrow."

The momentary awe created by the sudden conflict, and its almost miraculous termination was at an end. Scenes of peril and blood were too familiar to all present to drive away, for any length of time, their accustomed cheerfulness. The bottle circulated freely among them, and many a wild story of hair-breadth escapes from the Indians, or the wild beasts, filled up the intervals. Simpson was standing at the counter, his brawny chest and sinewy arms laid bare, while his host was rubbing his shoulder, with a hand as hard and horny as the skin of the alligator.

"I say, Tom," said he in a whisper, pouring on at the same time a fresh supply of whiskey, "that was a bad fight you picked up."

"Bad! I think it was," replied Simpson, through his

ground teeth, "Do you know there is but one thing keeps me from believing that fellow is the devil."

"What is that?"

"Why, if it was Old Nick himself, I am almost sure he would have been off to hell with Jim Black before this. Still I don't understand how anything of flesh and blood, could jerk my knife from my hand, without getting a scratch, and then tie me fast, hand and foot, in less time than it takes to tell it."

"Nor I neither, Tom. I thought you was a long ways the best man on the Mississippi."

"I would have sworn it, Williams, at the drop of a hat. Why, it was only last week that I caught a half-grown panther by the throat, and choked the critter lifeless before it could do more than tear the clothes, and a little of the hide off my arm and breast. Yet this fellow comes along here and handles me as if I was a ten-year old boy. I don't understand it, and I never shall."

By this time Black had returned with the poultice. Bidding Williams spread down a buffalo skin, he applied it carefully and skilfully to the battered shoulder of his patient.

"There," he said, as the last ligature was fastened, "all's right. Now lie down and be quiet."

"I will, Jim, though its nigh about the only thing in which I would like to follow your advice. They tell me you were a doctor before women and cards got into your head, and made you the devil's imp that you are. At any rate you cured me once before of a worse hurt than this, and it may be that same thing has more than once kept my knife from between your ribs."

"May be so," replied the gambler, carelessly, "but it is not dead certain. I do not think I could have got out of the scrape as easily as that fellow yonder did; still it is no five to one bet that every one who undertakes it is going to kill me first."

So saying, he turned on his heel and walked away.

Before the first light of the morning had gilded the east, the hunters had taken their way to the forest, and none appeared at the breakfast table but Lile, Simpson and Black. Bear meat and venison steaks were smoking on the board, with excellent corn-bread, butter and milk. There was, also, something called coffee, but it was muddier than the water of the Mississippi of which it was made. The biscuit resembled in shape and size the mud turtle, so common in the creeks and bayous of the South. In Mr. Black's opinion, however, it was a breakfast "not to be sneezed at;" and either the others agreed with him, or their appetites were something of the sharpest. Conversation there was none; unless a brief question, now and then, and a still more brief reply, could be called conversation. Between these three men there could be little in common, and neither thought fit to manifest any particular interest in the affairs of his companions. What the future might reveal, what antagonism, or what friendships it might establish, was unknown, and very probably uncared for. When the meal was finished, they sauntered into the front cabin, which, as we have seen, answered the purposes of sitting-room, card-room, and grocery.

"This is likely to be a dull day," remarked Black, as he drew a cigar from his pocket, and lighted it by one of the blazing brands of the fire. "The boys will not be back before night, and we shall have nothing to do but watch the steamboats as they pass. It is a pity your arm is hurt, but for that we might have a social game of cards to pass away the time."

"My arm is well enough," surlily responded Simpson, who did not exactly like the allusion to his discomfiture of the night before. "I can handle my rifle or knife easy, but I have no money, and I don't think I would play with you any more, if I had."

"Perhaps, sir," said Lile, addressing Black, "you would take a game with me."

The gambler's eyes sparkled. It was the very thing he had been longing for, but he stood too much in awe of that strange man to make the advance.

"Certainly," he said, "I do not know how else to get through the day."

Seating himself astride the long bench before the fire, he drew a deck of cards from his pocket, and shuffling them carelessly, asked,

"What shall we bet?"

"Anything you please."

"Well, I never bet very high, but a little stake makes the game more interesting. Suppose we say *ten* a game."

Lile pulled out a purse, well filled with gold; a coin remarkably scarce at that day on the Mississippi, when the whole country was flooded with paper money. In a short time afterwards this money became utterly worthless, making shipwreck of many a reputed fortune, and dragging down many a man who fancied he was beyond the reach of poverty.

The money was staked, and the game commenced. At first the gambler won. The stakes were doubled—he lost—doubled again, and again, until, in less than an hour, the redoubtable Jim Black was penniless. In his desperation, he pulled out his watch and diamond pin, and proffered to play for them.

"No," was the reply, "I have no use for your jewels. I am satisfied with the lesson I have given you. These cards are marked. I knew them as well as you did, having seen such things often in Paris. You thought to swindle me, and now that you have had your own trick turned upon you, must put up with your losses in the best way you can."

"Where is the mark?" asked Simpson, who had been watching the game with intense interest."

"There." Putting his finger on the left hand side of the card, about a fourth of its length from the top.

Simpson took the deck in his hand—ran his eye eagerly over them, and exclaimed ;

"By God! it is as big as a horse shoe."

"Yes, now that it is shown to you ; but you have been playing with this man for years without making the discovery."

Simpson laid down the cards, and in a tone of deep and stern determination addressed Black, who had remained perfectly silent during the foregoing colloquy.

"I told you that if ever I caught you cheating, I would introduce my knife to your heart strings, and as God is my judge I will keep my word."

The gambler's matchless impudence now came to his aid. He had long since recovered from the first confusion of detection. Looking Simpson steadily in the face, he said :

"You promised, I know, to cut my throat, or something of the sort, if you ever caught me cheating you; but it happens that *you* haven't caught me at all. I played a marked deck on a stranger who knew them better than I did, and I have got badly sucked in. But what is that to you? I never cheated you, or if I did you never caught me, and can't prove it."

"He is right," said Lile, "and if you will take my advice you will avoid him hereafter, rather than quarrel with him for what is past and gone. I assure you it is the better course. Let it drop where it is and walk a little way with me. I have something to say to you privately."

Slowly, reluctantly, and with frequent backward glances at the object of his resentment, Simpson followed the footsteps of Lile. When safe beyond the chance of being overheard, the latter briefly inquired,

"How much money has that fellow won from you?"

"First and last at least three thousand dollars."

Well, here is about five thousand dollars I have just won from him. Take it all, you are entitled to some compensation for the uneasiness he has made you suffer."

Simpson drew back, but Lile urged it upon him. "Take it man, most of it is yours. I do not want it, and played with him for no other purpose than to win what you had lost. Besides I want you to do me a service, and I do not know how I could have paid for it in a cheaper way."

The hunter pocketed the money, but it was clear he had many misgivings as to the propriety of doing so. His companion continued interrogatively.

"You know the road to San Antonio de Bexar?'

"Every foot of it, as well as I know the ground back of Williams's house."

"Well, I am going there, and I want some one who can guide me by the nearest paths through the forest, and over the prairies. Will you go?"

Simpson thought of the pile of gold he had seen—he knew the scarcity of that description of money—he remembered also that his companion had never uttered a syllable to indicate from whence he came, or what was his business, and a suspicion flashed over his mind that he was an emissary of the Mexican government. Under this impression he replied.

"Tell me first whether you have any dealings with the Mexicans."

"No, but I hope to have soon. The American settlers in Texas have declared for independence. They will have a hard struggle, and I am going to offer such assistance as a single arm can give."

"If that is what you are after," ejaculated the hunter, "you need not have paid so high for a guide. I would have done it for love. What is more, I will stand by you till the game's played out."

"Then we will consider it settled. When can you start?"

"Day after to-morrow. By that time my arm will be strong enough to stand a tussel with a bear. I have nothing else to do but send this money to my old father and mother in Tennessee, who reduced themselves to poverty in trying to learn me better things than roaming the woods three-fourths of the year, and associating with gamblers and cut-throats the other fourth. When I know they are provided for neither man nor devil will have much hold on me."

"I thought you had been better educated than the men with whom I found you."

"Yes, I learned English pretty well, and also a little Latin and Greek: but I have been among these people so long I have caught their language, as well as their manners, and I suppose it will stick by me to my dying day."

Without further conversation they returned to the house, and the same day Simpson took advantage of a passing steamboat to send his money to a merchant of New Orleans, with instructions to forward it to his father.

The night passed much as usual after the return of the absent hunters, except that there was no gambling. Black did not appear at all discomfited by his exposure, or out of spirits from the serious loss he had sustained. He laughed, drank, told stories with the rest, and was among the last to seek his bear skin couch.

With the dawn of morning the hunters again sought the

woods, and Black, contrary to his custom, went with them. Lile and Simpson were busied with preparations for their departure. The latter insisted on seeing everything. It was in vain the former assured him that he was himself an old hunter and soldier; that he knew all that was needful, and had provided it accordingly. Simpson urged that the woods were new and strange; the dangers to be encountered of a different kind to any to which his comrade had been accustomed. He examined his rifle; shot it at a mark to prove its accuracy. Tried the temper of his bowie knife by driving it through an inch plank; and finally inspected his powder horn and bullet pouch. The examination clearly pleased him. As he laid down the last mentioned article he gave vent to his satisfaction.

"You know more than I thought any man could learn in the settlements; and it is a real comfort in the woods to know you can rely on your companion."

CHAPTER IV.

"Weak, weak and vain our struggles to be free;
Before earth's atoms from dark chaos sprung,
The hand of fate had traced his stern decree,
And high in heaven the changeless tablet hung."

The sun had long passed its meridian, and was rapidly descending the western hemisphere. In the deep forest of cottonwood which nearly every where skirts the Mississippi, two men, with their rifles beside them, were seated on the trunk of a fallen tree in earnest conversation. The first was our old acquaintance Black, who was very busily engaged digging a trough in the decaying trunk with the point of his Bowie knife. The other was a tall and powerful man, with black eyes and sun-burned face. His thin and closely compressed lips, together with a certain fierce, devil-may-care expression of countenance, told of iron firmness, and a haughty self-dependence, resulting from many a danger encountered and overcome. In sleep, a physiognomist would have pronounced those features well suited to his manly form; but there was something in the eye—its cat-like shape; its constant watchfulness; its restless and uneasy roving from object to object, that spoke of crime more loudly than of daring. Not a dry branch cracked, not a bird fluttered but attracted his attention, and each time his hand was laid unconsciously on the long rifle by his side. At the time to which our story refers, Black desisted from his occupation, and looking fixedly at his companion, hissed through his closed teeth,—

"I tell you, Montgomery, it must be done."

"And I tell you, Jim Black, this is no child's business.

I wouldn't mind sending a rifle-bullet through the stranger, if he is as rich as you say he is, but Tom Simpson is too well known in this neighborhood. He will be missed. You and me will be suspected, and we have done a good many things in our time that won't bear searching into."

"Simpson must die too. He is dangerous. Every time he looked at me last night, his eye had the roll of the panther when about to make his leap. Besides, he knows all now, and will tell every trader that comes to the *Landing*, so that as long as he lives our game here is blocked."

"I know all that, and wish that d—m—d black-browed, say-nothing devil, had been in hell before he came this way. But how are we to help the mischief that is done without running too much risk? The law is weak in these parts, I know, but you and me have escaped a long time, and luck will change after awhile."

"Yes; *luck* will change. Men who rely on luck are certain to be swamped in the end, but sense and management seldom fail. They start to-morrow for Texas, and take the nigh cut through the swamp. I wormed it all out of Lile last night, when he little thought what I was after. For sixty miles the path can be travelled very well by horses. Now what is to prevent you and me from crossing the river to your cabin to-night—mounting our horses at daylight, and pushing on ahead for forty or fifty miles. There are plenty of hiding places for the horses as well as for ourselves, and the job can be done without risking a coroner's inquest."

His fellow-ruffian did not answer for some time. He was calculating in his own mind all the chances of risk and profit. At length he spoke,—

"I suppose I must stand by you, Jim, but I don't like it a bit. Tom Simpson has the eye of a hawk ,and knows the woods better than any Indian between here and the Rocky

Mountains. I can't tell what that stranger knows, but he's not been raised on carpeted floors, and that skrimmage of his, at Williams's, the other night, was not the first he's been in by a hundred. You say I shall have the five thousand?"

"Yes, that much any how, and if he is as rich as I think he is, there will be more to divide. Now let us be off. We have no time to spare, and need not stop at the Landing to make excuses for not killing any game to-day."

"But we must stop to buy a quart at Williams's. I don't think I ever left this side without taking some of the *red-eye* with me, and it would look rather suspicious if I went without it."

"Right; exactly right. I did not think of that. Buy half a gallon; and whisper to Williams, as a great secret, that I have determined to keep out of the way until that affair of the marked cards blows over. He will be certain to tell it to every body, and it will account for our absence."

As the sun was descending behind the tree tops, on his westward journey, the intended victims of this cold-blooded assassination were standing on the bank of the Mississippi, watching the muddy torrent rushing by with its mighty tribute to the ocean. To one of them all that he saw was too familiar to excite emotion. The dark forest of cottonwood had been his home for years. By day and by night he had threaded its most intricate paths. Each individual tree was a familiar acquaintance. Separately and collectively he looked upon them with that feeling of indifference to which use alike brings the free rover of the woods and the lordly occupant of a palace. In the river, indeed, he felt an exulting pride—the pride of patriotism. It belonged to America. Like Niagara, the lakes, or the wide prairie, it belonged to his country. He had come to spend a portion of every year upon its banks. In his heart he believed the commerce of the world could not be carried on without its aid, and that man would have been treading upon dangerous ground who ventured to say, in his presence, the universe contained any thing to equal or rival it. Its sucks, eddies, whirlpools, snags, sawyers, all were dear to him, and the faintest approach to a sneer would have been resented as promptly as an intimation that the battle of New Orleans was not the greatest recorded event in history.

To the other it suggested reflections of a widely different nature. He compared it with his own stormy and tempestuous life—rushing on in its headlong course, grand, majestic, turbid, terrible. Laughing to scorn the puny efforts of man to control and direct it. Threatening everything that floated upon its bosom with destruction. Whelming every obstacle beneath its waves, and finally cutting its way far into the Gulf, tinging even the deep sea with its own muddy hue.

"But at last," he murmured, "it mingles with its brother waters. The stain it has borne for a thousand miles is washed away, and in that vast home the wild torrent becomes clear and pure as the mountain rill. Will it be so with me? I know not, and I doubt. Yet, surely the feeling that urged me to revisit these shores was from above. It is not the promptings of the Evil One that, day after day, direct me to assist in striking the shackles of tyranny from human limbs, and the deadlier shackles of superstition from the human soul. Not his the hand that drew away the curtain from the star of hope. Not his the voice that whispers return, repent; there was pardon for the thief upon the cross, and the words of forgiveness converted his dying agonies into rapture."

A calm had come—the calm of despair. The winds that now ruffle those waves, could only have been unchained by the hand of *Him* whose mercy follows even those who have trampled on His laws and defied His power.

Slowly he turned to go away, but Simpson laid his hand upon his arm, and whispered,

"Wait."

Black and Montgomery were approaching from the direction of the house, with their guns and accoutrements. Walking in the Indian fashion, one behind the other, they passed by our two friends without a sign of recognition, undid the fastenings of a skiff, and commenced pulling rapidly across the stream. Simpson watched them in silence, until they had pulled out many yards from the bank, when his thoughts assumed the shape of words.

"There goes a precious pair of scoundrels. I wonder what devil's work is in the wind now. Every time, in my knowing, that they have crossed this river together, some traveler has been missed, or some other foul deed done."

"Their good intentions are directed to us this time, my friend," was the response of Lile. "Mr. Black, like most cunning people, betrayed himself last night. He was too inquisitive by half, and much too careless, seemingly, about the answers he received. Men situated as he and I are, do not ask questions of each other without feeling an interest in the answers. From his look and manner, an unsuspecting person would have been apt to imagine that my route, and my time of starting were the most indifferent things in the world to Mr. James Black. My conclusion was, that he intended to waylay and murder us both, if he could, and I have been expecting all day to see him do the very thing he is now doing."

"Like enough! Like enough! He hates you for exposing him—he knows that he has lost me as a customer, and may, at any time, feel the point of my knife. Besides, he would cut half a dozen throats, at any time, for a less sum than he thinks you have about you. I wish you had let me kill the murdering thief, as I meant to do, yesterday."

"I shall not interfere a second time, if my suspicions are correct. Is any change in our plans necessary?"

"Not if forty lions were in the path. We know something now, and will know more in the morning. If murder is what they are after, they will catch it themselves, unless Tom Simpson has forgotten his woodcraft."

Lile extended his hand, and grasped that of his companion cordially,

"Now I know you, my gallant friend; and as our lots are to be henceforth cast together, I may as well say that you need have no misgivings about my inexperience. True, I know nothing of the country we are to pass, but I am an older woodsman than yourself, and never in the forest, the desert, or the walled town, have I met that man who was my equal with rifle, with sword, or with dagger."

"I believe you; and what is more, if you were to tell me you could run and jump the Mississippi, I'll be d——d if I didn't believe that too. It would be no stranger than jerking me about like a cub bear of a month old."

"Forget that. I will do the same thing for your foes, if it should ever become necessary."

"Forget it! I might as well try and forget I had ever seen that river yonder. I shall dream of it for a year. Not in malice though. It was an open stand up business, with the advantages all on my side, and Tom Simpson is not a man to nurse ill-blood for a free fight of his own choosing."

The deepening shadows now reminded them that it was about the usual hour for supper. The thoughts of the hunter had again returned to their purposed journey, and as they walked towards the house, he said,

"We must pack up two days' provision. There is plenty of game on the way, but it will not do to let our rifles speak in the woods until we know what Black and Montgomery are after."

With this the subject was quietly dropped, and neither refered to it again. There was no bustle of preparation, no nervous restlessness. Calm and self-confident—relying with perfect faith on each other's skill and courage—conscious that both had been tried by greater dangers than any now threatening them, and certain that no proper precaution would be neglected; the knowledge that their pathway was to be waylaid by murderers, created no more uneasiness than a winter rain would have done in the bosom of an ordinary traveler.

The next morning a dense fog shrouded the Mississippi, and completely hid the opposite shore. At such a time the boldest shrink from trusting themselves upon the bosom of the dangerous stream. The wheels of the steamboat are stopped, and the sonorous bell continually sends forth its warning peals. The birds sit with folded wings on the trees, and the panther creeps with slow and fearful steps to the brink to lap his morning draught. The long moss hangs in gloomy festoons from the stirless branches. No breath of air is stealing over forest or wave; but every where there broods a still and awful calm. At one place the murky vapors shape themselves into the dim outlines of a grim tower, with its frowning battlements and guarded loop-holes—close by these rises a giant figure, whose proportions are those of an ante-deluvian race. Rapidly as the shifting scenes of a panorama these are swept away, and an old graveyard takes their place, whose hoary tombstones are covered with the moss of centuries. This in turn disappears, and another, and another, and another succeeds; but all sad, all sorrowful, all filling the mind with nameless dread and apprehension. The far-off hoot of the owl struggles slowly through the mist, and the long cry of the wolf sounds like the requiem of the water-wraith over the victims about to be swallowed up by the rapacious flood. Night has its terrors, but night and storm, and darkness, have no shapes of fear like those that people a fog on the Mississippi. Real dangers mingle with those imagination has conjured up, and reason aids the fancy to unman the stoutest heart. Yet our travelers stopped not for fog, or floating trees, or the hidden shore before them. Silently, but firmly, they stepped into the frail skiff, and pulled out upon the foaming waters. The light paddle-blades bent in the grasp of the strong hands that held them, and the little barque sped through the gloom with the swiftness of the sea-gull. Landing on the western bank, they followed the main road a short distance, and then struck off along a bridle path to the South.

"It is but a short mile to Montgomery's cabin," said Simpson, as they walked on, "and there we shall learn enough to decide upon our plans."

"You do not expect to find them there, do you?"

"Not if they mean mischief. In that case they were off two hours ago. Montgomery will shed no blood near his own door. The settlements here are too thick. He is suspected already, and a murder here would be troublesome."

A few minutes walk brought them in sight of three or four cabins in the forest, constituting the dwelling and out houses of Montgomery. As they approached, three large and powerful dogs sprang over the fence with the evident purpose of giving instant battle to the intruders. The hunter, however, was an old acquaitance, whose footsteps they had often followed through the woods.

At the first sound of his voice their fierce growls were changed into a glad whining, and all three leaped upon him, licking his hands and face in the exuberance of their joy.

"There, pups, that will do," said he, as he gave to each a rude caress. "If your master was half as honest and true as you are, he and I would pass through the world, and leave it, on better terms than I expect."

The noise of the dogs brought an old negress to the door, whom Simpson addressed with a cordial—

"Good morning, Aunt Sophy, where is your master?"

"Him and Massa Black, done gone huntin' dis two hours ago."

Letting the butt-end of his rifle fall to the ground, and crossing his arms over the muzzle, he questioned the old woman long, and closely. He asked particularly what time they started. Why they had not taken the dogs. What route they took, and whether they had gone on foot or horseback. Having obtained all the information she possessed he declined "Aunt Sophy's" invitation to stop and take breakfast—bade her good bye, and placing one hand on the topmost rail of the fence, he cleared it at a bound. His companion followed his example, and the two moved on in the direction of the deep forest skirting the clearing. In a short time they came to a path made by cattle or other domestic animals going to and returning from a water hole. Here they separated, walking on side by side, but at a considerable distance apart, and scrutinizing closely every foot of ground they passed. Hour after hour glided by. Absorbed in the business before them, not a word was spoken until near noon, when Lile called the hunter to his side, and pointed to the deep print of horses hoofs in the soft soil of the woods.

"Here is the trail at last; and one a blind man might follow."

Simpson examined it for a moment, and then spoke in a low musing tone, as if talking to himself.

"Well, Bill Montgomery is a damnder fool than I took him to be. Why, I can follow that track for a week and tell within five minutes of the time he crosses every mud hole on the way. Jim Black never knowed much about the woods, but *he* ought to have known better than to leave signs as plain as these when he goes hunting such dangerous game as you and me, captain.

Lile only replied by a brief inquiry as to the nature of the country before them.

"It is all open woods for thirty miles, with little or no undergrowth. Then there is a cypress swamp, for three or four miles. Beyond that is a canebrake. It is there they will wait for us, for there only can they hide the horses."

"Then we have nothing to do but follow these tracks for the remainder of the day."

"That's all. Do you take the path, I'll follow the trail, I reckon they run pretty much together, but I don't like to risk losing the scent, now we've found it."

The progress of our travelers now became much more rapid. It is true that with the habitual caution of men inured to the dangers of a wild and roving life their eyes continually roamed through the forest, searching out every suspicious object, and marking every moving thing, but this in no degree abated the speed of their progress. Occasionally a deer bounded past, and near nightfall a huge bear, within fifty yards, reared himself against the trunk of a tree, and commenced, leisurely, to pull off the bark with his claws. Beyond this no living thing disturbed the solitude about them. About dark they reached the lagoon agreed upon as the place of their night's encampment. A fire was soon kindled, and the rude supper brought with them was despatched with a relish the dwellers in cities never know. Their plans for the morrow were then arranged as far as practicable: much, of course, being left to be determined by circumstances. When this was done the hunter arose, and taking his rifle said,

"You may sleep here as safely as if you were in Williams's cabin. We are in a bend of the lagoon, and the gap is not more than forty yards wide. With this starlight it will go hard if a wild cat enters without my knowing it. I will rouse you at midnight if it is needful."

So saying he disappeared among the trees.

Lile spread his blanket upon the ground, and laid down upon it, but not to sleep. He gazed upward through the trees upon the calm blue sky, and the bright stars which everywhere spangled its vault. With what bitter reproaches did that scene of peace, of beauty, and of holy harmony speak to his stormy soul. In the mountains of Asia—amid the gorgeous civilization of Europe—in the deserts of Africa—on the heaving billows of the dark blue sea, a hundred, and a hundred times had those stars spoken to him before. But never until now had they so touched, softened and subdued his iron nature. Memory carried him back into the long gone past. He remembered himself a bright eyed boy, rising with the lark and warbling songs as blithe and gay as his. Now bounding with his young companions in joyous sport from hill to hill, or breasting with exulting strength the billows of the mountain stream. Then came a dream of love: sweet as it always is in youth, when we scarce dare name even to our own hearts the passion that consumes it. When we build an altar and place thereon a divinity of our own creation—robbing the archangels of their beauty, and stealing from heaven its sinless purity to clothe an earthly idol; before which we then bow down in blind adoration. Adoration that soon finds a bitter ending. Happy those who never dream: or whom an early death cuts off before the hour of waking comes. How or when that hour came to him none knew, but come it did, and war, famine, pestilence, the wild adventure, and the wilder revel had each taken him by the hand, but each in turn fled before the mightier demon who had taken sanctuary in his breast. Even now with his path waylaid by murderers; with the howl of the hungry panther in his ear, and none but a solitary sentinel to guard his lonely couch, he thought not of the dangers around, or the weary journey before him. Step by step he traced back the years of memory. Every joy he had known rose up before him, but the vision rested only for a moment, and brought no gladness in its train. Not so with its sorrows. They were seared in as by the lightning on his brain. Rapidly he ran over the terrible record until words came to syllable reflection.

"And now, what am I? An outcast and a wanderer: my father's honest name discarded that it might not be blackened by the deeds of his son. High talents unemployed. Genius bringing forth none but evil fruits. Strength, skill, and courage, more than mortal, sold year after year to some barbarian prince, in whose petty feuds were wasted energies sufficient for a nation's redemption. Exciting strife wherever I go, and dogged, even here, by a fatality that is never at rest except when my hand is red with human blood. Oh! could we only know to what the first sin leads how few would take that fearful step."

At this moment the cracking of a dry branch caught his ear, and springing to his feet, rifle in hand, he bent his gaze in the direction whence the sound proceeded.

"You sleep lightly," said Simpson, emerging from the wood, "the snapping of that stick would hardly have waked a slumbering panther."

Lile did not see proper to give occasion for painful questions by saying he had not slept at all. Throwing his rifle on his shoulder, and casting his eye upwards to the stars, he replied.

"It is past midnight. Show me my post, and I will keep watch until day-break."

"No further watch is needed. Indeed I did suppose not any was necessary from the first: but as it would do me no harm to sit up until midnight I thought I might as well keep an eye on the track those murdering villains had taken."

Fresh fuel was added to the fire, and the two friends stretching themselves side by side upon the ground, slept until the dawning morn had streaked the east with its rosy hues.

CHAPTER V.

"Such tools the tempter ever needs,
To do the bloodiest of deeds;
For them, nc visioned terrors daunt,
Their nights no fancied spectres haunt,

"Fell as he was in act and mind,
He left no bolder heart behind."

Let us return to Montgomery and Black, whom we left paddling across the turbid current of the Mississippi. The shades of night had fallen on the earth when they reached the collection of huts described in the foregoing chapter. They found the old negress at her solitary supper. Bidding her add something to it for a couple of hungry men, they divested themselves of their accoutrements; took a long draught from the stone jug Montgomery had brought with him, and set about building a huge fire upon the ample hearth of an adjoining room. This done, their rifles were discharged; carefully cleaned; their locks removed and oiled. Then followed another *swig* at the jug, and with appetites sharpened by exercise and alcohol, they sat down to the plentiful repast "Aunt Sophy" had prepared. Supper over, they took their way to the stable, in which were two horses of uncommon bone and muscle. These were thoroughly rubbed down, corn-cobs supplying the place of curry-combs, and plentifully fed. Returning to the house, the jug was again put in requisition for a "Night-cap." Some bear-skins were spread upon the floor before the fire, and the two were soon wrapped in slumber as profound, and apparently as peaceful as that of an infant in its cradle.

All this time their conversation had been about the ordinary events every day occurring in the forest, or on the river. There was no allusion to the murders they had that day agreed to perpetrate. No speculations upon the chances of success or failure in their undertaking. Their bearing throughout was calm, cool, undisturbed by fear, or by anxiety. In short, they were bold, hardy, and determined men, who, having once resolved upon the commission of a crime, permitted no weak misgivings to interfere with the execution of their purposes. The stirring life of the frontier had done much to drown reflection. They were also in the morning of existence, and at that age, the voice of remorse, though never silent, comes to us in comparatively faint and feeble notes. It is in after years, when strength begins to wane, and courage to fail, that conscience gathers its hordes of demons about the heart. It is then we look upon the sunbeam with horror, from its contrast with the blackness within. It is then we shrink and tremble at the night, and fancy that every shadow is a grinning fiend. The evil we have done not only clings to the human soul with a never-ending life, but year by year it exudes a deadlier venom, while year by year the power of resistance fails. The lost wretch feels as if he were chained on the brink of a burning lake, whose lurid waves rise higher and higher, as they roll in angry surges at his feet. One after another, mirrored on its fiery surface, the deeds of a lifetime spring up with startling distinctness, while to his ear, each separate one has found a voice and shrieks for retribution. Oh! how different do they seem at such an hour from the things that self-delusion painted, when interest, pride, revenge, ambition, avarice, with careful hands obscured the deeds they prompted. As yet the lawless ruffians, reposing beneath the roof of that forest cabin were unvisited by the torments of remorse. It might be they would never know them *here*. It might be that an All-wise Providence had decreed, they should rush suddenly and unprepared, upon the dread hereafter. Let us wait—the problem will soon be solved.

About two hours after midnight the gambler rose. Heaping some additional logs on the fire, he roused his companion with a gruff

"Come, Bill, it is time we were stirring."

Montgomery rose, and producing an iron lamp, fed with bear's grease, from a cupboard in the corner of the room, lighted, and placed it upon the table. Their rifles were again inspected, and the blades of their Bowie knives partially oiled, so as to pull easily from the scabbards. Black then undertook to prepare breakfast, while the squatter went to the stable to examine into the condition of the horses. The morning was frosty and cold for that low latitude, a circumstance Montgomery did not fail to make an excuse for helping himself to an "eye opener," on his return to the house.

"I have told you, Bill," said the gambler, looking up from the meats he was frying, "at least a hundred times, that if you mean to make your living by cards, you must quit that d—m—d habit of drinking in the morning. I am as fond of liquor as you are, but I never drink until after dinner. And no man ought to who doesn't want his brain kept as muddy as the Mississippi."

"Maybe you are right about *the papers*, Jim, but you and I have set about making a living with a different sett of tools, and, as liquor don't interfere with the use of the rifle or the knife, you needn't grumble now."

"It interferes with every thing, I tell you. Brains are just as necessary in a skrimmage with a bear, as in a game of poker; and yours will be of d—n—d little use to you the balance of this day. At least mine would be to me, if I had swallowed half the whiskey you have."

"Well, there's nothing but hard riding to do to-day, and to-morrow I'll humor your whim."

"That will do. Now let us eat and be off. It is past three o'clock, and it wont lack much of day-break by the time we get started."

Breakfast was despatched after the manner of men who regard eating as a necessary evil; not as a luxury to be prolonged to the latest moment. The horses were brought out, saddled, and packed with the few articles necessary for a short encampment in the woods. The two then mounted, and set out on their dark journey without a twinge of conscience, or one moment's reluctant pause.

"Keep well to the right," said the squatter, to his companion, who was a little ahead, "if Simpson and the stranger come straight from the landing, they will strike *the trace* about my water hole, and it is best not to let them see horse's tracks beyond that."

"Pshaw! they have no suspicion of us."

"I reckon not; and I should be sorry if they had. But Simpson knows, as well as I do, that there's mighty little traveling done along *this trace* on horseback, and it's not the safest thing in the world, to set him to guessing what it means."

Black mused for a moment, and then said slowly and earnestly,

"Bill, tell the honest truth, ain't you a little afraid of Tom Simpson?"

The squatter checked the throb of rising passion at the reflection on his courage the question seemed to imply; but his answer, though divested of anger, was given in that low, determined tone, which conveys a warning, as distinct as that of the rattlesnake before he strikes.

"Jim, if you had asked that question like a man who wanted to hurt feelins, I should have been tempted to try my rifle on your carcase before the other game got in sight."

"I meant no harm. I do not want to quarrel with you any where; and certainly not now, or here. I had good reasons for asking."

"Then I'll tell you. I don't think I ever knowed exactly what it was to be afraid—that is, what other men call afraid. I don't know how to explain it, but I'll tell you a story, and that will let you understand the rights of it. When I was a little boy, daddy lived up on the edge of the Indian nation. One evening there came a traveler along, and asked if he could stay all night. Daddy was gone hunting, and nobody knowed when he'd be back. So mammy told him he might stay, if he could take care of his own horse. I followed the stranger to the stable, where the first thing he did was to shuck himself, and go to rubbing his horse with all his might. I was standing looking on, whistling Yankee Doodle, when he turned 'round and asked me if I warnt afraid. 'No,' says I, 'what's here to be afraid of?' 'Oh! nothing,' says he, 'only I sometimes have fits, and then I'm dangerous.' I didn't know what *fits* meant, but I took it to be some wild varmint like a bear, or a catamount. So I sidled off to the house; gathered mammy's butcher knife, and a good sized rock, and then went straight back to the stable. The feller never let on like he seed me, but kept working away on his horse. After a while he begun to pile in the corn and fodder. I couldn't stand it any longer. 'Stranger,' says I, 'aint you going to have one of them things?' 'What things,' says he. 'Them things you was talking about,' says I. 'Oh! fits,' says he, busting out in a laugh, 'what the devil do you want me to have one of them for?' 'Kase

I never seed one of the critters,' says I, 'and I wants to see one.' He looked at me in a way I didn't then understand, and said, mighty solemn, 'I was only joking with you, my son. Put away your knife and rock, and remember what I tell you, when I am gone. With that bold heart in your bosom, you have only to lead an honest life, and this world will be no hard place for you to live in.'

"And now, Jim, the feeling I had, when I was going back to the stables, with that rock and knife, is the only kind of fear I ever felt. I didn't want to run away from the thing, no matter what it was, but I wanted to get something to hurt it.

"While I am talking, I may as well tell you something else. It's more than twenty years since that happened. I'm sure I haven't thought about it more than two or three times since; but yesterday, when we was coming down the bank, and that stranger turned to look at us, I'd a swore he was the same man who told me to lead an honest life. He's changed mightily. He's fuller, and his flesh looks harder, and tougher. He's had trouble enough, I'll be bound. But the first time I laid my eyes on him, I was certain I had seen him somewhere. I watched him when Tom Simpson was charging on him like a buffalo bull; and there was something in his eye I had seen before. I watched him when he was moping over the fire, looking as doleful as a gal whose sweetheart had got tired and gin her leg bail; and I was certain I knowed him, but I couldn't think where we had met. When he turned to look at us, as we were making for the skiff, it flashed on me at once. As certain as my name is Bill Montgomery, that man was in these parts twenty years ago."

Black listened to the narrative in silence, and from the careless manner he permitted the bridle to hang on his horse's neck, it was evident he was deeply interested, When it was finished, he asked, in a voice of some anxiety,

"Well, what has that to do with our present business?"

"Nothing. Only it looks a little hard, to waylay and shoot a man who gave me the only good advice any one ever took the trouble to waste upon me."

"Think of the five thousand dollars, Bill, and recollect this job makes you independent."

"I have thought of that, or I should not have stirred from my cabin this morning. No matter what comes, you needn't be afraid of any flinching on my part now."

Neither appeared to be disposed to continue the conversation. Montgomery had already spoken at much greater length than was his wont; and he now pushed on ahead, still keeping about a hundred yards to the right of the path, or *trace*, as it was generally called by the settlers. The sun was nearly up, when the squatter broke the unsocial silence of their lonely ride.

"We must mend our gait. I want to cross the Cypress Swamp before sundown; for I have no notion of floundering in that d——d bog after dark."

The horses were pressed into a rapid trot: a pace they preserved throughout the day, wherever the nature of the ground would admit of it.

It was yet early in the evening, when they approached the edge of a gloomy morass, that fancy might easily have converted into a vast burial place for some Aboriginal tribe. The bare, and stunted *knees*, scattered here and there, looked like tombstones, placed to mark where chiefs and warriors slumbered; and over all the dark Cypress, with its melancholy drapery of moss, kept up a continual moaning, as the wind howled through it, for the beautiful, and the brave, who had long ago passed to the Spirit land.

The scene was not without its influence on the hardened

natures of the lawless men who now reined up on its brink. The one was rude and unlettered. Beyond the first rudiments of his own tongue; he had learned nothing from books; but it was impossible to live, as he had done from early infancy, in the wild forest—to roam over the vast Prairie, and climb the snow-capped summits of the Rocky Mountains—without imbibing a portion of that poetry which gives to the language of the Indian, a beauty and a melody, rarely equalled by the cultivated eloquence of civilized life. Unknown to himself, a lovely flower had grown and blossomed amid the noxious weeds neglect had sown, and evil associations nourished, in a heart not naturally bad.

The other was of a different order. His intellect had been carefully cultivated, and he had at one time mingled familiarly with the most polished society. He was a student, at times, notwithstanding the absorbing nature of his pursuits. To a thirst for gaming, he had surrendered character, honor, temporal prospects, and everlasting hope; but to his active mind, books of some sort were a necessity. In addition to English literature, he was familiar with the infidel writings of France and Germany. A school whose baleful malaria has floated across the Atlantic, and is beginning to infect the purer atmosphere of our Western continent. He was one of those human compounds, by no means so infrequent as we are prone to imagine. With a keen perception of the beautiful, and a not unjust appreciation of all that virtue can bestow; he was dragged on, not blindly, or reluctantly, but willingly, and with a knowledge of the consequences, to the dark doom that sooner or later overtakes the criminal.

Morally, the squatter was infinitely the better man, for his was in part the sin of ignorance. He had but one talent to account for, while the other had seven. Different, however, as they were by nature, and still more by education, that gloomy swamp, with its funeral vegetation of cypress, waked kindred emotions in each, and tamed alike, for an instant, the tiger and the fiend.

"We must make in for the trace," said Montgomery, after a pause, "there is no other crossing place."

His voice was low—almost sad. His companion noticed it, and would not trust his own in reply, for fear of betraying a similar weakness.

The swamp was crossed by the horses slowly, and with difficulty. On the opposite side a wide cane-brake spread out before them. Following the trace for a short distance further, they came to an opening having the appearance of an old camping ground, used by either Indians or hunters, on former occasions. Here they halted—unsaddled, and so fastened the horses, as to enable them to feed on the young cane growing around. A fire was kindled; and, after paying their respects to the leathern bottle Montgomery had brought with him, the less important business of supper began to occupy their thoughts. The cooking process was simple enough. A young cane was cut from the adjoining thicket, one end sharpened, and run through a piece of raw meat. The meat was then held to the fire, on this primitive spit, until about half done, when it was changed, and the other side subjected for a like time to the operation of heat. A cold hoe-cake supplied the place of a plate, and a Bowie knife did the rest.

Reader, did you ever try it? If not, take the word of a man who has, that no supper served up in the most faultless restaurant of New York or Philadelphia, ever yielded a flavor so delicious as a day's exercise in the open air, where the winds of heaven are permitted to blow unobstructed by brick and mortar, added to a fast of thirteen or fourteen hours, imparts to this woodland cookery.

Under the genial influence of the beverage contained in Montgomery's bottle, the two became gay and noisy. Not unfrequently the loud laugh, ringing through the forest, disturbed the owl on his solitary perch. Now a rude song rises on the air, and the panther moves uneasily in his lair, as the night wind bears the unaccustomed sound to his ear. Who would have deemed that these men were bent upon an errand of murder? Alas! in this world the blackest crime often puts on the gayest seeming. It is not alone the sullen brow, and the gloomy mood, which speak to you of violated laws, and outraged humanity. If sin wore always its own unsightly covering, many of the young and inexperienced, who are first its dupes, and then its agents, would escape its snares; and many a human tear, wrung from the mother, the wife, and the sister, would dry up at the fountain.

"It will be two hours," said Montgomery, as they arose from a hasty meal in the morning, "before the game can reach the stand; but accidents might happen, and it's best to be at our posts. There are trees enough in the edge of the cane to cover us; and they must come out so close that we can pick them off before they know what hurts 'em. Do you take Simpson for your mark, I'll take the stranger."

Black assented to this arrangement. Each one selected a tree, sufficiently large to screen him from any prying eye in the direction of the swamp, and lying down behind it, awaited patiently the coming of their intended victims. They had occupied their hiding place but a few minutes, when the squatter's attention was attracted by a hasty exclamation from Black.

"Damnation, man! look yonder! Hell, and fury, we must have been bewitched this morning."

As he spoke he pointed to a column of smoke, rising majestically from their camp-fire of the night before.

"By God! you are right," answered the squatter, springing to his feet. "It will not do to have that smoke curling up among the trees when Tom Simpson's on the trail. But that blunder's soon mended."

With rapid strides he returned to the fire, and carefully extinguished every burning brand. It was already too late. A mile off, in the swamp, the quick eye of Lile had detected the smoke above the tree tops, and pointed it out to Simpson. The latter watched it for some time without giving expression to his thoughts.

"It is smoke, certain; and Bill Montgomery, and Jim Black built the fire that made it. There is mighty little credit, captain, in circumventing a couple of born idiots like them. In the first place they must leave a trail a counter-hopper could follow: and now they have hung up a sign-board in the clouds, to let us know exactly where they are. Curse their pictures, they must think they've got an easy job on hand, or they wouldn't be half so careless."

"The smoke has disappeared," responded Lile, who had continued to watch it.

"Worse and worse. If they had let the fire burn, a fellow who didn't know that two such lambs as they are, were in this neck of woods, might have thought it was built by some honest traveler, who had left it burning when he started this morning. But any man, with two grains of sense, would know that some devilment was afoot, when they take the trouble to put it out at this time of day. Well, Mr. Black, this game ain't 'seven up.' I reckon I have got about as many advantages of you now, as you have had of me for the last five years. And, by the eternal God," he continued through his ground teeth, "I will play them all. In one hour more, if you are not past robbing at cards, and murdering on the road, I will sign a lie-bill, and give you permission to paste it on my old father's door."

The hand that held his rifle was clenched with a force that almost glued it to the barrel; and the muscles of his arm swelled beneath the tight buckskin hunting shirt, until the limb looked gnarled and knotted as the trunk of the live oak. Lile watched him, with the interest a strong man always feels, in the physical development of another. In his heart he believed he had never seen a frame of such tremendous power, and capable of so much endurance; and he thought how easy it would be, with such a companion, to clear a pathway through a hundred opposing foes.

Notwithstanding the deep and concentrated passion boiling in every vein of the hunter's frame, he was calculating, with cool precaution, every step to be taken. Thinking over every tree, and hiding place on the margin of the swamp, where a foe might be concealed. Estimating every chance of surprise on either side; and calling to mind every inequality of the ground, that might assist or obstruct him in the fight. In such a struggle he meant to throw away no chance, however slight. The covering of a single cane stalk would not have been dispensed with. It was not that his pathway was waylaid, and his blood sought by assassins, which so roused and inflamed him. It was the five years of poverty and privation he had undergone—the consciousness that his parents had been deprived of the comforts of life, while all his gains went to line the pockets of a swindler.—This roused the ferocity whose very intenseness made rashness impossible. True the money had been restored to him, but the suffering could never be obliterated; and hate, the darkest and the deadliest hate, suppressed and almost mastered until now, found legitimate excuse for its gratification, and gave to conscience the power of clothing the act of vengeance with the mantle of self-defence.

A little farther on the swamp became harder and firmer. Here they left the trace, and struck off in a south-eastern direction, so as to reach the firm ground about a quarter of a mile below where Black and Montgomery were posted. To do this, wide leaps were occasionally necessary, and near the margin, a black slough, full twenty feet in width, seemed to bar all further progress. Simpson stopped and hesitated; but Lile, taking the hunter's rifle in his left hand, cleared it, with both guns, lightly and easily. Relieved of the weight of his rifle, his companion also essayed the dangerous leap. With his utmost effort he barely reached the outer edge of the bank. A strong hand grasped his collar as his foot struck the turf, and dragging him forward, saved him from falling backward in the slough.

"This is no time to thank you," he whispered. "A few steps puts us on firm ground; and yonder within twenty yards of that broken tree, we are certain to find our very particular friends."

No further time was wasted in conversation. Separating as had been before agreed on—the one following the edge of the swamp, the other skirting the cane—they commenced their advance with all the caution of men trained in the wiles of Indian warfare. Never exposing their bodies for more than an instant at a time; springing from tree to tree with lightning like rapidity, they approached noiselessly, the spot where the assassins were lying in wait. At length, in bounding from the shelter of one tree to another, Lile lighted upon a dry cane stalk which cracked loudly beneath his weight. Black and Montgomery, whose eyes had hitherto been bent chiefly in one direction, were instantly aware of their danger. They comprehended at a glance that they had been suspected,—that Lile and Simpson had consequently avoided the trace, and were now approaching their position from the flank with no very peaceful intentions. Surprised as they were, their conduct exhibited none of the cowardly meanness that usually characterises the assassin. Promptly availing themselves of the shelter of the trees where they were lying—opposing skill to skill, and courage to courage, they prepared to take the chances of the deadly struggle. By a quick change of position, Lile sought to expose Montgomery to the fire of his own or Simpson's rifle. With equal rapidity the squatter bounded to another covert. The thick cane on one side, and the morass on the other prevented any further manœuvering, and it appeared now to be a question of patience alone. All at once the squatter was startled by the fierce growl of a panther immediately behind him. Turning to face this unexpected foe, his head protruded beyond the shelter of the tree. The sharp crack of a rifle immediately rang through the forest, and Bill Montgomery fell to the earth a lifeless corpse. Black heard the growl of the panther, followed by the rifle shot, and his eye was attracted to the spot where his late companion stood. It was for a moment only, but that moment was fatal. Darting from the tree where he was sheltered, with leaps more rapid than those of the grey-hound, Simpson cleared the space between them. Black saw his danger when it was too late. He attempted to raise his rifle, but the hunter grasped it with one hand, while with the other he drove the long bowie knife to the hilt in his breast, forcing it through two ribs in its bloody passage. The rough edges of the bones grated harshly as the knife was withdrawn from the wound.—A glassy film came over the eyes of the gambler—an ashy paleness spread around his lips—without a word, without a groan he sunk down, dead even before his body touched its mother earth.

Simpson gazed upon the prostrate form with an expression half of pity, half of gratified revenge. Pulling off the handkerchief from the dead man's neck, he wiped away the crimson stains from his weapon, and addressed the inanimate body.

"I have known you, Jim Black, a little more than five years, and the most of that time, I have had a presentiment that I would kill you some day. You have brought it on yourself, when you had only to keep out of my way twenty-four hours longer, and I should have been gone beyond your reach. You electioneered hard for a bloody grave, and you have got it. If you were alive now you would own you deserved it. The only good thing any man can put into your funeral sermon, is, that you were game to the back bone—I never knew you stand by, and see the strong oppress the weak; and never heard of your cowering to an angry frown, if the devil himself wore it."

Lile, who had reloaded his rifle, now approached, saying.

"That rush was gallantly made, my friend, but it was very bad generalship. After Montgomery was disposed of we could easily have placed Mr. Black between two fires, where either you or I could shoot him without the slightest risk."

"There was no risk about it, captain, I knew that if I could ever catch his eye off me, he was gone. I had been wishing for five minutes that a limb would fall, or something would happen to make him look round. That panther did the business, and it has put me in such good humor with the critters, that I don't think I shall shoot one for a year to come."

"No panther was near."

"Why, I heard his growl as plain as I hear you now."

"Nevertheless there was no panther about. Nature bestowed upon me the gift of ventriloquism, and as I found it useful, I practiced it carefully when I was a sojourner in the far east. When I found that Montgomery had no notion of showing any part of his person for me to practice at, I concluded I would try what effect an angry panther at his heels would produce. It startled him, as I expected, and a half ounce ball through his brain, saved him from the mortification of finding out how badly he had been cheated."

"Well," replied the hunter, "this is the third wrinkle I've got within the week. First, I found out that I was no *pumpkins* in a scuffle. Next, that I couldn't jump for *corn shucks*. And now, after ten years' practice, it turns out that I am tolerable *ordinary* even at a bush fight. I shouldn't be surprised if it would end by your showing me the road to San Antonio, instead of my guiding you."

CHAPTER VI.

"Innumerous o'er their human prey,
Grim errors hang the hoarded sorrow;
Through vapors gleams the present day,
And darkness wraps the morrow."

OUR story now changes from the free forest to the crowded city. From the rude scenes and daring deeds of the West, to the velvet ottomans and the courtly vices abounding where spires and cupolas rise to meet the clouds, instead of the tall cottonwood, the majestic oak, or the towering chestnut. In one of those splendid mansions in the city of New York, whose decorations rival the gorgeous magnificence of an Eastern palace, a throng of pleasure's votaries had assembled. Diamonds glittered beneath the soft light of the chandeliers, and eyes, brighter than the jewels about them, reminded you of Mahomet's promises to the faithful, when the war-worn soldier of the Crescent passed from the battle-field to the arms of the Houris who awaited his coming. Music floated through the perfumed air of the crowded saloons, and now and then the low laugh of a young girl, richer and sweeter than all instrumental melody combined, fell upon the charmed ear, and made the listener dream of heaven. The camel-driver of Mecca was but half an impostor. The daring courage, the lofty genius, and the matchless wisdom that led him on to empire over shattered thrones and broken sceptres, were emanations from the God whose prophet he pretended to be, and stamped with probability the mission with which he claimed to be entrusted. He searched all the depths of the human heart—tried all strings, until, at last, his hand rested on a chord that throbbed alike in the breast of the peasant and the prince—the scholar and the boor. Discarding the temptation of gold for avarice, of glory for ambition, of luxury and ease for indolence, he seized upon *one* all-pervading, all-alluring passion. He held out *one* reward for danger and privation, for toil, famine and death. When the glittering stars of the Crescent waved over him, the soldier thought of the dark-eyed girls his prophet had described in language whose prose is poetry—whose poetry sings itself into music. Amid the deadly roar of battle, their songs were floating around him, and the lance's point was to him a bridal bed. Stretched upon the cumbered plain, he looked upward to the rounded forms, the swelling bosoms, and the love-lighted countenances which seemed impatient at his delay, and the bloody sod became a couch of roses, and wounds and death but lovely ministers to the softest pleasures. Mark Anthony threw away a world for Cleopatra's lips, and Mark Anthony was but a type of his race. Speculative school-men may talk about the fanaticism of the early Moslem, and attribute to religious zeal his daring and his triumphs. But men who have known the world, who have turned over page after page of the human heart, who have seen it in the sunshine and the shadow, who have watched its throbbings from the palace to the hovel, will form more correct opinions. Fanaticism was indeed burning within him, but it was the fanaticism of love. Woman was the goddess of his idolatry—her lips the nectar for which his soul was athirst—her embrace the heaven for which he panted. No wonder he triumphed. No wonder that, with such rewards before him, two continents were insufficient to stay his victorious tread, and, at last, the wild music of the Saracen mingled with the roar of the waves, beating on the Western shore of Europe.

In all our moods, in spite of all our struggles, the charms of woman sway and bend us as easily as the north wind bows the waving grass. Even frailty, in such a tenement, catches the hues of Eden, and the pleased senses lull the severer judgment to sleep. Look upon the lovely beings now gliding through yonder stately mansion. The very air they breathe has turned to incense, and all things about them are bathed in a glorious beauty beyond the artist's skill to paint—beyond the human tongue to syllable. Yet all were not unstained by something worse than levity. Few could expose a breast no touch of sin had ever darkened—while over many of the richest flowers blooming there the hot breath of passion had passed, leaving an adder's egg to be warmed to life among leaves whose outward seeming was unchanged, and whose fragrance still was sweet.

Reclining on a sofa close to the music-stand was a young officer to whom the reader has been introduced. He seemed like one upon whom the enchantments around had lost their power, and his brow was darkened by thoughts that had no business there at such a time. He was roused by a light tap on the arm, and a sweet voice murmured—

"You are melancholy to-night, Mr. Wilson."

He turned quickly, and beside him was one who might have served as a model for the Grecian artist, who wandered from isle to isle, whispered his tale of love in every maiden's ear, treasured up every beauty and every grace in his memory, and then combining them all, produced his ideal of the Goddess of Love.

"Pardon me, Mrs. Winter, but I knew not that you were here, and Paradise would be gloomy without you."

"Pshaw! I thought better of you. Quit compliments, or give them the spice of originality."

"That were indeed difficult. I doubt if there is a single

flower in that wide field Genius has not already gathered and laid at your feet."

"Upon my word, you improve. But give me your arm —I wish to take a stroll with you through these rooms; first to show you off as my beau, and next because I am dying of curiosity, and I know no one else who can relieve me."

"I take it for granted," he remarked, after advancing a few steps, "that your last motive is the controlling one. Pray tell me in what I can gratify you."

"Now, that is what I call coming to the point, and smacks of the soldier much more than the fashionable gentleman. But I am only a fashionable woman, and cannot afford to be so direct. Besides, you know but little of woman's nature if you suppose that even the gratification of her curiosity could take precedence of the vanity of being escorted by so faultless a gentleman as Mr. Robert Wilson. Stop," she continued, as he was about to reply, "the compliment was given gratis, and I want no return, at least not in the same coin."

Approaching a deep window, she drew her companion within the heavy drapery of satin and gold.

"There," she said, "we have done enough to be talked about for the next half hour. At least twenty of *my* bosom friends will be whispering to *their* bosom friends, that a desperate flirtation is going on between you and me; and more than one will contrive to let my husband understand, in the most innocent manner imaginable, that I am madly in love with a young officer of the army."

"A pleasant intimation truly. And pray what will he say to all that?"

"Say! Nothing. He will forget that he has heard it before supper is over. He never loved me enough to be jealous."

"And did you love him?"

"Fie! for shame. You will give me a horrid idea of your West Point training directly. I do not care, though, if I do answer *this one;* but, remember, you must ask me no more such questions. No, I did not. He had enormous wealth—I had some beauty, and more accomplishments. It suited him to have a fine woman at the head of his establishment; it suited me *to have* an establishment. The word love was not written in our marriage contract, and I do not think it was mentioned by the priest at the altar. I never loved any one else. I am sure he never did. I do all I can to make his home pleasant and agreeable. He humors all my whims, and so we are the best possible friends, while neither makes the slightest pretensions to more. There, sir," she continued, "you have the confession of a pretty woman, which can do you no good, and may cost you something; for I do not make confessions gratis, if I do sometimes pay compliments in that way."

"I can think of nothing you could ask that is not granted beforehand."

"Thank you. If you please, we will proceed to business after your own fashion—plainly, and without circumlocution. Rumor has it that there has recently arrived in this great city a Circassian or Georgian, or some other Asiatic Princess, beautiful as an angel, and rich as she is beautiful. It is added that you have been so fortunate as to make her acquaintance. Is the story true, or any part of it!"

It was well that the heavy curtains shut out the light of the chandeliers; for a tell-tale paleness spread over the countenance of the young officer, and any one endowed with half the shrewdness and knowledge of society possessed by his fair companion, would have read his secret at a glance. The question was so sudden, so different from any thing he expected, that the power of utterance failed, and he almost gasped for breath.

"You do not answer me. Has my first question proved too much for all your liberal professions?"

With difficulty he commanded himself sufficiently to reply. "I was thinking what interest you could possibly have in such a matter."

"None, it may be, or it may be a great deal. Is the story true?"

"It is. At least I believe so."

"One thing more. You must introduce me. Do not think," she added quickly, "that I do not see and understand all the folly and meanness of running after titled strangers, who accept our hospitalities with an air of condescension, and repay the kindness we lavish upon them by unmeasured abuse or unfeeling criticism. I feel the degradation of such vile sycophancy; but it is the fashion, and while it is so, I must swim with the tide."

Seizing eagerly upon the opportunity thus offered to change the conversation, Mr. Wilson replied, "Why not establish a better fashion? Why not lead the way in teaching our countrywomen to respect American merit and American virtue? Believe me, there is more genuine worth in one honest American heart, than in a hundred of the worthless scions of a rotten aristocracy."

"Perhaps so. But it is not *worth* we seek in society. An easy address and polished manners are worth a thousand virtues."

"Oh, what a commentary," answered the young man, with emotion, "upon that gay throng through which we just now passed. In the islands of the East there is said to be a reptile, whose glossy skin of blended colors emits a light so beautiful and exhales an odor so delicious, that the traveller cannot resist the temptation to gather it to his bosom, though he knows its touch is deadly. How like to that reptile is the fashionable world you describe; and surely you, who are its queen, must know it well."

"Mr. Wilson, if most of my acquaintances had talked to me in the strain you have done to-night, I should have laughed in their faces, or turned on my heel and left them to their own meditations. If I have not done the same thing with you, it is, partly, because I suppose you did not care one straw whether I did or not."

"You wronged me then. I should have cared a great deal; for it would have made me think less of you than I hope ever to do. It would pain me deeply to believe that so fair a shrine held nothing within, the pure might love, the good claim kindred with, or the enthusiastic worship."

The splendid woman he addressed looked down with unconcealed embarrassment; but when she spoke her voice was clear and sweet. "I ought to be angry, but in truth I am better pleased than I care to express. I *am not* the heartless thing the world, *my* world, believes me, and I am glad you know it. Excuse me, however, for saying this conversation is rather too serious for a young gentleman of twenty-three or four, and a young woman scarcely his senior. When shall I have the pleasure of an introduction to this Eastern Peri?"

It was now the lieutenant's turn to feel embarrassed. He hesitated, stammered, and at last said he was afraid his acquaintance was too slight to venture on taking such a liberty.

"Go and ask her, man. I never intended to run the risk of being turned away from her door."

"Mrs. Winter," he replied gravely, almost sternly, "you know not what you ask. Besides, if your object be what I suspect, it would be useless. Her faith is Mahometan—

she receives few visitors—goes to no public assemblages, and could not be drawn, by any earthly inducement, into the brilliant society over which you preside."

"Is this so? Then half my interest in her is already gone. I do not care to conceal from you that it was the *êclat* of first introducing a princess, young, rich, and of peerless beauty, to the exclusives of upper-tendom, which made me so anxious for an introduction."

"As that inducement no longer exists, I suppose I may consider your application withdrawn."

"Quite the contrary. I am a true woman, Mr. Wilson. I see there are difficulties in the way, and those very difficulties determine me to persist in my original purpose. Of course I may depend on your assistance?"

"Pardon me, madam; but in this matter I cannot aid you."

"And why not?" she asked, angrily. "I fancy that the acquaintance of Pauline Winter would bring no discredit even upon a princess, at least in this republican land; and that a young lieutenant of the army need not be ashamed of the slight intimacy implied by calling upon a stranger in her society."

"Now you are angry and unjust. I will not answer you with taunts, as I might do; for that young officer, obscure as you deem him, unfriended as he is, with no fortune but honor, a good sword, and a strong arm to wield it, stands far too high in his own esteem to wound a woman's feelings. I cannot do what you ask, and I will not. Neither will I stay and listen to insults I cannot resent. With perfect sincerity, I wish you pleasant slumbers, and a happy waking."

He turned, but her hand was on his arm. "Stay. We must not part in anger. Excuse my hasty speech; for indeed, indeed, I meant not what you have chosen to impute to me. But you must admit your refusal to grant me so slight a favor is very, very strange."

"Slight!" and his whole frame shuddered as he repeated the word. "Slight! I tell you, granting that favor would go far towards making me the thing I most loathe on earth—a villain, an ungrateful, teacherous villain."

"More mystery. I have heard too much, or not enough."

"Then hear more. Ever since I have known Zerah Lile, I have been conscious of a wild intoxication in her presence—something I had never felt before—something I could not understand. Still I persuaded myself it was not love. Self-delusion was easy, for it was pleasant. But at last the truth broke on me, though not until my veins were filled with a fiery poison, compared with which the adder's would be innocent. For such a malady there was no cure. There was, however, one way to preserve my own respect, and prevent her from discovering that I had cherished a hopeless passion. That course I adopted, and swore never again to enter her presence of my own free will."

"You love her. Why not tell her so, and sue for her's in return. I thought you held the opinion that an American gentleman might pretend to the love of a queen."

"So I do. Would to God there was no barrier but that. Unfortunately she is already married to an American gentleman, and," he added, with unconscious sarcasm, "loves her husband."

"Married!" ejaculated the lady, and the thought flashed over her mind that if she could not secure the princess, it would be no mean triumph to capture the husband. "Married! Who is her husband? where is he now? and what is he?"

"As to *who* he is, I only know that he is my benefactor. As to *where* he is, I am equally ignorant, except that he told me he was going on a long journey. *What* he is, can be more easily answered. He is a man of wonderful endowments—gifted beyond the sons of earth with strength, courage, genius—all that can allure, and all that can command. Long a soldier in other lands, he returns to his own in the meridian of life, to pass the remnant of his days on the free soil where his infancy was rocked."

There was a pause. The man was wrapped in his own bitter reflections: The lady was regretting the failure of her scheme to dazzle the fashionables of the good city of Gotham. She was the first to break the silence. "I pity you." (Perhaps she felt *some portion* of the sympathy she expressed.) "From my soul I pity you. Our conference," she added, "has lasted too long. Take me back to the music room, and try to look more cheerful, or they will swear I have blasted all your young hopes in the bud."

As they walked on he drew a card from his pocket, and, stopping beneath one of the lights, wrote on it the name and address of Monsieur Evadne. "I could not," he remarked, as he handed it to her, "comply with your request. But here is the address of one who probably can. He is a banker, and is doubtless known to Mr. Winter."

"You are very kind; but I am afraid I shall not have the heart to pursue the matter any further."

Nevertheless she put away the card carefully in her bosom.

And this is fashionable life. High capacities for good frittered away upon idle follies. Talents that might be employed to improve and enlighten a generation, wasted upon petty rivalries, where even a triumph leaves a sting, and the mortification of failure carries always the added bitterness of self-contempt. Where the heart is deadened, the feelings indurated—every pure and every lofty passion withered, and the holiest emotions crushed and trampled on by a selfishness so low, so mean, so despicable, that the haughty Lucifer turns in disgust from the reptiles crawling into his kingdom, and leaves to meaner instruments the task of torturing a littleness his proud and lofty nature cannot stoop to punish.

Let us turn from the scenes where splendor only wraps corruption in its gaudy mantle, to follow the footsteps of one whose mind is yet unpolluted—whose instincts are still upright and honest. Lingering a few minutes after his fair companion had left him, he made his way unobserved to the front entrance, and was soon upon Broadway, that great thoroughfare which silence and solitude have long since abandoned. Where the beggar and the merchant prince meet upon terms of equality—where the morning always dawns upon brows blackened by crime, or haggard with dissipation—where the frail of one sex and the restless and the wretched of the other make a continuous stream from the first lamp-lighting to the rising of the sun, when they disappear in dark alleys, or darker human dens, to give place to the sons of avarice,

"Whose hearts of human flesh,
Beneath the petrifying touch of gold,
Have grown as stony as the trodden ways."

Not once, but often, the pen of genius has been employed in describing a great city at night, and giving substance to the impressions it never fails to make. But it is in the early morning that its deepest secrets are revealed—its widest contrasts manifest. It is then that the laborer, passing to his daily toil, burdened with the implements of his trade, makes his way with difficulty through the gilded equipages, and liveried footmen about some rich man's mansion—looks up at the illuminated windows, and wonders how it happens that he, with all the attributes of a man — heart, brain, feeling, honor, virtue — should be doomed to unceasing toil, while the mere caricatures of men who fill those luxurious chambers, whispering soft nothings into ears incapable of comprehending the language of intellect; or moving with slow and mincing gait over Brussels carpets softer and warmer than the couch from which the laborer has just risen; or lounging on a sofa, fan in hand, to recover from the *excessive fatigue* of having danced two sets in succession; should live on in ease and indolence, staining the current of society with the vices that alike distinguish them from, and sink them below, the chattering monkeys of interior Africa. Pass on honest son of toil, and repine not at the seeming hardness of the dispensation. Yours is far the happier lot. No French cooks, and no artificial stimulants are needed to give sweetness to the food you have earned by the sweat of your brow. Sleep comes unbidden to the hard couch of poverty, while the downy pillows of the dissolute woo the gentle goddess in vain, and drugs and opiates purchase the fevered slumber that is not rest, nor even forgetfulness, but a heavy stupor peopled by the spectres of conscience. You may fold your wife to your bosom with the proud conviction, that, though the rough winds of winter may have played among her tresses, and the summer's sun burned its freckles upon her cheek, no lawless lust has ever sipped a single dew-drop from her lip. The little infant who climbs upon your knee, bears your image reflected in its tiny features, and when his young breath, sweeter than the odor of rose-leaves, is fanning your cheek, no dark suspicion checks the outpouring of a father's love, and turns to gall a father's fondness.

A few stars yet linger in heaven. Like the pale watchers by a dead man's corpse, they have looked down through the long night upon corruption, and now they are dropping away; one by one, worn, wearied, sad and sorrowful. The lamps still burn along the street, and the curtain of night is but half withdrawn. Mark that closely muffled female hurrying rapidly up the pavement. Her husband is from home. Her children have been left untended and uncared for. She has passed the night in a libertine's arms, and the trembling fears of the morning are treading on the heels of the guilty joys of the evening. With nervous haste she is returning to the bed she has dishonored, shuddering at every step lest her disguise should be penetrated by the prying eyes of some acquaintance, who, she knows, would not hesitate to borrow her plate for a dinner party, and publish the shame of the lender to give zest to the entertainment.

Here comes one of a different order. That opera dress proclaims that she too has passed the night from home. But on that brow, lovely as it is, sin has set its signet ring, and shame long since blushed itself to death. She has left her lover (what a revolting application of the word!) not because *she* feared detection and exposure, but that *he* did. And now she is walking leisurely to one of those palaces of prostitution, where a few short years of splendid sensuality are purchased by a death of misery, and an eternity of woe.

There is another, the heavy cross on whose bosom betokens that her faith is Catholic. She has lingered at the confessional, but the warm kiss and the double benediction at parting proves that the penitent's long visit to the priest's chamber has been a sweet one to him, and the expression of her countenance, as she trips homeward, denotes that the penance imposed was not severe or displeasing.

Issuing from yonder cellar is a knot of drunken revelers, who have been vexing the ear of night with ribald songs and ribald jests. Squandering the hard earnings of an industrious parent—wandering through life without an aim, without an object, save the gratification of beastly appetites. With no tear for the wretched—no word of hope for the despairing—no balm for the suffering. A foul blot upon the moral creation, festering and rankling, and only endurable to the beholder because he knows it is eating away its own existence. Decay and death are written in the blood-shot eye, and on the bloated face, and the worm is already hungering for his loathsome banquet.

A little further on you may behold a young man with downcast look and staggering gait. Intoxication has not caused that reeling weakness, or filled his swimming brain with fire. He has passed his first night at a gaming table, and the hell of earth has given him a foretaste of the hell hereafter. Within a twelvemonth his employer will be robbed—his own fair fame blasted—the gray hairs of his parents dishonored—and a convict's cell in the penitentiary his narrow dwelling-place.

But is there nothing pure and lovely—nothing upon which the eye may dwell without repugnance, or the heart treasure among its holiest memories? Yes, much, very much an angel might look down upon with gladness. Here the widest charity atones for the narrowest selfishness. The loftiest aspiration relieves the lowest instinct. The purest piety combats the blackest infidelity. Truth, Genius, Poetry, and Eloquence move with unstained garments among their debasing contrasts. A world is gathered here. A human world, and a world of beasts and reptiles. How delightful the one, if it could be separated from the horrors of the other!

Our hero paused not to speculate upon the moving mass with which he mingled. In his own bosom there was food enough for thought. A great temptation had sprung upon him—he had yielded, for he was human. To know Zerah and not to love her, was to him an impossibility. Rapidly and strongly that love had twined itself about his heart strings, and there it would remain forever. But he was not one to deceive himself with the vain hope that it could be returned, nor did he wish it. From him she was fenced round by a double wall of gratitude and honor. Had these defences not existed, it would still have been the same. For worlds he would not have breathed one word of passion in her ear. Duty and self-respect required him to avoid the object of his idolatry, and prudence assured him that distance was his best protection. In his solitary chamber he thought over the past, and pondered on the future. To say that no bitterness mingled with his meditations would be to exempt him from the frailties of humanity. Yet was there no wavering, no unmanly attempts at self-deception—no dishonoring dreams of a guilty triumph in a trusting husband's absence. She was to him "a crystal gilded shrine." Once the thought flashed over his mind that Lile might never return—that she might again be free But almost instantly followed the question. What of it? Would she love me then? And the answer came, from the inmost depths of his own self-partial bosom, NO. Like the proudest of England's Peeresses, she would turn from a second suitor with the haughty response, "Equal the deeds of Marlborough before you seek the hand that once was his." Hour after hour he paced his little room, and when the sunbeams stole through the window, he threw himself into a chair and penned a letter to the Secretary of War. He asked to be relieved from the recruiting station at New York, and ordered to duty on the frontier. Enclosing the letter to the Commander-in-chief for his approval, he summoned all his fortitude to wait with patience an answer to his application. In a few days it came. How eagerly he broke the seals! His eye glanced over it, an icy coldness shook his hand, and the paper fell to the floor. His request was granted, but his look was that of a condemned criminal, rather than of the successful applicant. Such is human nature. Yesterday he would have given his little all to be assured of the contents of that paper. To-day he read it as a sentence of banishment from the only light that beamed on earth for him. A banishment easy in contemplation, dreadful in reality. Every nerve was rigid, and the blood stood stagnant in his veins. *Thought* only lived. That dreary pause revealed a life of crushed and broken hopes—of blasted joy and gnawing agony. Oh! why should one so young, so noble, be so sternly tried? Was it that ages ago, before earth's atoms were collected from chaos, the doom of everything that moves, and has its being here, was written on a changeless tablet, and hung around the Eternal Throne? or was it that fire and torture were needed to melt away the dross from the gold of mortality, and fit it for the hands of a Workman whose ends we know not—whose justice we dare not question? Not here, amid the shadows of this lower orb, may the answer be read. The messenger of an unseen Power walks among us in darkness, striking down whom he listeth. We know not whence the blow cometh nor wherefore, and never can know until that great day when all that is dark shall be made bright, and all that is mysterious shall be revealed.

Other thoughts than those of an overshadowed existence found a place in the mind of Wilson. Dim and afar off a solitary light rose on his vision. Through the mists of the present it beckoned him on over a rough and stony pathway to the splendid fane it lighted. No sweet flowers reared their stems of beauty around its base. No offering from the hand of friendship filled the air with incense. No home endearments knelt and worshiped there. Pity turned from its scorching blaze, and Mercy stilled the notes whose power to charm was gone. But neither the toilsome road, nor the cheerless end could banish the fascination of that Altar's flame. In every age, man has owned its influence. In every age, the high and the happy have sacrificed contentment and peace for its sake. Then why should the wretched hesitate? Surely they are Ambition's fittest votaries. To them it curtains the past, and gilds the future. It beamed upon the young officer like the first star that kindled its rays over Paradise, and he welcomed its coming as the Persian welcomes the advent of his fiery god. The bowed head was raised from the hand on which it leaned. With firm and erect carriage he passed from the barrack room to the street. His heart had grown old and hoary: and he went forth to battle with the world with all the life and energy of youth, added to the cooler judgment and unbending purposes of maturer years.

That day he addressed a note to Monsieur Evadne, advising him that he was about to leave New York, for the head-quarters of his regiment in the West—requesting him to inform Mrs. Lile, and excusing himself for not calling in person, upon the plea of necessary preparations for his hasty departure. If he expected an answer, none came. It was long afterwards, when stretched upon a bed to which wounds and fever had confined him, among the everglades of Florida, that he heard once more from his strange benefactor and his beautiful spouse.

CHAPTER VII.

And tall and strong and swift of foot were they,
Beyond the dwarfing city's pale abortions,
Because their thoughts had never been the prey
Of care or gain, the green woods were their portions;
No sinking spirits told them they grow gray;
No fashion made them apes of her distortions;
Simple they were, not savage; and their rifles,
Though very true, were not yet used for trifles."

WE must again tax the reader to journey from the city to the wilderness. Our history lies mainly with that mysterious man whose destiny seemed akin to that of the fated Jew who struck the Saviour on his way to the cross, and heard the awful doom thundered in his ear, "tarry thou till I come." Centuries have rolled away since those words of fearful import echoed upon Calvary. The mighty empire, which, stretching out its arms from the shores of the Mediterranean, grasped a world in its vast embrace, is numbered among the things that have been. The four arches of the Forum have crumbled away, and the traveler searches in vain for the spot, where the goddess of eloquence, bestowed upon the young Cicero the baptism of eternal fame. The lightning of heaven has descended upon the Pantheon, and its scathed and blackened walls have been succeeded by a Christian church. The sun-beam no longer gilds the Augustan halls, and the outlawed bandit lurks amid the gray ruins from whence issued the mandates that swept over earth, and found none bold enough to disregard them. Arches, vaults, temples, and porticoes—the long colonnade, and the splendid mausoleum—are no more. The grove, where fauns and satyrs danced to the lyre of Ovid, is a dreary waste, where death is for ever riding on the malaria that rises from the steaming plain. The forest of Hymettus, where Virgil gathered the honey that filled his verse, has disappeared, and the sweet thyme and the odorous wild-flower sickened and died when the shadow of the green leaves passed away. New thrones have risen—new empires ceased to be. But the wretch whose tongue reviled, and whose hand smote a crucified Redeemer, lives on. Still wherever he wanders, travels with him the curse, "tarry thou till I come." One by one his kindred and his tribe laid down in everlasting sleep. One by one he followed them to their final resting-place, and the fierce agony of the damned, gnawed his heart-strings, as the hollow sound made by the falling earth on the coffin-lid, shaped itself into words, and murmured, "tarry thou till I come." Winter came and went, but brought no whiteness to his raven locks. The hoariness was all within. Years flew by. The Roman eagles had winged their flight from Palestine, and the silver stars of the crescent glittered through the land of Judea; but no change had come for him. Beneath the banner of Lusignan, he stormed the infidel fortress of Cæsarea; a huge stone toppled from the shaken wall, and crushed him beneath its weight. The senses fled, but on the very verge of eternity the spirit stayed its flight. Strong hands rolled the granite mass from the mangled form; the bleeding body was stretched upon a litter of lances, and from the hollow tread of the soldiers, who bore him to the leech's care came up the words, "tarry thou till I come." He sought another land, and entered a great city, where the plague had made its loathsome home. He sat down by the side of the stricken victims, and held their infected hands within his own. He rested upon the same couch with the putrid corpse, and lifted the dead bodies with his naked arms, into the burial cart; but the pestilence scathed him not, and the groaning wheels, as they rolled away, screeched—"tarry thou till I come." Again, he stood upon a beetling crag, and looked down upon the foaming surf that roared around its base. With a wild laugh he leaped from the dizzy height into the dark gulf below. The waters closed around him, but the next surge threw him, stunned and bleeding on the shore, and the winds that swept over the sea, howled louder as they passed, "tarry thou till I come." And so, from age to age, and zone to zone, he has wandered on; denied the last refuge of mortality, yet suffering all mortality can endure. Like him had Bernard Lile been a wanderer. Like him had he grown familiar with agony, but, unlike the Jew, the dark night around him might have a morning. From his own haughty and imperious heart was distilled the venom that had made his life a thing of gloom and terror. Let that heart be touched and softened by repentance; let it bow in humility at the footstool of a power no mortal may resist, and the star which rose in beauty over Bethlehem, will give peace and brightness to the shadow and the night. Already there were indications of a change. It might take years to effect it—it might never come; but there is always hope when the struggle between good and evil has once commenced. Even as he stood near the dead bodies of the baffled assassins, in the forest of Arkansas, thoughts crowded upon him that brought forth fruits at another day, and as he turned to follow the footsteps of his guide, through the thick cane-brake before them, the stern lines of his compressed lips had almost relaxed into softness.

Rapidly through the forest, and over the wide prairie, they pressed on their lonely journey. From the women and the children in the few scattered houses on the route, they learned that there was a gathering of the hardy pioneers on the frontier—that Burleson, Rusk, Fannin, Milam, and many others, were in the field. Blood had been shed, and more was soon to flow. When they approached nearer to San Antonio, they learned that the town and fortress were garrisoned by about fifteen hundred Mexicans, under the command of General Cos. The next day they entered the camp of General Burleson, and found his forces to consist of six or seven hundred men, tolerably well armed with rifles and knives, but very poorly provided with artillery. The new comers were gladly welcomed. Lile walked through the encampment; marking with a soldier's eye all he saw, and calculating all they could accomplish. Undisciplined they certainly were; but there was in each bosom an abiding conviction of the justice of their cause, an indifference to life, if unaccompanied with liberty, and a self-confidence nothing but an infancy rocked amid dangers can give, and nothing but death can take away. In that army there was no brawling, no gambling, no drunkenness. The first settlers of Texas were earnest and sober men. Their lonely lives had imparted a deep seriousness of character to the most thoughtless among them. They did not *plunge* into revolution. They *walked* into it, with their eyes open; knowing the odds against them, and scorning it, when Freedom gave the word. For such men fetters are never forged.

On the fifth of December, a tall, gray-haired man, whose firm tread and swelling muscles told that time had stolen away none of his strength, stepped from the ranks, and held brief conference with the general. Then turning to where the citizen soldiery were drawn up in rude imitation of regular order, his voice swelled bold and high as he exclaimed, "Who will join Old Ben Milam in storming the Alamo?" There was no preface; no stirring appeal to their patriotism; no glowing pictures of glory to be won in the perilous undertaking; but the simple question, repeated in a voice clearer and louder than the trumpet's call, "Who will join Old Ben Milam in storming the Alamo?" Storm the Alamo! Storm a stone fortress bristling with cannon, and defended by fifteen hundred regular troops! Storm it, and with what? With undisciplined militia, armed only with rifles and hatchets! Aye! it is even with such tools that iron man expects to pick his way through the granite walls of the enemy's stronghold. The question was so sudden—the men so unprepared for such a desperate proposition, that for a brief space no voice was raised in reply.

"If, sir," said Bernard Lile, stepping deliberately to the side of the veteran Texan, "you will accept a stranger's aid, there is one rifle at your service."

"You might have said *two*, captain," added Simpson; "for I wouldn't miss that sight for the best plantation on the Mississippi."

Three hundred more rushed to the side of Milam. Three hundred such as roused Ferguson from his eyrie on King's Mountain, and struck the death-blow to British dominion in America. They paused not to ask what means they possessed to accomplish the daring deed. One man had been found bold enough to propose it, and around that man rallied three hundred "children of the the chase," whose nerves of twisted steel had never been shaken by disease or debauchery, and in whose vocabulary the word *fear* had never been written With them to resolve, was to act; and in two hours from the time that old man's voice rang along the lines, they were on the march for the fortress that a few weeks later became immortal. Formed in two divisions, the first under Milam himself, the second under Col. Johnson, they entered the suburbs of San Antonio. A sharp fire of grape and musketry was opened upon them from the town. The heavy roll of a twenty-four pounder from the fortress succeeded. The iron globe hurtled, with savage ferocity, through the street. Another and another followed, until the house of Antonio de la Garza, in which the division under Milam had taken shelter, was riddled with cannon-balls. Unaccustomed to regular warfare—without scientific knowledge, or the instruments necessary to render it effective, the cause of the republicans looked desperate indeed. In this extremity, the miltary experience of Lile enabled him to render inestimable service. Seizing a crow-bar, he set the example of opening a passage from one house, through the partition walls, to another.

"Remember that trick, boys," shouted Milam, as he leaped through the opening; "it may help us at a pinch another day."

From house to house the daring pioneers burrowed their way. Once within rifle range, a close and deadly fire was opened upon the enemy's artillery. The Mexican gunners disappeared as rapidly as a swarm of insects is swept away by the wing of the tempest; and when the night closed in, every piece, within range of the Texan shot, was abandoned. Under cover of the darkness, the assailants employed themselves in strengthening the position they had gained. At day-light, they discovered that the Mexicans had occupied the house-tops in their front. Throughout the day the fire was kept up on both sides with little apparent advantage. As the shades of evening began to fall, Milam grew restless and impatient.

"This will never do," he said; "our powder will give out. We *must* make a rush."

"I think you can do better, Colonel," suggested Lile. "Yonder house to the right commands the enemy's position. If that is taken he must give way."

"By heavens! you are right," answered the old man, with flashing eyes. "Will *you* lead a detachment across that street? It takes a bold man to do it; for the bullets are flying as thick as musquitoes on the Brazos."

"No, Colonel. I came here to follow, not to lead; but if you will send an officer and five or six men to occupy it, I and my friend Simpson, will engage to make a way into that house, in five minutes, if the bullets were twice as thick as they are."

"Quick, then. Here's McDonald, who never feared the devil himself, shall support you."

With a rifle in one hand, a crow-bar in the other, Lile and Simpson leaped from the window into the street, They reached the opposite side, and the crow-bars, impelled by arms that gave them the force of a battering-ram, had shaken the solid door from its hinges, before the Mexicans seemed to be aware of their object. A shower of bullets began to patter around them. It was too late. The door fell, and the two friends leaped within the cover of the building, just as McDonald and his men descended to the street on the opposite side. A harder task was before the lieutenant. The first surprise of the Mexicans was over, and a hundred muskets were levelled at his little band. Two fell to rise no more, and two others were badly hurt. Without further loss, he gained the house, and the enemy lost no time in falling back to a new position. The night of the 6th was employed by the enemy in opening a trench on the Alamo side of the river, and strengthening a battery on a cross street. At daylight on the 7th, a continued roll of musketry from the trench, and the sullen boom of the guns of the battery, told that the work of death had re-commenced. A thick smoke settled over the Mexican lines, and sheltered the artillerists from the unerring rifles of the Texans. Incessant flashes of lurid light chequered the gloomy curtain, and the dense vapor rose and fell as the round shot tore through it, with a fierce, hissing sound, on their dreadful errand. For the first time the hardy yeomen felt the unequal nature of the contest they had so gallantly provoked. For the first time they began to experience that uneasy feeling which is so apt to afflict young soldiers who are compelled to sustain a galling fire without the chance of returning it effectually.

Milam saw the unwonted depression spread among his men, and all the lion of his nature was roused. "Stand to it, boys," he shouted. "Remember Zacatecas. Learn from her that unless you gorge the tyrant with his own blood, he will soon be lapping that of your wives and children. Keep behind your sand bags, and let him waste his powder upon them. We'll get to closer quarters when the sun goes down."

The gallant bearing of their commander dispelled the momentary panic of the troops, and a loud shout answered his cheering words. Satisfied with this encouraging demonstration, Milam turned towards the quarter occupied by the division under Col. Johnson. He gained the middle of the street—there was a quick roll of musketry—the old man stopped—reeled—fell, and his gray hairs, clotted with blood and dirt, were strewed upon the ground. Instantly a tall form was at his side. With a giant's strength, he lifted the dying martyr in his arms, and bore him back among his men.

"This is a dark day for Texas," said Bernard Lile, composing the manly limbs of the hero as he spoke. "We may take yonder fortress, and we will, for the earth that has drank the blood of Milam can never bear a foreign yoke; but a hundred fortresses would be insufficient to pay his country for the life that has fled."

So died the first great martyr to the cause of Texan independence. His death-couch was the unpaved floor of a Spanish hovel—his winding-sheet a soldier's blanket. But the cloth of scarlet and gold which covered Cœur-de-Lion on his kingly bier, hid no bolder heart; and the steel-clad nobles, who gathered around the dead sovereign, shook with no sincerer grief, than the rude forest children who bent above the lifeless form of the Republican Leader. There was no outward burst of grief—no maddening calls for vengeance on the foe. The fire of rage died out in the presence of a deeper and a deadlier passion. The light that gleamed from every eye was the cold, concentrated, merciless glare of the tigress, when the hunter's shot has drawn the life-blood of her cub. A hasty consultation was held, and Col. Johnson selected to take the place of their lamented commander. At ten o'clock that night, in the midst of a cold, drenching rain, they stormed the house of Antonio Navarro. Next morning the Zambrano Row was taken: the enemy being driven with murderous fury from every room. The priest's house now fell, and the Mexicans were completely shut up in the Alamo. To a soldier like Lile, it seemed that the most serious work of the colonists was now only about to begin. They had nothing with which to batter down the walls. There was nothing with which to cover their nearer approach. To scale them looked like madness, and yet to scale them was the fixed determination of every officer and every man in that dauntless band.

"We have hunted the wild beast to his den," said Lile to a rugged forester by his side; "but I do not see how we are to get him out."

"By God," replied the man, "if I hadn't seen you do things Gen. Jackson would study about before trying, I'd half suspect you of being a little cowardly."

"You are welcome to suspect what you please, if you

will only get over those walls as quick as I do. Still, I cannot see how it is to be done."

"Eat them down with our teeth, if there's no other way. Old Ben Milam will never rest in his grave until we do it."

"Well, I do not intend to eat any of those stones, but I intend to be the first on top of them, and my hand shall be the first to quell a foe beyond them. Will you mount with me?"

"I'll try; but to tell the truth and shame the devil, I don't believe I'm able to keep up with you."

He had hardly ceased speaking before a white flag was seen to emerge from the fortress.

"There," said Lile, pointing it out to his companion, "our bargain is spoiled. They are about to capitulate."

"Yes," was the bitter response, "the white-livered dogs have knocked under, and Milam's blood is not half revenged. Never mind—another day they shall pay for it."

True enough, the bearer of that flag, was the bearer of a proposition to surrender. General Martin Perfecto de Cos, with an army of fifteen hundred regulars, protected by a strong town and a still stronger fortress, surrendered to three hundred militia, and was himself the messenger of his own disgrace to his master. History records no more daring achievement, and contains *but one* more glorious chapter.

The volunteers, who had stormed the town and fortress of San Antonio de Bexar, dispersed, and returned to their several homes, leaving about a hundred men under command of Col. Travis, to keep possession of the post they had so gallantly won. Simpson, who had been badly wounded in the assault, was removed by Lile to Carlos's Rancho on the river below.

Our story still lingers around the spot so memorable in the annals of Texas. Early in February, courier after courier came in from beyond San Antonio, with the startling intelligence that Santa Anna had collected a great army, and was marching in person toward the revolted province.

"Bloody with spurring, fiery red with speed,"

these couriers rushed from post to post, to spread the news of the coming danger. The dictator proclaimed in advance his intention not to subjugate, but to destroy. From the Rio Grande to the Sabine, it was known to be his fixed resolve to spare neither age nor sex—to leave, in his own phraseology, "nothing of Texas but the recollection that it had been." Unawed by numbers—unappalled by the threatened doom, the citizen soldiers prepared to breast the advancing tide. It was well understood that the first fury of the tempest must burst upon the Alamo, and, as the little band under Travis were wholly inadequate to its defence, he was again and again urged to blow up the walls and retreat.

"Never!" replied the dauntless patriot. "When these walls are blown down, it shall be by Mexican cannon, not by American powder."

Again he was told that his force was insufficient to man the walls; that he must be cut off, and every man would be sacrificed.

"I know it," was the stern reply, "but I want to teach these barbarians what Americans can do. I know that we shall be sacrificed, but the victory will cost the enemy dear, and in the end be worse for him than a defeat."

On the 21st of February, the advanced division of the army of Santa Anna, under Ramirez Sezma, sat down before the devoted citadel. A flag was sent in, with a summons to surrender at discretion.

"Go back and tell your chief," answered the heroic

Travis, "that I have lived with unshackled limbs, and by the blessing of God, intend to die so."

Slowly from the church of Bexar now rose a blod-red flag. Upon its crimson folds no motto was written—no device appeared. Above the temple of the living God—in mockery of the Redeemer's precepts, there it waved, a dark and awful red.

"See," said Crocket, as the merciless signal caught the breeze, "they give us fair warning to expect no quarter."

"They had better wait till we ask it," answered Bowie, a stern smile spreading around his thin lips, and giving to his countenance that peculiar expression of deadly determination, before which, it is said, the boldest on the frontiers had quailed.

"You are wrong, Bowie," said Travis, bitterly, "for in that case they never would have had an opportunity of displaying this amiable trait of the Mexican character. But come away from the walls. Round shot and shell are not the most agreeable aquaintances in the world, and in five minutes more a swarm of them will be traveling in this direction."

The commander of the Almo was mistaken. The Mexican general was in no hurry. Slowly and deliberately he drew his lines, and erected his batteries. About three o'clock on the morning of the 23d, a rocket ascended from the head-quarters of the Mexicans: rising high into the air, it turned slowly and gracefully at the culminating point—the dry powder ignited, brilliant sparks for a moment illuminated the heavens, and all again was black. A half hour later, another fiery messenger went up towards the stars. Simultaneously, the roar of five different batteries shook the solid earth. Darkly, as the pestilence walks, the round shot hurtled on its way; with an angry kiss, the heavy shell sped towards its mark, leaving a trail of light behind.

But shot and shell had a common destination. For twenty-four hours, without ceasing, that blasting hail beat upon the doomed garrison. For twenty-four hours they bore up under the ceaseless storm of infernal missiles. Not an eye winked—not a cheek blanched. Calmly, fearlessly they waited for the nearer struggle. At length it came. A dark column, with the regiment of Tampico at its head, moved in double quick time to the assault. The fierce cannonade had ceased, and nothing but the tramp of marching men disturbed the silence of the early morning. Still as the copper snake in its coil, lay Travis and his men. Nearer and nearer came the tread of the stormers. At once a dozen fire-balls were ignited and hurled from the ramparts. The dark space over which the Mexicans were marching, was lighted up as if by magic. Even the buttons on the uniforms of the foe were distinctly visible. "Now let them have it!" shouted Travis, and a sheet of flame ran along the walls. Curses, dying groans, and the confused noise of armed men jostling against each other, proclaimed the fatal accuracy of the riflemen. Another volley succeeded, and the famed regiment, baptised "invincible" by Santa Anna, broke and fled in wild terror to the encampment, all that day, with a red spot upon his cheek, Sezma moved among his men. Threats of punishment were freely mingled with promises of reward. Their pride, their patriotism was appealed to. They were reminded of their former achievements, and stung by comments on the infamy of being baffled by a handful of raw militia. The next morning, two columns moved to the assault. One from Bexar, west, and the other from Lavilleta, south. The artillery of the garrison, under the command of Major Evans, ploughed bloody furrows through the advancing columns, but not until they came within rifle range did they falter. Upon that compact mass every shot from the garrison told. File after file went down in quick succession. They paused—huddled together like frightened wild fowl—a shower of grape swept through them—a volley of rifle bullets completed the panic—with a yell of terror they threw away their muskets, and fled behind their entrenchments.

The Mexican general had suffered too grievously, and his men were too much disheartened to venture upon a third attack. Again the roar of artillery swept over the Prairie, and frightened the wild deer to more distant pastures. On the first of March, thirty-two men, from Gonzales, cut their way through the enemy and joined the garrison. With these was Bernard Lile. He had left his wounded friend to take part in the game of life and death so boldy played by Travis. Never has the pen of history been called upon to record an exploit like that these devoted patriots had performed. Thirty-two men cutting their way through an army of four thousand! Seeking no reward—impelled by no hope of safety—guided and animated by no feeling but patriotism, and asking nothing but the privilege to die side by side with their countrymen. Desperate men have often been known to resort to desperate expedients for the preservation of life. But such was not the motive of the men of Gonzales. Outside the enemies' lines they were already safe. They cut their way in to die. It was the martyrdom of liberty they sought; and as long as the silver waters of the San Antonio glide towards the sea, they will have a voice to murmur their fame.

On the 3d day of March, Santa Anna himself, with strong reinforcements, arrived and assumed the command. A new battery of heavier metal was established, and lines of cavalry, to prevent the possibility of escape, were drawn between the entrenched camps that encircled the fort. Travis saw that his last hour was rapidly approaching.

Resolving to make one more effort—not for life, but for Texas—he called his men together, told them plainly that in two days, at farthest, unless succor arrived, certain butchery awaited them, and asked who would undertake to bear a letter, through the Mexicans, to the President of the Texan Convention. The men listened in silence and with folded arms. Not a man moved—not a voice was raised in reply. A shade gathered on the manly brow of their leader.

"What!" he exclaimed, "have I no one here bold enough to risk his life singly for Texas?"

David Crocket stepped from the ranks; his buckskin hunting-shirt was stiffened with clay, and blackened with powder-smoke, but his fresh and ruddy complexion gave no token of the fatigue he had undergone, and his bearing was as calm as when he walked down the aisle of the representative Hall at Washington.

"You see, Colonel," he began, "it's not because any of us are afeard to die, but because none of us wants to lose his share in what is coming. When I was in Congress, I noticed that all the fellows were striving for glory; but talking wasn't one of my gifts, and precious little glory fell to my lot. Now here, behind these rocks, the question is put in a shape that I feel able to take a hand. I'm arter glory, Colonel, mixed up with a sprinkle of Mexican hide and tallow. I reckon these boys are much of my way of thinking; and if you ain't got no objection we'll just stay where we are."

Amidst the applauding murmurs which followed the Old Hunter's harangue, Bernard Lile walked to the side of the commanding officer.

"I am comparatively a stranger, Colonel," he said, "and it is most fit the lot should fall on me. I came here to serve Texas, and it matters little to me in what capacity the service is rendered."

"Let him go, Colonel," shouted a dozen voices at once, "we saw him when he lifted old Ben Milam from the street, and if mortal man can get through yonder lines, he will do it."

So it was arranged that Bernard Lile should that night be the bearer of despatches to the President of the Convention, or to General Houston, (then supposed to be in Victoria,) as circumstances might determine.

When darkness came, Lile was ushered from the gate by Travis himself. "God bless you!" said the hero, grasping the hand of his messenger for the last time. "We shall meet no more. In a few days, I and the brave fellows with me will be food for the vultures. You, sir, are said to have a heart that never knew fear, and an arm that never met its equal. Use both for Texas, if you would have the blessing of a dying man. Say to our friends to take no thought about avenging our deaths. We will avenge ourselves. But tell them to learn from us that life without liberty is worthless, and if they cease to struggle while one hostile foot is left upon the soil of Texas, we will come back to curse it. Again, good-bye. In another world we may recall the memory of this hour. In this one we are parted for ever."

Lile returned the firm pressure of his hand. He spoke not of hope, for he knew that none existed. He offered no encouragement, for he felt such words would be an insult to that dauntless chief. But as he turned away, he resolved that more than one Mexican ghost should, before the morrow came, precede the gifted and self-sacrificing patriot to the spirit land.

Knowing little of those with whom he had to contend, and believing they would make an effort to escape during the night, Santa Anna had taken the extraordinary precaution of placing three lines of sentinels between his encampment and the fort. Approaching the first of these, Lile put in practice the arts he had learned among the Thugs of India. Throwing himself upon the ground he wound along with the noiseless motion of the serpent, towards his intended victim. Suddenly he stood erect by the sentry's side. Grasping the astonished soldier by the throat, he drove a long knife to his heart. Without relinquishing the hold upon his neck, he let him sink slowly to the earth, to prevent the clatter of his arms in falling. A gurgling noise escaped from the windpipe when the pressure was removed; a slight shiver shook the body, but nothing else gave warning that a soul had fled. At the second line, and again at the third, the same scene was reenacted. A thousand yards south-east from the Alamo, an entrenched camp lay directly in his path. Here he anticipated little vigilance would be exercised. With three lines of sentinels between them and the fort, and strong cavalry pickets in every direction outside, it was to be expected that they would feel tolerably secure. He was not, however, a man to omit any precaution where the least uncertainty existed. Stealthily he crossed the ditch and clambered over the earthworks. Profound silence reigned throughout the encampment. Slowly he passed through to the opposite side, assured himself that there was nothing in that quarter to interfere with his escape, and then returned among the tents. The first he entered he judged from its position to be that of a captain of a company. A dark lantern was dimly burning within. The solitary occupant slept soundly—from that sleep he never awakened. With the blood that gushed in a crimson torrent upon the camp-bed, Lile traced upon the canvas wall: "Remember the blood-red flag of Bexar." Softly he crept to another tent, and another, and wherever he went, the angel of death went with him. By accident his hand touched the foot of a soldier who slept less soundly than his comrades. Starting up he grasped the intruder, and fiercely demanded his name. Scarcely a second elapsed before the Mexican sank with a dying groan across the mouth of the tent; but the alarm was given—it spread from tent to tent; lights flashed through the encampment; and the "long roll" sent forth its startling notes. Swiftly as the flight of the night-hawk, Bernard Lile cleared the works and sped across the rolling prairie. The din of the camp rose behind him—squadrons of horse were galloping around—the sharp challenge of the pickets were heard on every side. Without winding or turning he ran the dangerous gauntlet, and was soon far beyond the reach of pursuit.

Through the 4th and 5th of March a heavy bombardment was kept up by the Mexicans. At day-break on the sixth they rushed to the final assault. They were met by a shower of grape and bullets too thick and deadly for any Mexican courage to stand,—they broke and fled in wild disarray towards the town. They were with difficulty halted and reformed by their officers. Again they rushed on; this time bearing the blood-red banner in their midst.

"Mark the man who carries that flag," said Travis to the powder-grimed rifleman by his side.

The sharp crack of the rifle followed, and the flag went down. Another hand raised it aloft, another rifle shot succeeded, and again it fell. It was caught up once more; once more the report of the rifle was heard, and the bunting fell for the last time. There was no hand in that host bold enough to raise it again.

"Toting that bloody rag aint so funny after all," muttered the grim rifleman, as he reloaded his piece.

The enemy had in the meantime gained the wall and

planted the scaling-ladders against it. Strong hands seized them, and hurled ladders and mounting Mexicans to the ground together. Rifle and pistol shots were poured upon the confused mass. Again the stormers scattered and fled over the plains. Santa Anna himself halted the fugitives. With bitter execrations of their cowardice, were mingled the most tempting promises of promotion and reward. He reminded them that the little garrison must be worn down by ten days' incessant fatigue and night watching, and spoke of the deep disgrace of being baffled by an enemy so few in numbers—so ill prepared for prolonged resistance. Strong reinforcements were brought up. The artillery played incessantly upon the fort to cover their approach. Thus protected and supported, they were driven once more to the assault. The rifles of the garrison made wide havoc in the advancing ranks. Ladders were thrown down, and stones toppled upon the struggling crowd below. But new foes succeeded; they swarmed up the wall and mixed with its defenders. Overborne by numbers—with no chance to reload—the Americans clubbed their guns, and fought on until the last man expired. None asked foi quarter,

"But each struck singly, silently, and home,
And sank outwearied rather than o'ercome."

Travis remained upon the wall until two shots passed through his body. He fell, and General Mora rushed up to dispatch him. The dying hero raised himself upon his elbow, and thrust his good sword through the heart of the Mexican. They were found side by side in death; the sword of Travis, clenched in his stiffened hand, and still remaining in the breast of Mora. Around David Crocket there was a horrid wall of human bodies. His death was sudden and without pain. The freshness of his features was unchanged, and a strange smile rested upon his rigid lips. Death had overtaken him before it faded, and glued it there till the worm came to eat it away.

Such was the dictator's first achievement in Texas. Fifteen hundred of his dead and wounded soldiers told the fearful story of "what Americans can do." Over that spot, some day, a monument will rise to meet the skies, with the proud inscription, "Thermopylæ had *one* messenger of defeat, but the Alamo had *none!*"

CHAPTER VIII.

"Yet though destruction sweeps these lovely plains
Rise, fellow-men: our country yet remains.
By that dread name we wave the sword on high,
And swear for her to live—for her to die."

Bernard Lile reached the Cibolo, and followed that stream to its junction with the San Antonio. Here he rested until the daylight would enable him to make such observations as his situation demanded. The direct route to Victoria would leave Goliad, where Fannin was stationed, considerably to the right; but that involved the necessity of crossing the open prairie, which would, without doubt, be continually scoured by Mexican horse. At another time the danger from this quarter would have had little influence on his course; but he knew not of what importance the despatches he carried might be to the Texan commander, and resolved to encounter no risk in their delivery that could be avoided. When morning came, he soon ascertained that the prairie was alive with light troops, and no alternative remained for him but to make for Goliad, keeping as much as possible within the protection of the timber. The toilsome distance was accomplished with a rapidity almost miraculous. Arrived at Goliad, he communicated to Colonel Fannin all he had seen at Bexar—the inevitable fate of the devoted garrison, and the probability that his own post would be the next point of attack. That gallant officer engaged to send Travis's despatches to General Houston, and Bernard Lile determined to remain at Goliad, and share the fate of Fannin and his comrades. This course was rendered more agreeable, by finding Tom

Simpson in the camp, completely recovered from his wound. The force under Colonel Fannin was composed almost entirely of volunteers from the States—men who had left the comforts and security of home, to do battle in the cause of liberty—not mere adventurers, who had no ties to bind them to the land of their birth, and who were willing to take any chance of bettering their desperate fortunes—not paupers, to whom the camp was a refuge from starvation—nor hardened miscreants, to whom war and butchery was a delight—but young men, for the most part educated and refined, who left peace, security, and plenty, for peril, privation, and death. In their boyhood, they had read the story of the revolution, and their little hearts bounded with indignant anger at the recital of the wrongs our fathers had suffered. In manhood the tale was borne to them, that, in a neighboring land, their kindred and friends were threatened with chains and the gibbet, and the generous impulse of the child swelled into the sterner resolve of the man. Urged on by that love of liberty engendered by American principles, they grasped their rifles, and rushed to take part in the struggle begun by freedom against the myrmidons of despotism. They were a glorious band: swayed neither by the lust of conquest nor of spoil, but frankly periling life and fortune that a people might be redeemed,

> "How sweetly on the ear such echoes sound!
> While the mere victors may appal or stun
> The servile and the vain, such names will be
> A watchword till the future shall be free."

Marching berefooted, not half clothed, and often not half fed, they had already gone through an amount of privation and fatigue which would have dispirited a veteran corps. Yet these young soldiers, fresh from the luxuries of home, bore up under every discouragement, with a fortitude unsurpassed by that of the army of Washington in the camp of Valley Forge. The high qualities they had exhibited in garrison were about to be tested still further in the open field. The Alamo had fallen, and its brave defenders—crushed, not conquered, had been swept from the path of the invader. The slightest acquaintance with military operations indicated Goliad as the next point of attack. On the 12th of March, Colonel Fannin sent Captain King, with his company, to bring in some unprotected families from the Mission of Refugio. To divide his force at such a time was not the act of a prudent military leader, but it indicated the presence of a higher and a nobler quality—humanity. The great Bruce, in one of his direst straits, halted his little band, and freely exposed his own life, and the lives of those who were with him, to English butchery, rather than leave a single woman in distress. Amid all the achievements that made his name immortal, none shine with a more enduring lustre. The hand that crushed Sir Henry de Bohun's helm—the courage no danger could daunt—the energy no despair could chill, and the wisdom that broke the yoke of England, may cease to be remembered, but the heart that melted at a woman's wail is embalmed for ever. Actuated by like feelings, Fannin sent King to the Mission, and by this act sacrificed, in the end, his own life, and spread mourning through Texas and the States. King encountered an overwhelming Mexican force at the Mission. Taking refuge in the church, with twenty-eight men, he defended himself with desperate courage until the arrival of Lieutenant Colonel Ward, with a battalion, to his relief. The Mexicans then drew off, but soon after, being also reinforced, returned and reinvested the church. Three several assaults were made, and successively repulsed with immense slaughter. Some boys, with a commissioned officer, occupied the yard of the church, and fought with such obstinate valor as to call forth the warmest plaudits of Ward. Against this point the efforts of the Mexicans were now directed. Formed in close column, firmly and silently they came on. At the distance of a hundred yards, they deployed into line—detachments from the two wings took the yard in flank, and the centre attacked fiercely in front. The fate of the "little brothers," as they were christened, appeared inevitable. A tall and powerful man glided among them; with a quick step he passed from one to the other; "Keep under cover, and hold your fire my little heroes; wait for the signal." The enemy approached within thirty yards—the rifle of Bernard Lile—for it was he—rose to his shoulder,—and the foremost Mexican bit the dust. Quick as thought, the boys responded to the signal. Their wasting fire speedily disordered the Mexican ranks. An officer in the uniform of a colonel rode among them, fiercely waving his sword, and threatening instant death to the fugitives. The shattered lines was reformed. They were greeted by withering volleys from the yard; still they pressed on steadily and sternly over the dying and the dead. The leading files were in a few feet of the stone fence, when another hurricane of bullets swept through them, and again they were broken. Again that daring officer checked their flight; again he renewed their disordered ranks; again he led them to the assault. "There," said Bernard Lile, "is the truest soldier I have ever seen in a Mexican uniform. It is a pity to harm him; but my little favorites here must not be sacrificed for a punctilio." Even as he spoke, his eye was glancing along the barrel of his rifle. A sharp report followed. The Mexican reeled in the saddle—grasped convulsively the mane of his horse, then tumbled heavily to the ground. A single volley drove the disspirited assailants from the field. Profiting by the leisure afforded him, Ward made a careful inspection of his command. Three of the boys were too badly wounded to recover. His losses in other respects were trifling. The inspection, however, revealed the appalling fact, that not three rounds of ammunition remained. The enemy had disappeared, but they were unquestionably close at hand, and were probably only waiting for reinforcements to renew the attack. To retreat was unavoidable, yet a retreat in the face of an enemy so greatly superior, across an open prairie, with no cavalry, and no artillery, was an achievement Xenophon would have hesitated to attempt. Night came, and the order to march was given; but first it became necessary to communicate to the wounded boys the painful fact that it was impossible to remove them. The reply of the little sufferers deserves to be perpetuated in tablets of gold: "Never mind us; put some water in reach, and save yourselves." The big tears came to the eye of Simpson, who had fought like a lion throughout the day.

"By the Lord," he exclaimed to Lile, "this shall not be. I'll carry one myself—wont you take another, captain?"

"Willingly," answered Lile, "would I engage to carry twice the weight to the Gaudaloupe, if it would save them; but it would be cruel to move them, Tom. The one who is least hurt has not three hours to live. It is best to let them die in peace."

A soft couch was made by spreading the blankets, taken from the dead Mexicans around the church, upon the floor. The dying boys were laid upon it—water was given them —with sobs and tears their comrades bade them adieu, and set out upon their hazardous march. Simpson was the last to leave the church. It was fearful to look upon the fierce grief that shook his sturdy frame. Kneeling upon the bed of blankets, he pressed a kiss upon each of their pale cheeks, and recorded a dark oath, which drew tears from many a Mexican mother and wife in after years.

"Them boys," he muttered, as he walked along, "will be chopped into sausage meat, by the d—d brutes who couldn't look them in the face when they had guns in their hands. If God spares me, for every drop of blood they've lost, I'll draw ten from Mexican veins, and I'm not sure but what it will git to be twenty, before I begin to be particular in counting."

Darkly the little band made their way towards Victoria. At the crossing of the San Antonio, Lile and Simpson who were attached to no company, and who, since their entrance into Texas, had fought whenever and wherever it suited them, abandoned the main body with the purpose of rejoining Col. Fannin, whose post, they had no doubt, was by this time beleaguered by the enemy. They reached Goliad to find that it had been abandoned by the Americans. In obedience to an order from Gen. Houston, Col. Fannin had evacuated the place on the 19th of March, and commenced a toilsome retreat to Victoria. Following in the track of the retreating force, our adventurers learned slowly, one by one, the events we shall condense into a continuous narrative.

Col. Fannin's command amounted to two hundred and seventy-five effective men. Four companies of infantry, under Captains Shackelford, Pettis, Duval, and McManeman, with a few regular artillerists under Captain Westover. The river was crossed with difficulty, on account of the inefficiency of the teams drawing the cannon. The guns were finally dragged up the bank by the men—the untiring Shackelford himself wading into the stream, and seizing a wheel, set the example of rolling it up with his own hands.

After passing the San Antonio, and when within five miles of the Coleto timber, a halt was determined on, against the earnest remonstrances of Captain Shackelford, for the purpose of resting the wearied men and cattle. That gallant officer, with a prudence even more commendable than the high courage that led him to the field, insisted upon continuing their march to the timber, where the Mexican cavalry would be useless, and the men in some degree protected by the trees from the overwheming odds the enemy were hourly expected to bring against them. He was unfortunately overruled, and the command halted where it was. In one of his letters to the president of the convention, Col. Fannin had said, that while he had no superior as a *company* officer in Texas, he had grave doubts of his own fitness for the command of a considerable force. Whether this criticism upon his own merits was just, or whether it flowed from too great modesty, can never be satisfactorily determined. He was cut off before time and opportunity were allowed for the solution of the question. It is certain, however, that he was one of the most gifted, as he was one of the bravest, of the early defenders of Texas. The two errors contemporary testimony ascribe to him were venial faults. The first was dictated by humanity—the second sprung from the lion-like nature that despised danger too much to guard sufficiently against its approaches. The one has its apology in the best feelings of the heart—a little experience in the field would soon have corrected the other. Still it is permitted to the friends of those who fell, to monrn a mistake that had so deplorable an end. Had the counsel of Shackelford been followed, the bloodiest page in the history of Texas might never have been written, and the lamented Fannin himself might now be alive, to enjoy the shelter of that tree whose infant roots his life-blood watered.

For an hour the halt continued. To the dweller in cities that space seems brief and unimportant. It is only another drop of life wasted—another talent buried. But how often has the fate of armies and of empires hung upon that little spot of time. An hour, and Fannin would have been in easy reach of the Coleto timber. An hour, and oh! how different would have been the tale borne to the widowed wives, agonized sisters, and bereaved mothers of a band as chivalrous as Rome or Sparta ever sent to battle. There were those in that little army who knew its importance, but they knew also the duty of a soldier too well to murmur. Gloomily and wearily they marked the minutes as they passed—gloomily they stretched themselves upon the long grass, inwardly chaffing, not at danger, not at the overshadowing doom, but of the probability of a defeat where victory might so easily be secured, or the more galling alternative of being surrounded on the prairie, and starved into capitulation, without a good blow struck, or a laurel gathered to twine about their distant graves. At length that hour of fate rolled by, and the line of march was resumed. For nearly four miles no enemy appeared, and the near timber awakened hopes that were soon to be sadly crushed. The bugle notes of a cavalry troop came floating over the prairie. There was a wild fierceness in the barbaric music borrowed by Old Spain from its Moorish conquerors. Slowly, in firm order, and with the unmistakable bearing of tried veterans, seven hundred of the lancers of Mexico filed from a skirt of woods to the front, and moved obliquely across the path of Fannin. Guidons waved gracefully in the passing breeze—gleams of light flashed from the steel heads of their long lances—gay uniforms and gaudy trappings lent their varied colors to the martial show. In this emergency the resolution of the American commander was promptly taken. To cut his way through to the timber, was the dictate of prudence as well as of manliness. Closing his men into a compact mass, he moved directly upon the intervening horsemen. But now emerging from the same point of woods where the cavalry had first been seen, a dark column of twelve hundred infantry stretched itself out upon the prairie. Here, also, the amunition wagon broke down. Captivity, or battle upon the enemy's own terms, were the only alternatives that remained. At once a hollow square was formed, and with little hope save that of a glorious death, the devoted band awaited the assault. The enemy began by firing at long distances with their escopetas. No shot was returned in reply. They approached nearer, and poured in another volley. Still no answer. Again they advanced, and fired. Several of Fannin's men were wounded by this discharge. A ball carried away the cock of his own rifle, and another buried itself in the breech. Calm and unmoved, he stood erect among the bullets—from time to time ordering his men not to fire yet. The enemy who had now closed within a hundred yards, halted. It was evident they did not intend to approach any nearer to the front face of the square, which was composed of the companies of Shackelford and Pettis. The impatience of the troops was gratified by an order to fire, and the battle began in earnest. The remnant of the Tampico regiment, which had survived the storming of the Almo, charged the left face. They were received by a murderous discharge from a piece of artillery, and when a little nearer were mowed down by the score by Duval's riflemen. Almost at the same time the rear face was charged by a body of lancers, yelling and shouting like so many fiends broke loose from hell. A sharp fire of canister arrested them in mid career, and horse and man went down together on the bloody plain. For six hours, without intermission, the battle raged. For six hours that little band of heroes held at bay a force of more than seven times their number. Assailed on every side by lance, and bullet, and bayonet—their guns useless for the want of water to sponge them—without a breastwork, or trench, or tree, or the slightest protection of any description, unshrinking and unquailing they fought on. Now a heavy volley from the enemy makes a horrid gap in that living wall. The dead and the dying are borne within—the square contracts, and again a solid front is presented to the murderous shower. And so on through the day, and when the shadow of the night came down, that square was unbroken, and the enemy drew off from a field over which the pennons of the volunteers still fluttered. Col. Fannin had been seriously wounded early in the action, but continued through the day to cheer and encourage his men. The unshaken valor they had exhibited was about to be rendered doubly illustrious. Under cover of the darkness, there was a fair prospect for those who were unhurt to reach the timber, and make good their retreat. It was soon ascertained, however, that, during the engagement, their teams had all been killed or scattered, and if they retreated, they must leave their wounded comrades, of whom sixty were lying in their midst, to the mercy of a merciless foe. With one accord they resolved to remain, and share together whatever fate might befall them. With the dawn of morn, it was discovered that the Mexicans had received a reinforcement of five hundred men—they had also erected a battery beyond the range of Fannin's rifles. The volunteers were now in some sort protected by a slight earth-work, thrown up during the night. Carefully husbanding their ammunition, they received the Mexican fire without attempting to return it. Cannon balls whistled over them, and around them, but no answering echo came from the shallow trench and fragile breastwork. Deliberately, and beyond the reach of harm, the enemy kept up the work of murder. After a while they hoisted a signal for negotiations. Major Wallace was sent out to them. Gen. Urea insisted on treating with the commanding officer in person. Sorely wounded as he was, Col. Fannin determined to comply with the request. As he limped by Captain Shackelford, nearly one-half of whose company had been killed or wounded on the day before, that gallant officer, his tall form unbowed, his bronzed cheek not a shade paler, his voice clear, and without a tremor, addressed him in the determined language of a man for whom death has no terrors, when honor and duty gild its coming.

"If you can save our wounded, colonel—obtain fair and honorable terms, and such as you can rely on, capitulate. If not, come back among us—our graves are already dug—we know how to make them immortal before falling into them."

The Mexican general not only offered terms fair and honorable, but more highly favorable than Fannin had a right to expect. How he *intended* to keep them, can only be known to his God. How he *did* keep them, will be seen hereafter.

It was the 20th of March. The sun had not far to travel on his westward journey, when Lile and Simpson crossed the San Antonio. Before leaving the skirt of wood that runs along the river's bank, they looked out carefully upon the prairie. A strong body of Mexicans was marching towards them. Secreting themselves carefully, they waited its approach. It was the guard of Urea driving the unwounded volunteers, who had surrendered with Fannin, back to Goliad. Straggling parties of Mexicans continued to pass until the sun went down. The two then emerged into the open prairie, keeping a little way from the direct track to Victoria.

"It is all over," said Lile; "there has been a battle somewhere near, and the Mexican army is still encamped about the spot, or else they have murdered the wounded."

"That's what they've done," replied Simpson, with a fierce oath, "and here have I let at least three hundred of the devils go by without drawing a lead on the first one."

"Never mind," rejoined his companion, "there is time enough for that. Fear not that I will leave this neighborhood before you have an opportunity of shedding blood enough to satiate the deadliest revenge."

The long stride of men accustomed to pedestrian exercise, carried them rapidly over the level country. Far ahead the camp-fires of a considerable army blazed up along the edge of the Coleto timber.

"They will keep poor watch to-night," said Lile; "for they know that the last troops on this side the Gaudaloupe are either dead or captives. It will be easy to crawl near enough to mingle mourning with their rejoicing."

No proposition could have been more acceptable to Simpson in the then temper of his mind. It was agreed to approach within rifle-shot of the nearest fire, select each one his own mark, and make their escape before the confusion would enable the foe to begin a pursuit. Diverging to the left, they reached the timber above the encampment, and cautiously, through the shadows of the dark wood, drew near and nearer to the blazing fires.

"Look," whispered Lile, laying his hand on Simpson's arm; "look through this opening. There is an object moving backwards and forwards between us and the light. It must be a sentry."

"I see it," was the reply, in the same low tone; "but it's no trouble to get rid of him."

"Not much. Still we must wait—perhaps an hour—perhaps more."

"Why? I can stop that fellow's breathing in ten minutes, without disturbing the whippoorwill on the tree above his head."

"Very likely. But we do not know when the guard will be relieved, and if they should come around before we had effected our purpose, and find a comrade dead upon his post, an alarm would be given which would make our situation more exciting than agreeable. This man may thank his stars for the good fortune that has placed him on duty at this particular time—the one who takes his place will have less cause to be grateful."

Approaching as near as they could with safety, they took advantage of the screen afforded by a fallen pecan-tree, and waited for the relief to come round. Very soon the quick challenge of a sentry was heard—the countersign was given—a new man was put upon the post—his instructions communicated in a whisper, and the relief moved on. When the tread of the marching guard died away, Lile rose, and said:

"Now is our time. We have two hours before us. Give me your rifle until the sentinel is quieted."

Without a word Simpson handed him his rifle, drew his knife, and disappeared in the direction of the sentry. In less than ten minutes he returned, whispered "all is clear," and resumed his gun. The two then made directly for the nearest camp-fire. As they passed the spot where the sentry had been posted, Lile noticed that he was sitting with his back against a tree, apparently sound asleep; but a dark tide that welled from his bosom, was making its way slowly over the ground. Nearing the fires, they discovered that no tents had been pitched, and they judged rightly that the halt in that place was intended to be a brief one. Gathered about some blazing logs, ten or twelve Mexican soldiers were intently engaged in the fascinating game of *Monte*. Indicating by signs the different objects at which they meant to fire, their rifles rose together, and together the sharp echoes rang through the forest. Turning instantly with the speed of the wild deer, they bounded back along the margin of the little stream. To the noise and confusion prevailing in the camp they gave little heed, well knowing that no continued pursuit would be attempted in the dark. At the distance of half a mile they halted, and deliberately reloaded their guns.

"They will not move now before sun-up," said Lile, "for they will never believe two men would have ventured on such a deed, if unsupported. It will give Ward two or three hours more time, if he is not already captured, as I fear he is. For him we can do nothing more. Let us back to Goliad, we may help some of the prisoners to escape."

Simpson gladly acceded to the proposition. Aside from his willingness to share any danger his companion chose to encounter, he had another motive. When kneeling by the side of the wounded boys in the Mission Church, he had recorded an oath in heaven. Whenever he closed his eyes he fancied he could see thin silken locks clotted with blood—thin beardless faces disfigured by a brutal soldiery—their fair bosoms gashed with unnumbered wounds. Gloomily he brooded over the fate he believed, and believed truly, had overtaken them. Revenge is a natural instinct of the human heart. In the gentlest of our race it takes years of watchful training to soften and subdue it. Long and bitter must the struggle be before we receive, without ripening, the divine precept, "Vengeance is mine: I will repay, saith the Lord." The duty of forgiveness was one Simpson had never learned. His separation from civilized life and his association with the Indian tribes, had, on the contrary, cherished and strengthened the vengeful feelings of his nature. To him there was nothing holier than the blow that sent the murderer after his victim; and he would have scorned himself if, at any time, he had hesitated to take life for life. In the present case there was much to palliate, if not justify the bloody resolution he had formed. The invader had entered Texas with the avowed purpose of extermination, and his acts thus far had been in accordance with the proclamation. Butchery of the living had been accompanied with the foulest indignities to the dead. The bodies of the slain had first been mutilated, and then left to rot where they fell. The only wonder is, that the feeling thus awakened was arrested where it was.

Without rest or refreshment the two friends again struck across the prairie for the San Antonio. For days they skulked around Goliad, subsisting on a deer Simpson had killed, and wild onions in the river bottom. Once Lile formed the resolution of killing the sentries, and penetrating the town during the night. A little reflection taught him this would be superflous, and might give the Mexicans a pretext for murdering their prisoners. On the 25th they saw Ward and his companions brought in. At daylight on the 27th, Lile, who was sleeping at the root of a tree, was roused by Simpson.

"What's in the wind now? They are marching our men out towards the river with their knapsacks on. What does it mean?"

"It means treachery and murder," answered Lile. "Cold, black and heartless murder!"

A little distance from the river the prisoners were made to kneel down with their faces to the river. A suspicion of the truth flashed over one of the men. He sprang to his feet, loudly exclaiming, "Boys, they are going to kill us!—die with your faces to them like men!" A volley of musketry silenced his voice forever. Another succeeded. With a shout of hell the Mexicans rushed on with lance and bayonet to complete the work. Dying groans mingled plentifully with the brutal curses of the slayers, but not a craven cry, not a prayer for mercy issued from the mangled mass. The agony of torn sinews and crashing bones made itself heard; but no begging, no whining, no sign of terror added to the infernal gratification of the murderers.

As Simpson looked upon the scene, the veins of his temples swelled and worked like writhing serpents. Twice he raised his rifle, and twice his comrade laid his hand upon the lock, and sternly muttered "be still!" When it was over, they both turned away and penetrated deeper in the wood. An hour later they were at the ford of the San Antonio. A troop of Lancers was approaching. As the foremost files entered the stream they were greeted by that peculiar report of the western rifle, (sharp, quick and deadly,) no other fire-arm ever gives out; two bodies floated down the river—two steeds struggled masterless to the bank. Promptly the officer in command gave the order to charge—but the ford was deep and difficult, and before the passage was effected two more saddles were empty. Emerging from the river and finding that in consequence of the tangled undergrowth, as well as the swampy nature of the soil, pursuit on horseback was impossible, the Mexican officer dismounted the greater part of his force, and proceeded to scour the woods in every direction. This was exactly what the Texan scouts had foreseen and desired. Trained to the woods, they knew all the advantages they possessed and purposely drew the enemy further and further down the river. Frequent vollies of escopetas sounded through the woods. Occasionally only the rifle spoke in reply, but its every tone was a funeral knell. The Mexicans soon discovered that a longer chase held out no prospect except that of their own destruction, and commenced a rapid retreat. Lile and Simpson had no idea of parting company thus. The relative position of the parties were reversed. The pursued became the pursuers. With dogged pertinacity they hung upon the steps of the retiring foe. Breathless with fatigue and pale with terror, the Mexicans at length regained the road. Mounting their horses they fled with disgraceful speed from the fatal spot, leaving fifteen of their number weltering in blood. Upon examining the horses of the slain, the two Americans found a small quantity of dried beef, and a much more considerable supply of parched meal, mixed with grated sugar. Transferring these to a couple of the best steeds, and supplying themselves with two Mexican blankets each, they mounted and set off in a gallop to join the main army of Texas. It was known that General Houston had retreated towards the Brazos. A column under Sezma was hanging on his rear. Santa Anna was moving across the country with a strong force, due east from San Antonio. Ninety or a hundred miles to the south, the division that had destroyed Fannin and Ward, were also moving eastward. In all direction clouds of light troops scoured the open country. The whole distance is prairie, broken only when a running stream makes its way to the Gulf. The timber on the Colorado is the widest and that is only about seven miles in extent. Lile's object was to avoid the roving bands of Mexicans, and reach General Houston's camp with as little delay as possible. The open nature of the country made this a work both of difficulty and of danger. The first day their horses were completely knocked up. They were abandoned, and the journey continued on foot. It now became imperative that they should hide during the day, and travel only at night. The prairies of Texas are frequently dotted with small islands of timber, called in the phraseology of the country, "Motts." Near these there are usually low, marshy places, where the water collects during the rainy season, often remaining through the summer heats. On the third day, impelled by the desire of concealment, as well as for the convenience of water, the two friends had taken shelter in one of these motts. Long continued fatigue and watchfulness had done its work even upon their toughened sinews and iron frames. About noon they awakened from a deep sleep to find that a party of ten mounted Mexicans were within a few hundred yards of them. Flight would inevitably result in discovery and probably death. Concealing themselves as well as they could among the bushes, they waited for any advantage the chapter of accidents might offer. From the careless manner the Mexicans approached, it was clear that they were wholly unsuspicious of the presence of an enemy. Their horses were watered, and "staked out" on the prairie to enable them to graze, when the party piled their arms, and began to prepare the noon-day meal. While thus engaged, at some distance from their guns, two rifle shots echoed from the timber behind them—two bodies fell forward on the little fire, extinguishing it with blood. With drawn knives and a fierce shout, Lile and Simpson rushed upon the survivors. Panic struck at the suddenness of the assault, the Mexicans scattered and fled precipitately. Lile halted when he reached the pile of arms. Not so did Simpson. With terrible speed he followed in the track of the fugitives. The foot of the hindmost caught in the tangled grass, and he fell. As he struggled up the knife was sheathed in his back. The next one sank upon his knees and begged for mercy. "Yes," was the fierce reply, "such mercy as you showed Fannin." The blow descended, and the blood from the main artery of the neck spouted in the hunter's face. Deliberately he wiped away the crimson stains and rejoined his companion.

"I reckon," he said, "we've about paid for the boys; but it will take a life time to pay for Goliad."

Two of the best horses and all the provisions, as on the former occasion, were appropriated without scruple. The next day they learned from a scouting party of Texans, whom they accidentally encountered, that General Houston had received the news of Fannin's defeat on the evening of the 25th of March, and had fallen back to some point on the Brazos, believed to be San Felipe. Communicating, in their turn, the story of the massacre they had witnessed at Goliad, they pursued their way towards the head-quarters of the "Army of Freedom." On the evening of the 6th of April they reached San Felipe de Austin, and found its smouldering ruins occupied by the Mexican army; the Americans having burned it to the ground when compelled to evacuate it. Here they lost all trace of General Houston, and skulked in the neighborhood for several days before learning that he had gone in the direction of Harrisburg. It was the evening of the 20th of April that Lile and Simpson rode into the camp of the last army Texas was able to muster. The two armies lay in sight of each other, each occupying a body of timber near Lynch's ferry on the San Jacinto river, with an open prairie between. There had been firing throughout the day, and Colonel Sherman had made a daring, but unsuccessful, charge with sixty-eight men upon the enemy's artillery. Being unsupported, and finding himself opposed by an overwhelming force of cavalry, infantry and artillery, he drew off in good order, with the loss of only two men badly wounded. The main body of both armies had been busily employed during the day—the Texans in cutting away the brush and undergrowth in front of their encampment—the Mexicans in throwing up a breastwork of timber and earth. It was the obvious policy of Santa Anna to remain where he was without striking a blow. He had between six and seven thousand soldiers scattered over the country in his rear, and was hourly expecting reinforcements. On the other hand, Texas had collected the last man she could hope to muster. The Fabian policy heretofore pursued by General Houston, was abandoned at the urgent solicitations of his officers, and the next day was fixed for the decision of the fate of Texas. Lile and Simpson found the Americans silently and sternly preparing for the morrow's battle. But one fear was felt among them, and that was that their commander might still judge it prudent to draw off without hazarding a general engagement. Around every fire was gathered a knot of rough and hardy backwoodsmen, too much excited for slumber, too gloomily anxious and uncertain for conversation. Some were cleaning their firelocks—others were carefully rubbing the rust from their knife-blades. An old man on the verge of sixty, who had put one gun in order, was industriously engaged on another.

"What do you want with two guns," asked a comrade, who was near him.

"I want to use them," was the reply; "my son and son-in-law were killed at the Alamo, and I shall fight for both to-morrow."

"It's not certain," was the moody rejoinder, "we'll fight at all to-morrow. We've had so many orders to retreat that, by God, I wouldn't be surprised if we got another before morning."

The old man looked up with an incredulous stare. "Not fight! Not fight, and Santa Anna in less than a mile of us! May I be eternally damned, if 'Old Sam' does retreat, if I don't charge that army by myself, and go to join my murdered boys!"

"And may the devil fly away with me," said Simpson,

who had been listening with folded arms to the foregoing conversation, "if I don't charge with you."

"There will be more fingers in the pie," muttered two or three of the weather-beaten group.

Lile had spread his blanket upon the ground, and was half reclining upon it. His voice was clear and cheerful, as he said:

"It is wrong to doubt the General, comrades. He is too good a soldier not to know that further retreat must end either in exile or the grave. Sleep, and husband your strength. You will need it when the sun rises."

At every camp-fire scenes similar to that just described were being enacted. The very intensity of their desire for battle made them doubt the realization of their hopes. At intervals impatient ejaculations, half stifled curses, and dark and dismal resolutions, were fiercely muttered; but for the most part men were wrapped in their own meditations, and silence brooded over the sleepless host. The morning dissipated all shadow of doubt. Coolly and deliberately the American commander had weighed the chances of the doubtful struggle. Again and again he had passed in review every possible contingency. Prudently and thoughtfully his resolution was formed—promptly and fearlessly it was executed. The order for battle was given. With that order came a mighty change over the spirits of the troops. The men who a few hours before were sullen, gloomy, angry, almost mutinous, now sprang to their places with joyous alacrity. The light laugh, and the lighter jest, were freely interchanged, and bets were offered as to who should *cut the first razor strap from the back of Santa Anna.* The musicians caught the infection, and that army of daring patriots, whose friends and relatives had been butchered by the hundred—whose houses had been burned down—whose wives and children were homeless, and whose own destruction, to all human calculations, was imminent and certain, moved to battle to the soft melody of

"Will you come to the bower?"

Sherman began the fight on the left. Pouring in one deadly volley, he shouted "Charge! and remember the Alamo." The wild cry ran along his line, and was caught up and prolonged to the extreme right of the Texan army. It was not a *charge*, but a *rush*, or as one historian has called it, "a universal assault. The Mexican lines swayed and bent before the hurricane of steel. With terrible strength it tore through them, drowning prayer and shriek, and dying groan alike, in its awful roar. In fifteen minutes the field of San Jacinto was a vast slaughter pen in whose crimson mire lay the bodies of six hundred of the tools of tyranny, while far away over the wide prairie, north and south, east and west, rang the glad shouts of the victors; and old men, women and children—the homeless and the destitute, caught the echoes and answered, WE ARE FREE!

When the rout of the enemy was complete, and it was certain they could not again be rallied, Lile desisted from the pursuit, and walked slowly back over the battle-field. The first body that attracted his attention was that of General Castrillon. He had used every effort to prevent the flight of his men, and when that failed, deliberately folded his arms—sullenly refused to ask for quarter, and met his fate without a tremor. Three rifle balls had passed through him, but the dark frown was still upon his brow, and the face, even in death, was firm and unquailing.

"This at least," muttered Lile, "was a man. He asked not for the mercy he had never shown, and redeemed, in dying, the cruelties that had stained his living career."

Passing on, he observed that most of the Mexicans were lying on their faces. Not fifty of them had taken their wounds in front. He sat down upon a block of wood in the heart of what had been the Mexican camp. Silence brooded over the spot. The victors and the vanquished, mixed in a headlong race, had rushed on. He was alone among the dead. Darkly yet distinctly the stupendous results of that day's victory rose up before him. A blow had been struck at the foundation of every throne on the American continent. Along the pathway of the future he tracked the giant march of freedom. Well he knew, when once begun, that onward march knows no retreat. With a prophet's eye, he saw the shackles of the slave shivered from his limbs, while from province to province—through storm and tempest—through blood and tears—the spirit of Liberty held its resistless way; striking the pampered priest and the lordly tyrant together to the dust—evoking from the ruins of the gorgeous cathedral a purer and a holier religion, and proclaiming from the rent fragments of the stately palace, that the law has no superior—that all alike must bend to its mandates, and all alike are entitled to its blessings.

CHAPTER IX.

" High up in heaven one lovely star
Pours in upon my soul its light:
As, nested from the world afar,
A dove, with eyes clear, fond, and bright,
Gazes with earnest, mute delight
Upon its young, that all its life a treasure are.

TWENTY years ago the island of Galveston was a mere sand bank. Four or five fishermen's huts dotted the beach, and a few scattered dwellings of not much greater pretension, marked the site of the present city. Some distance down the island three trees rose in a cluster,—the only green things that grew upon the barren waste, except a long wiry grass with which it was partially covered. Near the entrance of the harbor were the remains of a rude fortification, built by Lafitte, when his piratical flag waved over the waters of the Gulf. At this place a fisherman had erected a temporary dwelling, and here Bernard Lile had obtained permission to remain until he could procure a passage in some one of the light coasting vessels trading to New Orleans. A treaty of peace had been concluded with Santa Anna, who was then a prisoner of war at Velasco; and all prospect of active operations being at an end, Lile was about to return to the beautiful being he had left for the purpose of taking part in the fierce struggle that had begun so sadly, and terminated so gloriously for the cause of Texas. Three days after the battle of San Jacinto, a messenger had brought him a letter from his wife. It was an answer to one he had written from the bank of the Mississippi, and ran as follows:

"So, Bernard, you thought it useless to write, as no letter could reach you in the wild land to which you have gone. I have surmounted greater obstacles for a less reward. What if there is no regular post? Here, as elsewhere, there are men who will do anything for money, and what sum could I deem extravagant that secured communion with you? There is a wild bliss in every thought that turns towards you, and when my hand has traced the letters that form your name, I can gaze for hours on the characters, finding in every one a beauty and a glory it is impossible for it to wear in any other connection. To pour out my full soul—to tell you all I have seen or felt, enjoyed or suffered, this is, indeed, a privilege denied to written intercourse, because all written words are weak and powerless to express the throbbings of a heart where love has made its home. Still the very act of writing has its rapture. The knowledge that your hand will hold the paper—that your eye will run over the lines—that you will think of me more often after its perusal, is a joy of which nothing can deprive me, and which nothing in the wide world but your presence could give. It is well I believe not in the faith your fathers taught. It is well I grew up in a land where it is not deemed sin for a woman to worship her husband. Your Allah may demand of the Christian wife divided devotion on earth, and a sole dominion hereafter. Mine asserts no such claim; nor would it be accorded if he did. In this bosom there is no room for another passion. Call it love, devotion, worship, idolatry, what you will; all, all is yours, and yours I would proclaim it on the arch of Al-Sirat if I knew the words would plunge me into the burning gulf below. But not so is it written in the Koran. In the third of heaven set apart for the faithful of our sex, and presided over by the mother of the prophet, its highest honors and its sweetest enjoyments are the rewards of those who have loved most intensely below. Think, Bernard, what bliss will be mine; when centuries hence that haven shall at last be reached.

"Do you remember when we sat down at the feet of an old man beneath the sky of Syria, and drank in the lore he had gathered through many, and many a year of fasting and of vigil? Do you remember how he traced out, step by step—from star to star—through the countless thousands that thronged the blue space above us, the soul's illimitable career? Beginning on this lower orb where disease and death, poverty and crime, disappointed hopes and blighted aspirations, the vexing littleness, and the sterner torture beset each hour of the cloudy journey, and travelling on through brighter spheres, losing at each progressive step some care, some pain, some grief that had afflicted us before,—gaining from each new capacities for enjoyment, new love of the beautiful and the good—gathering a host of feelings higher, purer, holier—listening to melodies that grow softer, more enchanting, and more delicious as we advance, until all we now know of bliss is lost, and all we can conceive of beatitude is forgotten, amid the inexpressible delights of the reality. Do you remember he foretold such a destiny for us, and when he led us through worlds on worlds to the seventh heaven, I asked: 'And then, what then? Shall I be separated from Bernard, there?' And the old man drew his mantle about his face, and answered not; and you folded me to your bosom with a sad smile, and said, 'love me while you can, Zerah! the future is a dark riddle, that the sage may read imperfectly—you and I not at all.'

"Well, Bernard, that question revealed a love that most men would have shrunk from as fearfully as the sting of the asp; but you drew the passionate thing who uttered it nearer to your heart, and from that hour I knew that Eblis had no power to tear us asunder.

"My pen has run back into the past, and I am forgetting there are many things in the present you are desirous to know. That the first days of your departure were dreary enough I need not say. Unhappily for himself, your young friend, Robert Wilson, thought it his duty to pay me many attentions. Day by day I watched the growth of a passion I knew not how to check, and whose existence, to do him justice, I believe he did not himself suspect. But it is a knowledge that cannot long be hidden, and when it came to him he acted as became the man who called you benefactor. If he had breathed one word of passion in my ear—if he had avowed the feelings I knew were burning and struggling in his bosom, and sought to win even pity or compassion in return, I would have scorned and loathed him more than the ugliest toad that defiles the earth. Not so did he act. Promptly, almost rudely, he tore himself away, vainly fancying that he carried his secret with him, and no doubt, supposing me indignant at the seemingly cold and formal announcement of his departure, through Monsieur Evadne. Then I pitied him. Then, if it could have relieved a single pang he suffered, I would have sent for him and soothed him with words of affection and regard, but I knew this would be idle, or rather it would be adding torture to torture; and so I let him go, trusting to time to soften the blow, and hoping that the active duties of a profession which leaves little time for melancholy thought, would blot out the memory of the wild and hopeless dream he had unconsciously nourished. If ever the day comes when we can meet without pain on his part, I will gladly tell him how much I honor the upright manliness he has exhibited—how much I feel for the misery he has endured. That day may be afar off, and I fear me it is; but let us hope that though the flower may be struck from the stem, the plant may continue to grow and flourish not the less vigorous and useful after its sweetness is gone for ever. In the meantime, I have directed Monsieur Evadne, to keep an eye on his every movement, and see that he wants for nothing money can buy. I had hoped also to procure him promotion to a higher rank, but our good friend tells me neither money nor influence avail any thing, for such a purpose, under this singular government of yours, and that he must carve his way with his own right hand from grade to grade. All, therefore, has been done I could do; the rest remains with you.

"A few days after Mr. Wilson's departure, I was surprised by a visit from a lady, who, I was told, occupied the highest rank in New York society. She is certainly beautiful. Her voice is low and sweet, and her manners are indicative of a head strong enough to sustain the consciousness of many surpassing attractions. I have been forced to see her often, and would willingly be rid of her, for I like her not, and yet find it difficult to discover what it is that repels me. You will naturally attribute it to the different customs and observances of our respective creeds. I think not. Much as I detest the constant exposure of female charms permitted, if not enjoined, in your society, I have learned how to make allowances for indelicacies which must result from such a course of training, and which from the very unconsciousness that they are indelicacies, in point of fact, cease to be so with those who are habituated to them. The Indian or the African maid, who daily associates with the opposite sex in a state but little removed from nudity, is not necessarily immodest, but it cannot be denied, that her sensibilities are much less acute, and her liability to error much greater from the custom. Your habits of promiscuous association are not so bad, and while

I see in them much that is repugnant to my taste, I am sure I have so far got the better of prejudice as not to judge them by the standard they would infallibly be subjected to in Mahometan lands. It is not that Mrs. Winter goes unveiled. It is not that her ordinary dress exposes more of her person than I think modest or becoming—it is not that she is constantly intimating her wishes that I should mingle in scenes I detest, or visit places whose publicity makes me shudder, that has created an aversion not easy to be concealed. You remember the little serpent that twines among the flowers of Persia, and when the bulbul comes to court the rose, hushes its song is death. Soft and beautiful and seemingly gentle and harmless, you might take it for the plaything of a child, and yet a giant's strength would be instantly withered by its venom. Even so does this woman seem to me. Lovely as she is—robed with graces that would adorn a sultan's throne—always affable in manner—always kind in words, there is still something to recall the serpent among the flowers. There is a spark in her bosom that has never yet been awakened. When it is struck, it will be deadly, and woe to him on whom her love or hatred lights. She asks often of you, and when you will return. I cannot tell her, for I do not know, and I would not tell her if I could. I cannot dwell upon your meeting with her without a feeling of uneasiness as far removed from jealousy as midnoon from midnight, but as full of agony as the darkest jealousy could inflict.

"Let me turn to a dearer theme. Rumors of coming battle daily reach us. I do not tell you to shun the foremost rank, for well I know that post is yours by right, as it will be by choice. Nor do I tell you to win new laurels to swell the pride of a woman already too vain of her lord to believe that fame has other gifts to bestow; and who loves him too much to doubt that others hold the same opinion. I pretend not to judge when or where the sword should be sheathed. The sense of duty that led you to the field must be your only guide. But if you cannot come to me soon, let me come to you. There is a terrible beauty in watching a single arm drive back a quailing host, and unwomanly as the wish is, I long once more to see you clear a pathway through the ranks of war. Not long since I caught myself wishing I were a man that I might share this peril with you, as I had shared those of other climes: but in a moment came the thought that if I were I could not be the wife of Bernard Lile, and the foolish whim fled away rebuked.

"Send back my messenger as soon as may be, with such tidings as you have to convey to her who is waiting to receive them, neither murmuring nor repining, nor gloomy, nor impatient, but loving and dutiful as ever."

To this letter he had despatched an answer announcing the probable close of the war—the capture of Santa Anna, and his own immediate return. Procuring a sail-boat on the head of the bay, in company with Simpson, he landed on Galveston island, for the purpose of taking passage to the United States. In the hut of the fisherman he again drew the letter from his bosom, and re-read the passages which referred to Robert Wilson, with absorbing interest.

"Poor boy," he muttered, "must I and mine bring blight and sorrow upon all who bear your name? Sorrow when I meant kindness. Decay when I meant to infuse new life into a vigorous shoot. There is *fate* in this. The shadow is over my pathway yet. The fearful race is not so nearly run as I had begun to hope. God grant that I may not, as of old time, rebel at the hand of the chastener, and relapse into the sullen calm of impenitent despair."

The opportunity he had waited for at length offered.

The light boat of the fisherman was ready to convey him to the vessel. Walking along the beach with Simpson he conferred with that worthy upon his future plans.

"You will not go with me, Tom?"

"No, captain. If I did not suffocate in the thick air of the towns, or sicken and die right out from inaction, I should be eternally fretted and annoyed by finding myself an object of curiosity and dread to all the children and little *niggers* we met. Besides, what the devil could I do in the settlements? I should be as much out of place as a bear at a bran-dance, and about as welcome."

"Go back to books and study, Tom. You have higher capacities than you deem, and are not yet too old to serve mankind in the closet, as you have done in the field."

"It won't do, captain. I had some such dreams in my youth; but that was before I had ever felt the wild freedom of the woods. It is all forgotten now. I must remain upon the border—at least until my eyes grow dim, and these strong limbs stiffen with age. If you want me at any time seek me in the west. I shall be somewhere along the Gaudaloupe or the San Antonio, unless the Mexicans or Camanches contrive to send me on a journey to the happy hunting-grounds. There will be wild work there for long years to come, and whenever you hear of a daring deed done, be certain that Tom Simpson has neither forgotten the wounded boys of the Mission Church, nor the cowardly murder of Goliad."

"And so you think this peace will not last?"

"Last! It will never begin. As soon as Santa Anna is safe he will laugh at the treaty. Filisola will halt where he is, and the work must be begun afresh."

"In that event you may count upon my speedy return. In the meantime can I do any thing for you in the States?"

"Nothing, but to write to the old man, and the old

woman that you left me well, and contented: and that I mean to come and see them before they die."

"That shall be attended to. And now good-bye. Our first meeting gave little promise of future friendship: but we have frankly periled life together since; and I say to you as I shall say to your dearest relatives, that a bolder, truer heart, or a stronger arm never served his country or his friend at need."

"Thank you. Thank you; not so much for myself, but it will make the old man feel proud of his son, and I have caused him trouble enough to make me wish to bring him some comfort in his old age."

Lile stepped into the boat. The hunter watched it, as it rose and fell with the heaving waves, until it neared the vessel's side.

"There goes a man," he said, wiping a tear from his sunburned cheek, "whom a pet lamb might love, but whom a run mad tiger might fear to meet. We shall see each other again I know. He's not made for towns, any more than I am."

Thus, upon the lonely beach, the two friends parted. The one to tread the dusty thoroughfares of civilized life —the other to mingle in the wild excitements of a border warfare.

Arrived at New Orleans, Lile soon found himself engaged in consultations with agents of the Texan government, who were devising means to start the infant republic prosperously upon its new career. As a naval force was one of the first and most important requisites, he engaged to man and arm a vessel at his own expence, stipulating only that he should himself have the selection of the officers and crew. This done he procured a passport for Cuba, and in a few days was again upon the blue waters of the gulf. The wind was blowing fiercely, and the angry waves dashed high up against the walls of the Moro Castle, as the vessel entered the harbor of Havana. Lile was standing upon the deck with a fellow passenger, (whom he had learned was an English engineer,) examining the celebrated fortress with as much attention as the surging billows would allow.

"Your republic," said the Englishman, "is reported to have cast a longing eye on the queen of the Antilles. That castle looks like an ugly obstacle in the way."

"I do not know what my countrymen may desire," answered Lile, "but if they should resolve to invade Cuba, that castle will prove a weak defence."

"Weak! You have nothing in your republic that approaches it."

"Perhaps not. You doubtless remember the story of the Spartan, who, when asked, 'where are your city's walls?' promptly answered, 'the bosoms of her sons.' We build no such fortifications. *We take them.*"

"When you take this one the day of miracles will have arrived."

"I have witnessed a greater miracle within a few months past. I have seen three hundred volunteers, without a siege train or any of the aids of science, take a stone fortress garrisoned by fifteen hundred just such soldiers as yonder castle holds; and if ever the American Union sends a hostile force against this island, the Moro battlements will not delay its conquest for a single week."

"You speak sanguinely, sir, for one whose theory is opposed by all the rules of scientific war. We, in Europe, do not entertain such extravagant opinions of the prowess of your countrymen."

"And yet a handful of raw recruits, drawn hastily from the plough, and the workshop, tore the laurels gathered in the peninsula, from the brow of Packenham, and drove his veterans in disgrace and terror to their ships."

The captain of the ship now interposed, and directed the conversation to other topics.

It was night—the soft night of Cuba. The moon was riding in the heavens clear, bright, and brilliant. Its rays appeared to rest with fond delight upon the lofty spire, and the gilded cupola, while it was easy to fancy them shrinking with disgust from the dark, narrow, and filthy streets of the island metropolis. From the plaza, in front of the palace of the governor-general, a band of music sent forth its delicious strains. Hurrying *volantes* filled the streets, and crowds of pedestrians thronged the little footways, all flowing towards the place of nightly recreation.

The luxury of a moonlight promenade in that scorching clime, added to the Spaniard's passionate fondness for music, never fails to draw together on such occasions "the beauty and the chivalry" of Havana. But distrust and suspicion are for ever hanging like a dark cloud above the scene. Here every tone of the voice, and every gesture of the hand is watched and noted. Even the laugh of the young Senorita is robbed of its mirth, for she knows not but the spies of the despot may report it as treason. Love, which elsewhere scorns the shackle and the bolt, finds himself fluttering with crippled wing, beneath a sky whose very air might fill an Iceland heart with fire. The maiden listens to the soft tale she loves to hear—the orange groves are blooming about her—bowers which the wild flower and the evergreen have united to form, are gently stirring in the balmy breeze—peace is in the heaven above, and sweetness in the earth below, but a horrid doubt comes to drive away the trembling ecstacy, and blast the fragrant beauty of the hour. As she listens an inward monitor whispers that the pleading tongue, whose accents had almost won her beating heart, is that of a paid informer—that the jealous suspicions of tyranny have rested on a loved father, or a darling brother, and that he who is kneeling at her feet is *hired* to win her love, in order to betray more easily the father, or the brother to the dungeon or the *garote*. Yet she dares not spurn him. She must listen and pretend to believe. From a hypocrite she becomes in turn a betrayer; and thus through the whole net work of society the deadly venom is diffused.

Lile lingered not among the promenaders, but threaded his way to the billiard saloon at Delmonico's. Glancing around the room, his eye rested on a bronzed and weather beaten seaman, who was watching the game with evident interest. Walking up to this individual, he quietly proposed to try his skill at an unoccupied table. The seaman looked up—a flash of recognition illuminated his countenance—it disappeared as quick as it came, and he answered,—

"I'm sorry I can't amuse you. You see I'm a cripple;" and he pointed to his right arm resting in a sling.

Lile took a seat on one of the cushioned benches, and continued to watch the game for some minutes in silence. He then rose and walked into the refreshment room. Seating himself at one of the little circular tables he lighted a cigaritta, and called for a glass of iced lemonade. While thus occupied, the seaman also entered. Ordering some cigars, as soon as the servant was out of hearing, he whispered, "Follow me when I go out." The cigars after some chafering were paid for, and the seaman sauntered towards the street entrance. Lile also discharged his bill, and walked slowly to the door. Keeping some distance apart, but constantly in view, they proceeded leisurely along the street leading to the Bishop's Garden. After awhile the houses grew thinner. Scattered patches of open ground allowed the moon-beams to light up the surrounding objects. The seaman now halted until his companion approached.

"We can walk on together now; but keep in the middle of the street. It is never safe to go near a dark wall in Havana."

"I hardly hoped to have met you, Velasquez," said Bernard Lile, "though I came here for the purpose."

"Hush!" responded the person thus addressed; "call no names until we are safely housed. You might as well talk in the ear of Dionysius as among Cuban winds."

They soon reached a large and seemingly deserted mansion, surrounded by an iron railing. The gate was unlocked by Velasquez, as we shall now call him, who stopped to secure it again while Lile walked on towards the house. A large blood-hound was sleeping on a mat before the door; rushing towards the intruder with a fierce growl, he sprang directly at his face. Sudden and ferocious as the assault was, Lile was neither surprised nor thrown off his guard. Stepping a little back, he caught the infuriated brute by the throat—held him for a moment in his deadly gripe, and then dashed him to the ground with a violence that forced the blood from mouth, eye, and nostrils.

"Damnation," exclaimed Velasquez, hurrying up, "has the infernal brute torn you badly?"

"Not at all," was the calm reply; "he is himself the only sufferer."

"I hope you have not killed him. He is worth his weight in gold, and it was all from my d—n—d carelessness in letting you go on without thinking of the dog."

"No; that gasp is not the gasp of death. Pour a little brandy and water in his mouth—the fresh air will do the rest."

A sharp ring brought an ill-looking servant to the door. The dog was given into his charge, and Lile entered the house with his host. Entering a room dimly lighted by a single lamp, Velasquėz invited his guest to be seated, and unlocking a crypt in the wall of the room, drew forth a bottle and drinking glasses.

"Now," he said, as he arranged them on a table, "we can talk freely; and here is something better than the wishy-washy stuff at Delmonico's."

Lile imitated his example, and helped himself liberally to the brandy and water.

"It is now more than twenty years," he said, turning the glass on the table slowly with his fingers as he spoke, "since I took passage on the good ship Nantucket, for Cadiz."

"I haven't overhauled the log-book lately," was the reply; "but I guess your reckoning is about right."

"You bore another name at that day, Juan Velasquez, and followed nobler pursuits than at present."

"According to my recollection, Bernard Lile," was the serious but not angry reply, "*both* of us sailed under different colors from those we now carry at the mast-head."

"True! but have you no wish to go back to the old home we loved so well—to wander by the little stream whose clear, pure waters seemed as if they had trickled from Paradise—to walk through the old grave-yard, and read upon the marble tomb-stones, where, and when the venerated fathers of our native village had passed away—to learn what young shoots had sprung into existence, and sickened and died before the mildew of vice had spread along their leaves—to stand where the humble school-house was hid among the clustering trees—to listen once more to the song of the nightingale, in the shady groves where our young loves were told, in that early time when the heart mistakes admiration of the beautiful for love, and knows not the stormy nature of the passion which rends the bosom of the man. Have no such dreams visited your midnight pillow, Juan Velasquez, and made your ocean couch more restless than the billows you rode?"

"Often, Bernard, often. But why ask! Why torture me or yourself, by recalling a happiness we can never know. A dark red stream is flowing between you and your native land. Wild deeds ashore and afloat have thickened around my path, and a halter would be the most probable welcome of the wanderer home."

"Not so. You would never be recognized. Besides, although a slaver, your trade has been confined to the Spanish coast, where it is not piracy."

"So says my log-book; but there are those whose notions of geography might vary from it."

"I have been home, and no one knew me. Nay, more, if I had proclaimed my name and lineage, they would have taken me for a lunatic."

"You!" exclaimed the sailor, starting suddenly to his feet. "You have stood upon the soil of New Hampshire! You have listened to the pealing organ in the old stone church! You have knelt among the moss-covered graves! You have drank from the little brook that goes dancing to the Merrimac! You have done this, while I have been sweltering in this accursed Isle of slaves and pirates! Good God! the thought will drive sleep from my eyelids for a month to come."

"Sit down, and let us talk calmly. Try a little more of this brandy and water. By the time another glass is finished, you will be in a better state to listen to what I have to tell."

Briefly, but clearly, Lile related all that had befallen

him since they had last met three years before. Ending with a glowing picture of the infant republic in whose revolutionary struggle he had fought so gallantly and so successfully. When he had concluded, his listener raised his head from the hand whereon it leaned, and said thoughtfully,

"This accounts for the strange stories I have heard, of a wonderful man who baffled armies with his single strength, and glided unseen through waking hosts, destroying as he went. I thought it some tale invented by the priests to amuse the fools, who imagine that heaven can only be reached over turnpikes where the holy fathers gather the tolls. I knew not you had left Palestine to give lessons on American prowess to the half-breed Spaniards and Indians of Mexico."

He paused a moment—sipped his brandy, and resumed,

"But to what does this tend? I know you have not sought me for nothing. You would not have come upon such an uncertain errand without strong motives."

"The errand was not so uncertain. You might not have been upon the Island, but it was certain that I should hear of you, and secure eventual communication. Still you are so far right, that I would not have come without a strong motive. Of those who knew me in boyhood, not one, save yourself, is living who would recognise me now. When I was driven a blood-stained outcast from my native shores, it was your ship that received me. A hundred ties have since been added, and now, when I see, or hope I see, the dawning of a brighter morn, I have come to point it out, and ask you to share it with me. What say you, John Abbott, to throwing the gyves, and fetters, and grates, and all the other implements of your accursed traffic into the sea; and launching on an honorable career, beneath an unstained flag?"

"What say I? What would the parched traveler on the desert of Zahara say to a gushing spring from our native hills? Even so say I; that it *would be* as welcome, *and is*—as unattainable."

"Listen, John. When a boy the swollen Merrimac closed over you; but a hand was stretched forth to save. When wounded, bleeding, faint, in the dark morass, near Sierra Leone, a cutlass was raised to dispatch you, the arm that held it was severed from the trunk, and you were delivered. When your vessel was sunk by a man-of-war—when all you had was gone, and you had hardly escaped with life in the canoe of a Kroo-man, another vessel was supplied you—your broken fortunes were mended, and you became the richer from the disaster. When the deadly fever at the mouth of the Senegal had turned your blood to fire, care and nursing brought back the pulses of health. Surely you are in no worse strait now."

"I remember it all; and forget not that I owe it to you. But this is not a case where your interference would avail me. I am a marked man. I am known as the most daring slave trader between Africa and the Spanish colonies. Fame adds, the most bloodthirsty and remorseless; but in that fame lies as usual. Go where I will, that brand will cling to me. It is only here, where the traffic is legal, that I can find associates. And even if I abandoned it to-morrow, I must either make my home on this Island, or become a hermit."

"All that has been thought of. I have agreed to fit out, at my own expense, a ship for the Texan navy, stipulating for the selection of the officers. Take the command of her—drop your Spanish name—resume that of your boyhood, and when a few years have rolled away, you can return to your own land, honored and respected, while I must continue to be known only as Bernard Lile."

"I will think of it. My head is strangely confused just now. Another glass of brandy will do us no harm, and then we must to bed, for the sun is stealing through the lattice-work, and it will soon be too hot for anything but slumber."

Lile had noticed that, soon after passing his own gate, the arm of Velazquez was removed from the sling in which he had carried it in the streets, and a long knife, that had evidently been concealed in the folds of the India shawl, was returned to his bosom. He now quietly remarked,

"I thought you were a cripple."

"My good friend," was the response, "assassinations in this delightful climate, are about as frequent as prayer-meetings in New England. In order, I suppose, to give the lovers of this agreeable pastime as much impunity as possible, the law makes it highly penal for any sojourner here to carry arms in his own defence. Now I am no subscriber to the theories of non-resistance, which I learn have taken root in our old country since I left, but, at the same time, it does not suit me to quarrel with the decrees of the captain-general. I have, therefore, adopted the little *ruse* of twisting an India shawl about my neck, and giving out that my right hand is disabled, when I think it prudent to have a bit of bright steel in my grasp."

"One other question. Why do you consider it necessary to take so many precautions in your intercourse with others?

"With *all* others I do not. But I am known to every government spy in Havana, and every stranger who approaches me is watched. I have dealings with many persons to whom a more intimate acquaintance with the authorities would be disagreeable; consequently, I recognise no one—am seen with no one, until I know what his business is, and how far he has reason to dread investigation.

"But yourself; have you nothing to fear?"

"Nothing to fear, but a good deal to *pay*. When I return from a successful cruise to Africa, my first care is to present the captain-general with a number of slaves—my next to distribute appropriate presents of slaves, ivory, or gold dust, among his favorite officials. After that I am safe."

"Your pictures of life in Cuba are gloomy ones."

"They are true; and that is a merit most pictures do not possess."

"With your permission," he continued, "we will postpone further conversation until the evening. There is your couch. You must be content to occupy the same apartment with me, for there is no other about the house that will be endurable two hours hence."

The sultry day of the tropics at length wore away. The sun went down clear, unclouded, brilliant to the last—burning with meridian lustre on the very edge of the glowing heavens. The silver moon walked along the sky, robed with a beauty unknown to colder climes. The dark forest of mangos, beyond the city walls, was vocal with a thousand melodies. A thousand insects whose life would wither at the north-wind's breath, glittered in the moonbeams, or sang within the shadow of the trees. The nightly saturnalia of the animal world had returned. Even man, restless, dissatisfied, impatient—fevered by ambition or avarice—trembling with guilty fears, or rapt in lofty meditations, owned the witchery of the hour, and forgot to struggle, to shudder, or to hope. From the back piazza of the house the two friends looked out upon the enchanting scene.

"This island," said Velasquez, "will some day own the dominion of the 'stars and stripes,' and then it will be a paradise."

"Nothing is more certain," rejoined his companion; "party feuds, and sectional jealousies may keep it out for a time, but it must inevitably become a part of the American Union, and you and I will probably live to see it."

"I hope so; for I love it despite the blasting tyranny that crushes its industry, and poisons its happiness; and I would have it free and prosperous, albeit that then it would cease to shelter the Rover of the African Main."

"If you accept my proposition it will matter little to you whether the slave trade is permitted or forbidden."

"Let us in, Bernard," was the agitated reply; "I know not where you schooled yourself to speak ever in that calm, unruffled voice; but I believe not your feelings are as dead, and waveless as they seem; and I know, that before we converse further on last night's topic, *I* must have brandy."

Without a word Lile followed his host to the apartment they had occupied during the heats of the day.

"Now," said Velasquez, after supplying himself with the needed beverage, "hear my answer, and ask me as few questions as possible; for you can ask none that will not give me pain. I have thought over all you said; I feel the kindness that dictated it, and acknowledge the hopes it holds out; but it will not do. The office you desire me to take would be sure to excite inquiry, and rip up by-gone events. I will go to Texas, not in your ship, but my own. Not as an officer of the national navy, but as a 'Down East trader,' who is willing, *for a consideration*, to take a few guns aboard his craft, and sail for a time under Texan colors. Doubt not that I will place that *consideration* at a figure the Texan authorities will gladly close with. The engagement once entered into, I will serve her with whatever skill I possess. By the time she needs me no longer, the exploits of Juan Velasquez will be forgotten, or swallowed up in those of some new adventurer. In the meantime, I can prepare the simple villagers for my return by purchasing a small property there, and giving out that the wild sailor, whom they supposed buried in the North Pacific, is cruising along the coast of Mexico, and expects to settle among them to enjoy the little wealth his labors have gathered. This will lull inquiry, or direct it into channels I need not fear. In four or five years I can go back with safety. If this satisfies you, let us turn to other subjects, for I love not to dwell upon promised happiness with maddening years of doubt and trouble intervening.

"I wished it otherwise, but I am content. Are you rich enough to carry out your plans?"

"I have enough, and more than enough. If I should need money at any time, I will apply to you."

"I shall claim your hospitality for one day more, and then I go to Zerah. You and I have done many deeds, John Abbott," he continued, "that will not bear overhauling by the Great Captain above. Mixed with them there has happily been something of good; but there is much yet to atone. Earnestly, and sincerely, let us enter on the work."

"Bernard Lile, if all the diamonds of Brazil were piled before me, I would not take them and exchange the feelings of to-day with those of yesterday. I owe you more—love you more than any human thing—beyond all human things together; and come what may, from this time forth the name of John Abbott shall be stainless. Resume your own; you have done enough already to redeem it, and may wear it with pride."

"Never! never! My punishment would be incomplete could that sweet hope be cherished."

We draw the veil over what followed in that lone mansion in the Island City. Long and fiercely had these two battled with the world. They had riven human statutes and mocked at human punishments. Their fellow-worms could invent no terror to daunt, no torture to appal them, but the shadow of the Archangel's wing rested upon them, and they became as pleading infants before the Eternal Throne.

CHAPTER X.

"How narrowly we miss the road
That might our future life decide!
So many paths are vainly tried!
So many but the right one trode."

"The slightest thing shall turn the scale:
The music of a distant chime,
The visions of an older time,
The weariness of things that fail."

A BRIG lying in the harbor of Havana, was alive and active with the bustle that immediately precedes departure upon a distant voyage. The monotonous, but not unmusical, song of the sailors, as they hoisted in the anchors, floated over the still and glassy waters. The flapping sails already began to catch the gentle breeze, as the parting words of John Abbott and Bernard Lile were spoken.

"Good-bye," said the former, placing his foot on the topmost round of the descending ladder. "Of Juan Velasquez you will never hear again; but in three months, tidings of John Abbott will be borne to you that I hope will please you."

"I doubt it not. For you and I another morn has dawned; and if the cloud comes between us and the sun, we must remember that, to hearts as stubborn as ours it is needful the chastening hand should sometimes be manifest."

The flashing oars dipped in the briny deep—an arrowy ripple spread over its still and waveless surface, and the little boat glided like a thing of life to the mole.

Soft and balmy blew the breezes that wafted the wanderer to his natal home. Alone with his own thoughts, upon the trackless sea, resolutely and impartially he scanned the pages of his existence. How needful is such a task for the purest of the children of earth! and yet how few undertake it! how few of those who do, succeed! Pride and self love are forever interposing a deceptive mist between us and the past. We look upon what has been done always with a feverish anxiety to have it appear as if done for the best. What we know has been done wrong—so palpably wrong no delusion is possible—we attribute to causes beyond our control, or to a blind and undistinguishing destiny. In some form, or in some shape, the spirit of evil is ever present, making self examination a mockery, and blasting the redeeming fruits of repentance, by clothing that repentance in the debasing garb of a weak and cowardly humiliation. Not in this spirit did Bernard Lile disinter the deeds he had committed. Firmly and justly he held the scales—honestly and fairly he weighed them one by one—humbly and penitently he acknowledged the wide errors he detected—nobly and manfully he resolved to amend them. In the rigid impartiality of the trial he had instituted, he discovered a hundred ways in which the most fatal of his mistakes might have been avoided, and its gloomiest consequences robbed of their bitterness. At the time it seemed to him impossible not to have acted as he did without loss of character or self-respect. Now he perceived that he was the victim of the same sin that hurled the rebellious angels from heaven. That a little more of patience and forbearance—a little less of pride and wilfulness, would have changed the whole current of his life, and left him free to exert the high powers of his mind and body, to adorn and ennoble the country he still loved with a yearning tenderness, even in the stormiest periods of his exile, or the blackest of his despair. He saw it all, neither magnifying nor diminishing its unsightly deformity; yet he indulged no unavailing regrets. His repentance was not of that character that weeps over gone follies, but makes no provision against the coming of new ones. Deeds, not tears, were its fruits. A better life, not a gloomier one, its promise.

With a clear sky and favoring gales the good brig tarried not on her voyage. Amid the din, and rush, and bustle of a New York wharf Bernard Lile leaped ashore. A carriage was called, and he was soon rolling over the stony streets to the dwelling of Monsieur Evadne. On his meeting with Zerah we will not dwell. Such scenes are sacred from the vulgar eye. He who loves, and has been separated from all he holds most dear on earth, may easily picture the fondness of the hour—the burning kiss—the close embrace—the earnest question repeated again and again—the loving gaze that wanders over his features, or rests among his locks, to see if time, or war, or toil, have left the impress of their whitening steps—the renewed caress—the speaking face, now pale as the lily, now flushing with the hues of the rose—the swimming eye, and the ruby lip, lighted by smiles as brilliant as the sunbeams that fell on the garden of Eden the first morning of creation—these may be dreamed of, cherished, hugged to our heart of hearts, but not described, revealed or pictured to the gross senses whose channels are of clay. To his young wife he was something more than life and love on earth combined. For him she had abandoned country, kindred, friends. To him she had surrendered heart, imagination, judgment. Beyond these and above them, he had become her religion. On the strong wing of an Asiatic fancy, she had soared from world to world, until she reached and rested among raptures the prophet of her faith was powerless to describe, and sought not to penetrate beyond; but even there, no flower bloomed, no stream glided in silvery beauty, no bird warbled, no incense burned, unless beauty, and music and fragrance were enjoyed by him. How she met him, or how that man of outward calm, and inward fire, returned the greeting, is a secret that those will deserve to be happy who penetrate, and those who do not, never can be.

Days passed, calmly and sweetly in the quiet seclusion of the banker's house. Care, toil, grief, struggles, poverty and crime were around them, but they knew it not. The outward world was forgotten, or remembered only as an unpleasant acquaintance, with whose presence and society they gladly dispensed. It was the season when the "fashionables" have deserted the dusty city, for the more dissipated life of the watering places. Mrs. Winter had taken wing with the rest, and undisturbed by her teasing importunities, Zerah gave herself up to happiness. Lile had communicated to Monsieur Evadne his desire to purchase and fit up a suitable residence in his native village, and that gentleman, with his usual business promptitude, had set about the necessary preliminaries.

The first cold days of Autumn, brought back the summer emigration, and Zerah was startled from her dreams of bliss by an unexpected call from Pauline Winter. With consummate art she affected never to have heard of Bernard Lile's return. Spoke of her meeting with him as an unhoped for pleasure, the greater, she added, from her expectation of converting him into an ally, with whose assistance Mrs. Lile might be induced to mingle in that society she was formed to adorn.

"I should fear, madam," was the courteous reply, "to attempt anything in which you had failed. Besides these are matters I understand little about, and in which I never interfere. Zerah must consult her own taste, as she has always heretofore."

"And that taste," added his wife, "leads me to prefer

the seclusion that early training and habit have made a second nature. You must pardon us, Mrs. Winter; I should bring a cloud upon your gay circles by attempting to move within them."

"That were impossible. But if you will not come yourself, I hope you will occasionally surrender your husband to my keeping. He at least has not habit and religion to plead as an excuse."

"Certainly," said Lile, "I could not wish for a fairer conductress through the mazes of fashion; and none but the most imperious motives could induce me to decline so tempting a proposal. Really, though, Mrs. Winter, my habits are almost as lonely as Zerah's. It has been long since I mingled familiarly with any society except that of the camp."

"So much the better," was the rejoinder. "I am told that long abstinence from the enjoyment of any favorite taste, or appetite, redoubles its pleasure. You shall come to me soon, and make the experiment."

"Perhaps so. But I make no promises. My stay in this city may not be a long one. My duties may at any time call me away; and you may judge how unfit I am for fashionable life, when I venture to plead *duty* to a lady as an excuse for not at once complying with her request.

"I judge nothing now; but shall reserve the question for decision and discussion, when we meet at one of my 'evening reunions.'"

More passed in the same vein. The lady took her departure, believing she had at length succeeded in her long cherished scheme, but without the exulting pride she once thought that success would bring. There was thought upon her brow as she entered the splendid equipage at the door, and there was more of feeling than she knew, or meant to express, in her voice, as she said,

"Good bye. Before many days I shall ask you what you think of life in New York."

An hour before she was burning to introduce him to society. Now she would gladly postpone it, if she could invent any other scheme to secure his society untrammelled by the presence of his wife. A strange riddle is the human heart. Like the little child, who cries and frets because its mother will not let it play with the burning taper, so we grown up children, grow angry, impatient, and rebellious, when any object of desire is beyond our reach. Let the protecting care of the mother be withdrawn from the child, and it learns, through the agony of blistered fingers, that brightness and beauty are not always harmless playthings. Happier than the adult, its punishment is temporary, while the lesson endures for a life-time. For our delusions, on the other hand, there is no cure; because the discovery that they are delusions, is fatal. We go on drawing thread after thread from the inmost core of the heart, and twining them into a glossy drapery, on which we hang the hopes and joys of existence. If the support to which they are attached should give way, the life-blood is dragged out by the falling thread, and all human feeling hurried to a rayless tomb. From such lessons no wisdom is ever gathered, no amendment ever follows. They are sent in judgment, not in mercy, and, to add to the bitterness of the punishment, they are clothed in the semblance of boons we have importunately demanded, and impiously reproached the hand that withheld them.

Alone in her carriage, Mrs. Winter became seriously and gloomily thoughtful. The curtain of a hitherto hidden mystery in her existence was beginning to be withdrawn.

"He is singularly handsome," was her inward reflection. "So calm, so self-possessed, and withal so gentle in his manners, who could believe his life had been passed in camps, with a rude soldiery for his only tutors. Mr. Bernard Lile may tell me what he pleases, but that soft and refined politeness was learned in the peaceful courts of kings, not in the rough tents of war. But it is his voice that moves me most; low, and sweet, and musical as an Æolian harp; oh! how much better is it fitted for a lover's pleading in a lady's bower, than a chieftain's harsh commands amid the vile din and butchery of a battle-field. Why did I not meet him before such impassable barriers had grown up between us? How madly I should have loved him! How different would my existence have been from the aimless thing it is?"

Poor self-deceiver, you love him now. The burning taper is before you. With the child's simplicity you are longing to play with the graceful flame. The boon you seek is death; and if left for another week to the guidance of your own judgment, woe and doom are before you.

When Lile returned to the room where he had left his wife, he found her standing on the floor. She approached, and placing her hand on his shoulder, inquired anxiously,

"Will you go to these public parties, Bernard?"

"No, Zerah. For many reasons, no. First, and that would be enough alone, it would cause you uneasiness. You have not mentioned Mrs. Winter's name since my return, but I have forgotten no word of your letter. Besides, it does not at all comport with my plans to become an object of curiosity to all the idle people of New York. I meant to leave here very soon, at all events. Mrs. Winter has hurried our departure. To-morrow we will go, if you can put up for a time with the discomforts of an unfinished house."

He took her hands in his, and, drawing her nearer to him, stooped to imprint a kiss upon her brow. The shadows of doubt and foreboding anxiety, which had gathered there, were dissipated, and a glad smile lighted up her angel features, as she replied,

"I can put up with anything where you are, but in truth there is nothing to put up with. It will be a pleasure, rather than an annoyance, to try a more primitive mode of living than is allowable under Monsieur Evadne's roof. You will think me childish and foolish," she continued, "but I cannot drive from my mind the conviction, that Mrs. Winter will some day work you harm. I had a strange wild dream, while you were gone. I thought she had come between you and me, and I had stabbed her as she slept. When I waked, I could scarcely shake off the impression that the warm blood still covered my hand. I shudder even yet to think of it."

"You must strive to give brighter colors to your fancies, Zerah. The fact that Mrs. Winter stiil lives, in excellent health, ought to teach you the fallacy of trusting to dreams."

"Nay, I believe not in dreams as the vulgar interpret them: but if read aright they have a voice of wisdom not to be despised. Once, when a little girl, I wandered forth with my father to gather the flocks from the hill side. We met an old man weeping bitterly. His life had been so blameless and affectionate that he was known throughout the tribe as the 'favorite of Allah.' Wondering what it was that had wrung such bitter tears from the patriarch, my father approached and inquired into the cause of his grief.

"'I had a dream last night,' was the reply, 'that disturbs me sorely. I dreamed I had murdered the friend of my early days.'

"And my father spoke, as you did but now, and said, 'Why weep for that? you know it was all unreal; your friend still lives.'

"'Yes, so the young and strong always reason; but the

spirit, that trembles on the verge of eternity, is gifted with a clearer vision. Allah sends no messenger on an idle errand. That dream came to warn me to guard well the future—that I had within me impulses and passions that *might* lead to murder—that under the influence of interest, ambition, or anger I had the capacity to dye my hands in the blood of my dearest friend. Therefore I weep to find that old age, and a life of self watching, have not conquered the innate baseness of my nature, and that I must go on trembling, and guarding against myself to the tomb.'

"The old man's language has abided with me to the present day. I shudder to think there are things that would make me shed blood."

"Is that all," replied her husband, in a lighter tone than was usual for him. "Then be at rest, sweet one, for that is a knowledge no dream was needed to impart. Unless my memory is greivously at fault, you have shed blood, and shuddered not when it flowed."

"But that was by your side and in your defence."

"Yes, and I little thought when, to amuse you, I spent months in teaching you to wield the light yataghan of Asia, that one day the lessons would be turned to so good an account. If you had dreamed of that beforehand, I should have had more faith in your visions now. For the rest, be assured that all of us need self watching; but there is no reason why that supervision should not be exercised without bringing gloom and disquiet to the mind. Henceforth let the clouds be mine, and the sunshine yours. I must go forth to prepare for our departure. Make your preparations also. In a few days, among the green hills of New Hampshire, you will forget this idle dream."

She said no more; but she *did not* forget. It had taken too strong hold of her fancy to allow reason to combat it successfully.

In a little village of New Hampshire, whose name and exact locality, the curious reader must excuse us for withholding, weeks and months of undisturbed and tranquil happiness flew over the heads of Zerah and her husband. Gradually Lile had worked himself into the regards of the sturdy villagers. No ostentation of wealth—no assumption of superiority proclaimed the wide difference between the rich and gifted stranger, and his unpretending neighbors. Daily he mingled with them familiarly as an equal, receiving and bestowing the hundred little kindnesses that sweeten the intercourse of adjoining farmers. His wife, too, had thrown aside her eastern garb, and not unfrequently was seen wending across the fields to the old homesteads around, or listening with grave attention to the advice of the thrifty house-wives who insisted on instructing her in all the mysteries of the kitchen and the pantry. By and by she was prevailed upon to attend the old stone church, whose erection dated back beyond the revolution, and though she never neglected the observances of her own faith, she exhibited a reverential respect for those of her Christian neighbors, and the venerated pastor already began to speak of her as "a brand snatched from the burning." Her husband knew her better. He knew that soft nature was harder than steel in all matters connected with her religion, but he listened to the old pastor's words without attempting to correct his error. To her he said,

"I feared greatly these people would annoy you with their preaching, for I knew of old that it is the nature of a Yankee to feel more interest in everybody's soul than his own. I am rejoiced to see how easily you have accommodated yourself to circumstances, and how good humoredly you submit to their obtrusive intermeddlings with your conscience."

"Love, Bernard," was the reply, "is a gentle teacher,

and a happy heart finds no difficulty in banishing ill temper. These people are kind to you. They are trying to be kind to me, and it would be cruel to tell them by word or act they are only impertinent."

"You are right, and I was wrong to mistrust the spirit in which you would receive it. Remember, if at any time hereafter you should grow impatient with them, there is nothing that so delights a genuine Yankee as wearying heaven with prayers for some person who stands in less need of them than himself, or some thing about which he is in profound ignorance, yet imagines he understands a little better than his Maker. Every community has its follies. In New England seven in every ten are afflicted with the belief, that the Almighty has placed them here for the special purpose of enlightening and redeeming the rest of mankind, and that in order to do this, it it quite immaterial how many vices and immoralities they leave uncorrected, and unrebuked at home, so they only declaim loudly and long against those they discover, or imagine to exist, elsewhere. Bear with them until it becomes really offensive. In that case I know how to put a stop to it. In any case consult your own heart, and that alone, it is a truer and a holier guide than you can find in all New England."

A new subject for gossip now engrossed the attention of the villagers. An agent had come up from Boston and bought the old homestead of Ephraim Abbot. It was soon known that this purchase had been made in the name of John Abbott, the wild sailor boy, who had gone off on a whaling expedition and never returned. Rumors were rife that he had amassed a considerable fortune by gainful traffic with the Pacific islands, and was now cruising as a privateer under the flag of Texas, against the commerce of Mexico. None knew exactly when he would return, but the purchase of his father's former mansion was regarded as conclusive proof that he intended soon to settle for life in his native village. Everywhere there is magic in wealth. Here, where titles of nobility are forbidden, and coronets and ducal crowns, are not allowed to divide the admiration of the populace, we look at the rich through magnifying glasses of intense power. From one end of the republic to the other, they are treated with a subserviency whose universality is all that redeems it from baseness. The satirist may ridicule, the moralist bemoan, and the orator denounce this patent meanness; but men who have read the poem with delight, and the essay with a feeling conviction of its truth, or listened with rapt attention to the burning words of the speaker, will, the next hour, run across a crowded street to shake a rich man's hand, when virtue and intellect clothed in rags, if met upon the same pavement would struggle in vain for a passing notice. It was wonderful with how many virtues the reported riches of John Abbott had clothed him. Those who a month before had forgotten his existence, and those who spoke of him as a graceless scamp, for whom the devil had an especial fondness from his cradle, now remembered a hundred anecdotes of his goodness of heart, and energy of character, and more than one gray headed wiseacre was heard to say, in tones of self-gratulation, "I always knew there was backbone in the boy." Bernard Lile was the only person in the village who appeared to be unabsorbed by the momentous event. He listened to all the others had to say, but made no comments on the various stories he heard.

Winter came—the hard winter of New England. Cold and bitter as it was, Zerah gladly welcomed its coming, since it afforded a never-failing excuse for the seclusion she loved to indulge. Her husband went forth as usual, but she stirred not beyond her own door. Early in April Lile entered her apartment and handed her an open letter. It was from John Abbott.

"Your accounts," he wrote, "are so favorable, that I have changed my original purpose. I shall be with you in two months after this is received. You know all that is needful to be done, and I leave it in your hands."

"I am so glad," she exclaimed, glancing over the brief contents of the letter; "I love that man, though I saw him but seldom."

"And you were right Zerah. The instincts of the good are the truest wisdom after all. Show me the man upon whom young girls and children love to fondle, and I will show you one who, whatever the world may say of him, has a kind and upright heart. John Abbott has long followed a traffic forbidden by the laws, and reprobated by the philanthropists, but he is sterling gold nevertheless."

Before those two months had rolled away, the rose had faded from the cheek of Zerah, and the springy lightness of her step was gone. The winds of the White Mountains had swept over the sun-born flower of Asia, and mingled with its warm life the icy chill of consumption. Care, skill, and nursing, were lavished upon her, but her step grew weaker visibly, and the hollow cough, too surely indicated the fatal nature of the disease. Lile would sit by her side, and talk for hours tenderly and hopefully, but alone in his own room he paced the floor with uncertain steps, often raising his clenched hand, and uttering a fierce groan of mingled agony and defiance. About this time John Abbott made his promised appearance. He was warmly welcomed by the villagers, and days were given up to receiving their visits, and listening to their congratulations. At length an ill-natured gossip, anxious to ingratiate himself with the rich man, inquired if their new neigbor, Mr.

Lile, had called to pay his respects, and upon being answered in the negative, was proceeding to comment harshly upon the seeming discourtesy, when he was interrupted by another, of better heart, who suggested that the serious illness of Mrs. Lile might well be her husband's apology. This gave Capt. Abbott the opportunity he desired to make inquiries without exciting remark, and he soon extracted a full history of Bernard Lile and his wife since their settlement in ———. At the close of the conversation he announced his purpose to "drop in before long and take a look at the stranger." Whatever Capt. Abbott did was right of course; and "everybody" exclaimed, "what a kind, good heart he has!" when they saw him next day deliberately walking towards the house of mourning.

Their meeting was that of stern, strong men, who love each other, and have been brought together in a period of trial and of sorrow. Scarcely a word was spoken—not a tear gathered in either eye, but their hands were clasped with a force that would have wrung the blood from fingers less sinewy and hard. At once Lile led his friend to the room where Zerah was reclining on a sofa, by the open window, to enjoy the breezes of summer. Gently and tenderly the sailor greeted her, regretting that he did not find her in the same high health as when they parted at Timboo, but speaking cheerfully of her speedy recovery. He made many minute inquiries of the places she had visited since, and listened with deep interest to all that had pleased or gratified her in her journeyings. When he rose to leave it was with the assurance that he would call every day she was willing to receive him. Lile walked a short distance with him down the green lane.

"I think I know all," he said, "but it is possible my

love for her frightens me too much. Do you think there is *a chance* for her recovery."

"Bernard, if you were a weak man—nay more, if fate could deal any blow that would make you shrink and cower; in a word, if you were not my brother, I would tell you to hope."

"Hush! Breathe not that word. Even she knows it not. While I live it must be blotted from your vocabulary. When I am gone the secret is yours; do with it as you will."

"You think then," he continued, "she must die."

"Before another crop of flowers have scented the air, the loveliest bloom that ever gladdened the earth since Adam and Eve were driven by the flaming sword and waving wing of the angel from Paradise, will be hidden beneath the turf in yonder church-yard."

"So my own judgment tells me. I shall see you to-morrow."

"Yes; and the next day, and the next. Never in gloom or peril have you fallen away from my side, and though I cannot avert this grief, I can, and will share it with you."

John Abbott was true to his promise. Every day he was at his brother's door. Every day he sat by the side of Zerah, and beguiled the weary hours with the wild stories he had gathered in his adventurous career, until at last the stricken victim began to look for his coming with as much impatience as her husband. The villagers soon found that good-humored and frank as Capt. Abbott generally was, there were some subjects with which it was not safe to meddle. Above all he brooked no allusion to his brother's wife, or her religion. One day he was walking with a deacon along the street. It was the hour when the factory operatives were released from the noon-day meal. A company of volunteers were parading at the time. The little children, pleased with the show, paid little attention to any thing but the soldiers. One of them, covered with cotton from the factory, heedlessly ran against the prim deacon, and soiled his best suit. With an angry "mind what you are about," the deacon rudely applied his huge paw to the little fellow's delicate cheek. In a moment Abbott caught his arm in the gripe of a vice, and said sternly,

"Give that boy a dollar."

"What should I give him a dollar for?"

"Because this muster is the only glimpse of sunshine the poor thing has seen in a month, and you have clouded that by your brutal treatment."

"I guess I have no dollars to give away."

"And I guess," was the prompt reply, "that if you don't do it, I will wallow you in the mire, until every rag on your back is too filthy to carpet a pig-stye."

This threat, and the manner of him who made it, could not be resisted. The dollar was slowly and reluctantly handed to the now grinning urchin.

"So far, so well," said Abbott; "but night before last, at prayer-meeting, you took occasion to put up a long petition for the 'poor, pagan wife' of Bernard Lile. If he had heard you, he would have broken every bone in your body, if the life of a generation had died with you. And now let me tell you for myself, that, if ever you breathe her name again in public meeting, I will get up and expose your conduct of to-day."

The deacon walked way, and John Abbott had an enemy for life: but John Abbott cared very little for that.

At another time he was listening to one of those pious gentry, whose charity is too expansive to be confined to their neighorhood or state, discoursing upon the horrors of southern slavery, and solemnly averring that he believed it to be a holiness in the sight of God and man to assist a slave in escaping from his master.

"Have you ever been in a slave state?" asked Abbott.

"I am happy to say I never have," was the pert reply, "and I trust I never may be."

"Well, I have: and I am happy to say there is no state south of the Potomac, where a man could do what you did three weeks ago, without being shunned as a leper."

"What did I do, sir?"

"You employed a man to mow in your meadow, and when he accidentally cut himself dangerously, you not only refused to send for surgical assistance, but refused to feed him, and turned him from your door, bleeding as he was. I, sir, the upholder of slavery, took him in; fed, nourished, and tended him. Which do you think rendered the most acceptable service to heaven?"

The man slunk off, but another, who was not disposed to yield the argument so readily, entered the lists with the air of a man who is about to propound and unanswerable interrogatory.

"You cannot deny, Captain Abbott, that southern slavery is fatal to female virtue?"

"I do deny it. Like every human institution, it is liable to abuse; and that it is sometimes abused in this regard, I do not question. But that is the fault of human nature, not of the system. If your life was pried into as closely as you are desirous of prying into the lives of our southern brethren, it would be easy to prove you a panderer to prostitution."

The man was one of the most sanctimonious members of the church in ———. He reddened with anger as he replied,

"I defy you to make good your insinuation."

"That is exactly what I mean to do," was the cool rejoinder. "You had a poor orphan girl engaged as a 'help' in your family. In trying to avoid treading on your little child, who had crawled in her way, she stumbled, and broke a handful of plates and dishes. You turned her out of employment, gave her a bad name, refused to pay her wages, and left her no alternative but starvation, or prostitution. She is now the inmate of a den of infamy. Do you think a just God will permit you to be singing in heaven, while she is shrieking in hell?"

If John Abbott had been a poor man, he would have been perfectly unendurable in ———, but he was rich, and his bitter sayings were all set down to the account of a sailor's "eccentricities."

In the meantime, Bernard Lile was in happy ignorance of all that was passing around him. Occupied with attentions to his suffering wife, he never bestowed a thought upon the outward world. Her's was the common history of consumption. At times the hectic flush of the disease spread over her cheek, and gave it the rosy hue of health. At times she felt better and stronger, and walked forth into the fields, leaning on the arm of her husband, to enjoy the sweet scenery of a New England summer. The hopeless nature of her complaint had been hidden from her, but one evening as she looked out upon the setting sun, she turned and said,

"I am going before you, Bernard. Like yon glorious orb, darkness will soon be about the places where I have loved to dwell; but remember the sun shines on, though we see it not, and when the shadow comes to us, another hemisphere is bathing in its lustre. So when the worm is eating our earthly tenement, the soul only goes to be robed by angel hands with a higher loveliness."

It was the first time she had alluded to her approaching end, and accustomed as he had been to suppress every sign of human emotion he shuddered as the trembling tones fell upon his ear.

"I do remember it, Zerah; and I remember also the prophecy of the Syrian Sage. I do not, indeed, believe in the sweet dream precisely as he painted it, but my soul tells me we shall meet hereafter, and be the happier for the meeting."

"Oh, yes! But for that, death would be very dark, and very dreary. As it is, I think of it as a long parting, which must take place, and which it is wrong to sadden still more by repining."

"You view it justly, my own love; and I will try to bear this blow with a portion of your own sweetness; although it is far heavier than all that have gone before. God placed you upon earth as an instrument to redeem a bold strong man, whose feet had wandered widely from heaven. Your mission is accomplished, and his ministers are waiting to bear you to your native skies. I must await his good pleasure before I rejoin you. I know not what work he may have for me to perform, but I am sure it will not be denied me to pray earnestly and fervently, that it may be a brief one."

"Trust all to Him. I see before you days of usefulness, and deeds of high and holy import. Happy here you cannot be when I am gone, but you can pave the way for a happiness that knows no end, *and you will.*"

A week later, Bernard Lile, and John Abbott, were standing over a new made grave in the old church-yard of ———.

"Let there be no name," said the former, "upon the tombstone. Engrave on it, the simple line, 'The beautiful has departed.' When I also am dust, have our names linked together on the slab." I have made you a deed," he continued, "of the little farm, and all that pertains to it. Lock up the room in which she died, and let no one enter it until my return. Take the little cimeter in the armory—it was hers, and saved my life once in her hand—hang it up in your own bed-room, and see that neither rust nor dirt defiles it. With all else do as you think best. If you should marry, and need additional funds for your family wants, draw upon Evadne. He will have instructions to honor your drafts."

"But, Bernard," said his companion, "I have no ties to bind me here, and see no reason why I should not go with you."

"There are many. In the first place you are a sailor, and unfit for the woods; but the unanswerable reason is, that if you go, there will be no one left to do all that is proper and right for her who found Bernard Lile a hardened devil, and left him *a man.* Besides, I shall not be alone. I left a friend on the frontier, as bold, as strong, and as true as you are, John; and that is saying a great deal. The forest and the prairie have long been his home. I shall seek his cabin and abide with him for a time. You will hear from me as often as circumstances will permit. For this night I claim the shelter of your roof. Mine would bring up thoughts it is better not to awaken. To-morrow I go."

The long absence he contemplated, and the many things that demanded his attention before his departure, protracted his stay in New York, far beyond his original expectations. To his surprise, he received a note from Mrs. Winter, condoling with him on his recent bereavement. It was written kindly, and in excellent taste, but it recalled events that were painful, and he would have prefered that it had not been received. There was, however, no alternative but to answer it, and he did so with graceful courtesy. He heard of her no more, until they accidently met upon

Broadway. He was about passing, with a mere bow of recognition, when she called him by name, and made some inquiry he could not avoid answering without rudeness. Mrs. Winter had far too much tact to allude to his former evasion of her hospitalities, but she remembered it, and was determined not to be foiled a second time.

"You are going to Monsieur Evadne's?"

"Yes. My outdoor business for the day is completed, and I was returning to address some letters to a few friends before my departure from New York."

"My purchases are also finished," she said, "and as I am going in the same direction, we will walk on together."

With easy self-possession, she dropped into the current news of the day—making not the slightest allusion to Zerah, or to the fashionable world, with which her existence had heretofore seemingly been bound up. She wished him to remember neither the one, nor the other. With the instinctive quickness of a woman, she felt that Bernard Lile had loved for the last time, but she knew that the very loneliness that follows the going down of the bright star, from which we have drunk in all of gladness and beauty, that has cheered our mortal state, prepares the heart for the reception of kindly emotions; and that words fitly spoken at such a time, are sure to win friendship, if they kindle not the flames of a new passion from the ashes of the old. Love was represented by the Ancients as a blind divinity. If so, his other organs are endowed with a delicacy and keenness that make ample atonement for the defect. Mrs. Winter was in love, and with exquisite skill she was careful to say nothing to scare away the bird she wished to entice.

"You spoke but now," she remarked, "of your speedy departure from New York. Do you indeed leave us soon?"

"Such is my present purpose. I have been delayed already beyond the time when I had hoped to be on my journey."

"It would be impertinent," she said, slowly, "to question the entire correctness of a purpose, whose controlling motive I do not know, but not impertinent nor intrusive, I trust, to regret the pleasure of which it threatens to deprive me."

"I had not the vanity to suppose," he replied, "that my going, or remaining, would bring regret or satisfaction to one surrounded as you are with enjoyments."

"The enjoyments may not be as real as they seem."

"Those of this world seldom are. But I should judge that *you* had few wishes ungratified."

"In truth there are very few: still the conviction that there is one cherished object beyond our reach, is sufficient to embitter all the blessings that are granted. I say not this is my case. I but enunciate a truth in which I am sure you will concur. We part at this corner," she continued, hastily, as if unwilling to hear a reply, "I shall be rejoiced to see you again before you leave. Monsieur Evadne can furnish you with our address."

To an invitation so conveyed, it was difficult to frame a refusal, and Lile had given his promise to call upon the Syren before she walked away.

Why Mrs. Winter should perseveringly seek the society of a man who did not love her, and who her reason told her never would, is a question philosophical speculators may settle among themselves. It might be a sufficient answer to say she loved, and with those who do, hope rarely dies. We may think it extinguished. We may examine our bosoms again and again, and *say* that it is; but like the little stream that winds its living path hundreds of feet below the earth's surface, it flows on, unseen, unknown, buoyant with life, and seeking only some narrow crevice to bubble into light.

Still another question may suggest itself. Why should she, who was bound for life to another, by vows plighted at the altar, encourage the growth of a passion which, whether successful or unsuccessful, must bring woe, and might bring suffering and disgrace together?"

> ———————— curious fool be still,
> Is human love the growth of human will?"

Nearly always we are hurried into errors, where the heart is concerned, without the least perception of the consequences. The dream is too sweet to permit us to reason of its uncertain results: or, if we reason at all, reason itself is colored by the love it is evoked to destroy. As long as the threads are of gossamer, we think it ridiculous to guard against fetters a breath can destroy. By the time we wake to the necessity of a struggle, those threads are of hardened steel, and the captive is bound forever. Nay, more, he has lost the *wish* to be free. The growth of such a passion is often as rapid as the gourd that sheltered Jonah on the plains of Nineveh. Happy, thrice happy, would it be, if it withered and died as soon. Mrs. Winter began by thinking she could love Bernard Lile, if there were no barriers between them. The step he had taken of leaving New York, suddenly, and without warning, connected him inseparably with her thoughts. In the interval of his absence, she discovered that she was madly in love; for the first time her heart had been touched. She knew it, and she *said* to herself that she rejoiced he was gone. She even tried to believe that the wearing dissipation of fashionable life would soon blot his image from her memory.

"How is it possible," she inwardly asked, "that I, hackn'ed in the world's ways, and daily wasting mind and heart upon its mean ambitions, should be capable of loving to a degree that might be dangerous? When younger, with feelings fresh and untutored by experience, I played with the gentle passion; what have I to dread now?"

Mrs. Winter knew not that Cupid himself had suggested this mode of reasoning, and she went on thinking of Bernard Lile, more and more, until his manly form was ever before her, and his musical voice eternally ringing in her ear. Often she awakened from slumbers in which he had mingled with the bright things that thronged around her dreaming pillow, and then she would close her eyes, and try to sleep again, hoping to enjoy once more the sweet and cherished madness of the vision. By and by she heard that his young and lovely wife had returned to heaven: and her heart throbbed with startling vehemence, when she reflected that a mighty gap had thus been made in the wall of adamant that separated her from the object of her absorbing passion. What obstacle now remained? None, she thought, but the formal vows her husband had purchased at the marriage altar, and these were but little likely to restrain her from the gratification of the intense delights imagination had pictured. Anxiously she revolved many different schemes for bringing about a meeting without seeming to seek it; and when chance at length effected it, she hailed that chance as a happy augury for the future.

Not many days had elapsed before Bernard Lile was at the door of the stately mansion of Mr. Winter. The lady received him alone. An hour passed in pleasant and agreeable conversation. When he departed she bade him adieu with winning courtesy, but nothing more. She did not walk to the door with him, but turned to the music-stand, and examined, or seemed to examine, the contents of a new volume, until he had descended to the street. Then she sat down on the little stool, and buried her face in her hands, not to weep, but to think. After a while she rose and walked from the room, muttering, indistinctly,

"He will come again. I am sure of that."

He did come, and, as he found he was not to be annoyed by invitations to attend her public parties, his visits were repeated. Gradually her manner towards him became more tender. Gradually she led him away from intellectual topics to softer themes. She contrived to let him understand, not suddenly but by partial glimpses, how loveless her life had been, and gently wooed compassion to her joyless lot. Admirably her game was played. With the calculating skill of a finished chess player, she touched no piece it was dangerous to move. Any other man would have been subdued; and even he with all his wide experience, and lofty intellect, owed his safety alone to the memories that clustered about the grave of his departed wife. He began to suspect that her feelings towards him were of a warmer nature than prudence would justify, when one evening as they stood alone at a window watching the sinking sun, she laid her hand on his arm, and looking inquiringly in his face, said,

"Will nothing persuade you to abandon the thoughts of roving away from a land as lovely, and as happy as this?"

"I can hardly say that a choice is left me," was the reply. "Here I might do some good, but that is problematical—At all events I know where there is a field of labor for which I am fitted; and I must not permit pleasure to lessen the demands of duties my judgment tells me are imperative."

"Do you then think that in our pilgrimage through life it is wrong or improper to gather such enjoyments as are to be found by the wayside?"

"Certainly I hold no such opinion. On the contrary I

believe every innocent enjoyment is an acceptable offering in the sight of heaven. I only mean that *for me* no enjoyments are left—that nothing but duties remain."

"Why so? Rich as you are, and gifted with capacities for the keenest intellectual and social delights, why should you not sip the honey that is presented to your lips, rather than wander afar off for the gall and wormwood that taxes your industry to find?"

The sun had gone down, and the evening star was shining alone in the heavens. He answered not directly but pointed to the solitary sphere and said, mournfully,

"Look at yonder star. Notwithstanding all its brilliancy it is denied companionship with its celestial sisters. A little later when its fellow orbs begin to glimmer in the blue vault it will sink below the horizon's edge. So it has done for ages that are gone; so it will do for ages that are to come. To me, as to that star, the doom of solitude has been spoken. I know not the purpose, but I know that it must be obeyed. Wherever the happy and the beautiful are, my stay must be brief. Already I am beginning to feel that I have needlessly encountered the risk of receiving another bruise upon a withered and broken reed.

"Your simile may be just as far as it goes, but it is imperfect. Look now again to the right of yonder star whose solitary brilliancy you bemoan. Do you not see a little orb whose rays are almost lost in the splendor by its side? Sweet and lovely in its retiring modesty it clings with undying tenacity to its glorious mate; together they traverse the remaining segment of the circle; together they sink into the ocean wave."

There was a dead silence for many minutes. When she looked up, there was a lustre beyond that of the stars in her speaking eyes, and sweeter than the flutes of angels floated the soft syllables—

"Do you understand me now?"

The step of Mr. Winter sounded in the entry. To her it was as hateful as the sentence that condemns a felon to the gallows—to him it was as welcome as the pardon that reverses the stern decree.

When alone in his own apartment he passed in review the events of the last ten days, and wondered at his blindness. He thought now that he ought to have perceived she loved him from the beginning, and he reproached himself for permitting the illusion to last so long. How to remedy the evil was his next care. With the decisive promptitude of his character he rang the bell, and requested the presence of Monsieur Evadne. Upon the entrance of that gentleman, he calmly remarked,

"I have not given as much attention to our business matters, my good friend, for the last few days as I might have done, and I have sent for you to know if it is possible to close them up by ten o'clock to-morrow."

"Everything," replied Evadne, "is possible with energy and industry."

"I may then count upon its being done?"

"Assuredly. It will only cost the loss of a few hour's sleep, and that my clerks are as well accustomed to as myself."

"I am obliged to you for your promptness. There is but one other thing I wish attended to. When I am gone write to Robert Wilson—advise him to resign his commission in the army, and engage in some civil pursuit that holds out the promise of greater, and more immediate usefulness. Tell him that you have instructions to honor his drafts for whatever amount may be necessary to start him in business, and that it is my earnest wish he should consult with you as to the future, and regulate his conduct in some degree by your advice. You know how to do this kindly and well, and I trust it to you. Say to him that I shall be absent for a considerable period. I know not how long. You may add that I am alone now, and that Zerah sleeps in the old church yard at ———."

With difficulty the man of business drove back the choking sensation he felt rising in his throat and inquired, huskily,

"Is there anything more to be done?"

"Nothing now. I will hand you some papers at breakfast, together with written directions where to find me when it is needful. Good night."

The banker left the room, and the strong man kneeling in his solitary chamber, sought relief from the wild war of his own rebellious passions in earnest and fervent supplication at the foot stool of the Most High. There, alone with his God, new hopes sprang into existence, and his soul drank in the beginning of the promise.

"Behold, I create new heavens, and a new earth; and the former shall not be remembered, nor come into mind."

CHAPTER XI.

"If thou hast crushed a flower,
The root may not be blighted;
If thou hast quenched a lamp,
Once more it may be lighted.
* * * * *
"But if upon the troubled sea
Thou cast a gem unheeded;
Hope not that wind or wave will bring
The treasure back when needed."

PAULINE WINTER knew not the effect her words had produced. She knew she had given pain, but from that very circumstance she extracted hope, since it indicated that whatever other difficulties she might have to overcome, she would not be required to combat the sullen calm of passionless despair. She was neither surprised nor uneasy at his absence the next day, and she made no inquiries into the cause of it. But when another and another passed, and brought no tidings, she grew restless and fearful. On the fourth morning a letter was put into her hands from Philadelphia.

"After our last interview," it ran, "I found it absolutely necessary to leave New York at once. It can matter little to you where I go, or what fate awaits me; but I cannot find it in my heart to make so churlish a return for all your kindness as to set out upon a journey of years without a word of leave-taking. In the busy world you will have no leisure to think of one who has crossed your path for a moment only to sadden it, and long before I come back again you will have forgotten my existence. With warm thanks for the hours not unhappily passed in your society, and still warmer wishes for your welfare, I bid you adieu.

"BERNARD LILE."

She read this note repeatedly with close attention. At one time she thought she could trace in it evidences of a heart not altogether untouched by the arts she had employed to win it. At another she crushed it in her tiny palm with a feeling of agonised despair. Then again she smoothed the crumpled paper, and pressed it to her fevered lips. Finally, it was deposited in her bosom, with the inward resolution to write to him as soon as she could extract the necessary information as to where a letter would reach him from Mons. Evadne, revealing all the wild fervor of the love that consumed her, and begging him to return if he would not have the stream of her existence dried up at the fountain.

In the meantime Bernard Lile was floating down the beautiful Ohio, towards its junction with the turbid Mississippi. On the western borders of Texas there was pressing need for the bold and strong to protect the families of the settlers from the constant incursions of Indians and Mexicans. The treaty of peace and limits signed by Santa Anna had, in a short time thereafter, been declared a nullity by Bustamente, and a merciless war had recommenced, more apparently for the purpose of harassing and annoying the Texans, than with any hope of ultimate subjugation. Large armies were no longer poured upon her territories, but from Metamoras, Reynosa, Camargo, and other towns along the Rio Grande, frequent expeditions were sent secretly and suddenly across the border, plundering and burning detached settlements, small towns and villages, and then rapidly retreating without waiting to try the issue of a battle. In this way the country beyond the San Antonio had been completely desolated. One family resided at Live Oak Point, between the bays of Aransas and Copano, and another at Lamar, across the bay from Live Oak Point. With these exceptions the wild animals were the only inhabitants of the vast region stretching away from the San Antonio to the Rio Grande. Even along the former river the settlements were few and far between. Some miles below the point where the road from Lamar to Victoria crosses the San Antonio, Tom Simpson had erected his cabin, and surrounded it with a rude palisade of logs. On the eastern side it was protected by the river bottom, whose waters almost washed its base. From every other quarter the approach was over a level prairie, and Simpson had too much confidence in himself and his rifle to doubt his ability to defend it against any predatory party, while the river bottom afforded a never-failing means of escape from any more considerable force. He had another security also in the absence of any thing to tempt the cupidity of either Mexicans or Camanches. Living altogether upon the produce of the chase—raising no herds, and cultivating no crops, there was nothing to be gained by disturbing him except rifle bullets directed with wonderful accuracy towards the vitals of the assailants. He was widely known on the border, and as widely feared and hated by his country's enemies. Many a scheme had been laid to entrap him without success, but they shrunk from an open assault upon his slight fortress, well knowing that it must be attended with a heavy loss, and would moreover very probably result in failure. One evening in June he had ascended to the roof of his cabin for the purpose of looking out upon the prairie to mark if any rising smoke, or other sign, indicated the neighborhood of an enemy. Two horsemen were approaching from the direction of the Victoria road.

"They must be some of our people," he said, after ascertaining that they were certainly alone. "No two men in

Mexico would undertake to enter Tom Simpson's den, if the gate was wide open before them."

He descended deliberately, and drawing the block from the port-hole, examined the new comers with close attention. When they had approached within thirty yards, he suddenly threw open the gate, and, with a shout of wild joy, rush out to meet them.

"I knew it would be so," he said, clasping the hand of Lile, and wringing it again and again, "I knew we should meet on the border once more."

Cordially and kindly Lile returned the warm greeting of his friend. The party then entered the enclosure, and Simpson, after closing and barring the gate, assisted in removing the saddles and bridles from the horses—shook down a quantity of hay cut from the long grass of the prairie, and left them to wander at will within the palisades. To questions propounded by Simpson, Bernard Lile said,

"I remembered your parting words on the beach at Galveston, and made my way at once to the West. In Victoria, I fortunately met with this gentleman, and prevailed upon him to guide me to your dwelling."

Lile's companion was no stranger to Simpson; who now turned to him, and said with animation,

"And let me tell you, Bill Stokes, that you have done many a worse day's work. I shall remember this as long as I am above ground, whenever you need a helping hand. If it ever happens that the Mexicans or Camanches light upon your cattle, or mustangs, I'll follow the trail to the Rio Grande, or the Rocky Mountains, but what I'll have them back."

All this time the hunter was busily engaged in the duties of hospitality. The fire had been replenished, and a plentiful supply of venison was sending out its savoury smell from the hearthstone. The cooking utensils were few and rude, but the most fastidious epicure would not have objected to the flavor of the repast. When it was ended, the three gathered around a blazing fire, which is not uncomfortable in that climate, after nightfall, during the hottest seasons. Many questions were asked and answered on either side, and several hours of the night thus glided almost imperceptibly by.

Something outside attracted the hunter's attention. He rose and stood at the door for awhile in silence, then fastening it securely with two heavy bars, he inquired in a low tone,

"Did you hear that?"

"Yes," answered Stokes, taking down his rifle, and bullet pouch, "the Camanches are about."

"I heard nothing," said Lile, "but the hooting of an owl."

"It was a Camanche," responded Simpson, "as certain as a gun is iron."

Lile imitated the example of his companions, and armed himself without delay; observing, however, as he did so,

"I am afraid I have become a little rusty. Tell me why you are so certain that sound was made by a human being at all—if so, why by an Indian, and, particularly, why by a Camanche? for I am told there are many roving tribes in this vicinity."

"Listen," said Simpson, "do you hear it now?"

"Yes."

"Do you hear the echo from the river?"

"Yes."

"Well, the human voice has an echo, but there is none to the hoot of an owl. Besides, that sound comes directly from the west. The nearest timber in that direction is a little *mott* two miles off. I never heard of an owl's lighting in the grass to pitch his infernal ugly tune. It is not a Mexican, for they know that five thousand Greasers couldn't catch me at night, with the river bottom in ten feet of my fence. It is not a Tonkawa, or Caroncahua, because I am on friendly terms with them, and they would have had more sense, too, than to agree on a signal they know I understand. It is a Camanche *sure*, and there are not less than fifty to back him. They will waste a full half hour, before they begin the attack, in prying around to find out whether I'm asleep or awake. The first notice they git will be apt to be a bullet through the short ribs."

So saying, he led the way to the top of the house, the roof of which was nearly flat, while the outside logs, running several feet above it, formed an excellent breastwork against small arms of any description. The three sides of the house, commanding a view of the prairie, were occupied by the defenders; that next the river being left unguarded, as no danger was apprehended from that quarter. The moon was shining brightly, and from the height where they were stationed, everything was visible that elevated itself above the waving grass. Eyes less practiced than those now watching it, would soon have discovered that it was agitated by something more than the light breeze coming up from the gulf; but the exact locality of the moving objects was too uncertain to justify the risk of a shot. After a while, Lile thought he detected a slight scraping noise against the palisades on the side of the house where he was stationed, and in a few seconds the head and shoulders of an Indian rose slowly above them. Raising his rifle with a quick aim, he fired before half the body of the savage was exposed. The Indian sank down, still clinging with his hands to the top of the split logs. In this way he hung for a brief space, when his hold relaxed, and with a deep groan he fell heavily to the ground.

"Keep close," shouted Simpson, "they know they are discovered now, and a flight of arrows will come next."

The words were hardly spoken before thirty or forty arrows stuck in the log breastwork, or whistled over the heads of its defenders. At the same instant a wild yell rang over the prairie, and a rush was made upon the defences from three sides at once. The Indians, beyond doubt, supposed Simpson to be alone, and calculated that by making a rush from several points at the same time his attention would be distracted, so that they could easily effect an entrance by catching the tops of the palisades with their lassos, and thus dragging themselves up. Ignorant of his interior defences, they imagined if they could once succeed in getting inside, his fate was sealed. They were grievously surprised when, mounting almost at the same moment, from different points, three rifle shots hurled as many assailants lifeless to the earth; but other lassos were thrown, and other warriors clambered up. Lile, who was armed with two of Colt's revolvers, in addition to his rifle, found no difficulty in clearing his side as rapidly as they showed themselves above the timber, and also in materially assisting Stokes, who was next to him. Simpson had shot down three of his enemies in quick succession, but as he was ramming home a fourth bullet, two Indians scrambled up together, eight or ten feet apart. The death dealing rifle pronounced the doom of one of them, as he straddled the palisades, and, falling forward, he was caught upon the sharp points, and suspended there a ghastly spectacle, in the clear moonlight, to his kindred and tribe around. The other succeeded in dropping within unhurt.

"You have got in my good fellow," muttered Simpson, "let us see how you are to get out."

Then turning to his companions, he said.

"Do the best you can above here, while I take care of that fellow below."

He was half way down the ladder before the words were fairly spoken. The Indian as soon as he touched the ground had run to the gate for the purpose of throwing it open, and in expectation of such a movement, the warriors had suspended their attacks, and were clustering to that point to take instant advantage of the daring manœuvre. This was a contingency Tom Simpson had foreseen and provided against long ago, and the savage, to his dismay, found that the heavy bars securing the gate were kept in their places by an iron chain and rings, which in its turn was fastened by an enormous padlock. While he was looking about for something to shiver the lock, the hunter descended to the ground floor of his cabin and bounded into the yard. With equal weapons the contest must have resulted in a victory to the white man. Tom Simpson made no idle boast when he asserted that no two Indians that ever walked the forest were a match for him in a hand to hand encounter. Apart from his superior skill and strength, he had a terrible advantage in the long "Arkansas tooth pick," that gleamed in his brawny hand. The butcher knife of the savage was turned aside with scarcely an effort, and the bubbling blood fringed with a light edging of foam covered the hilt of the white man's weapon before it was half withdrawn from the naked body. Dragging an axe from a recess where it was hidden, he ran around the interior of the palisades, severing every lasso that was suspended to them. This done he again ascended to the roof. The enemy had entirely disappeared. From the long delay in opening the gate they readily guessed the fate of their comrade, and disheartened by the heavy losses they had sustained they had crawled off through the grass. It was scarcely more than a half hour later when a dark line was seen to emerge from the "mott" of timber to the west and move rapidly northward.

"There they go," said Simpson. "Their horses were hidden in that clump of trees, and now they are off with a new grudge against me, and a new caution to be particular in indulging it."

"We can go below," he continued. "Is either of you hurt?"

"I've got an arrow in my shoulder," replied Stokes, "but it don't hurt much, and I don't think the bone is touched."

A blaze was soon kindled, and Lile skilfully extracted the arrow, and bandaged the wound. Picking up the feathered missile he examined it attentively, remarking,

"This must have been sent by a feeble hand, or it would have hurt more sorely."

"It struck the log," answered Stokes, "and deadened itself scraping through the bark. D—n 'em, they don't shoot them things for fun. They shot my brother on the San Marcos, and when I found him the head was sticking out at his back, and the feather was jam up against his breast."

"You have paid the debt with interest to-night."

"I paid it long ago; but I shall keep on paying it whenever I have a chance. It's different from any other debt I ever owed. The more it's paid, the better a feller feels. I left the States between two days to keep from settling a few little contracts I had made in Mississippi, but no man can say I ever dodged when there was an opening for a settlement with either Mexicans or Camanches."

Whatever opinion Lile may have formed of the morals of his new acquaintance he kept it to himself, and the party sought the repose they so much needed. When morning came, and they had partaken of a meal prepared with their own hands, Stokes indicated his purpose of returning to Victoria. His wound he treated as a mere scratch, whose chief inconvenience would be that he would be compelled "to tell every feller" he met, how the hurt was received With Simpson's aid his horse was caparisoned, and he rode away whistling "old Rosin the beau."

As soon as he was out of hearing, Simpson said,

"There's a pretty fair specimen, captain, of the wild characters who have come out among us since the revolution. He will fight from sun-up to sun-down by your side for the love of the thing—will ride ten miles any day to do you a favor—will cling to you through the worst times, and could not be bought by all the gold of Mexico to betray you. Yet, as he told you, he once run away to avoid the payment of his honest debts. To-day he would kill a Mexican without scruple for his blanket, or a Camanche for his horse, and to-morrow, if he could find whiskey enough to get half drunk, he would practice carving with his bowie knife on the body of his best friend for the slightest offence. I do not like this new stock half so well as the old, and I have been thinking of pulling up stakes, and squatting way out on the San Saba."

"I will go with you," answered Lile, "for I love not such characters any better than you do: though they are a hundred times better than the smooth silken villains of cities, who rob with professions of friendship, and murder character and happiness with the blandest of smiles.

"Let us go within," he continued, "and talk over our plans deliberately. I have brought two steeds of different mettle from the sorry jades we rode over the prairie after the massacre of Goliad, and I have also brought some new weapons which in our hands will reduce an odds of ten to one against us to an equality."

"By the Lord," put in Simpson, "it strikes me that

wouldn't make much more than a fair fight any way. We have been in worse scrapes than that, and got out of them without losing a hair."

"Yes, it was worse at Bexar; and a great deal worse at the ford of San Antonio. But we had stone houses to shelter us at the first, and trees and swampy ground at the last. We may be caught some day without these advantages, and in that case we must rely upon superior arms to make up the loss."

The horses were first examined. Simpson had been a bold rider in his youth, and though long accustomed to trust to his own limbs in preference to any four footed animal, he had not forgottten his early training, and pointed out with unconcealed satisfaction the excellent points of each steed in turn. Full sixteen hands high, broad boned, and strong; they had been selected from the best hunting stock of England, and were unmatched on the American continent for speed and endurance.

"They'll do *certain*," ejaculated the hunter. "If them weapons you were talking about, are half as good, we can ride to the Pacific ocean without finding men enough to stop us."

They entered the cabin, and Lile drew from the holsters the pair of revolvers he had brought for Simpson. They were "five shooters," of the calibre manufactured at that day; not so large or so deadly as the cavalry holster which came in use during the Mexican war, but more convenient, from the facility of carrying it in a belt when the horseman has dismounted. The present pistol doubtless surpasses it in perfection of workmanship and material, but it is difficult to find an old "ranger" who believes in the possibility of any improvement to the original arm.

"Our boys," said Simpson, "are beginning to use these things out here, and they say there's nothing like them;

but for my part I have always thought they was intended for weakly people. When I get close enough to use a pistol, a good knife does the business quicker and more certain."

"Judging this pistol by such as you have known, your conclusion is a natural one. But, my good friend, this short weapon, in a hand as firm as yours, will kill at forty yards with as much certainty as your rifle; and that is a good deal too far off to use a knife effectively."

Simpson turned it in his hand and eyed it incredulously.

"I see," continued Lile, "you must have a practical lesson. Bring out that puncheon, and rub a little wet powder on it until you make a mark half the size of your hand."

When this was done, he placed it against the side of the palisades, stepped off forty yards, and raising the pistol fired the five charges in quick succession without lowering his hand.

"Now look where those balls have struck."

"Every bullet's in the black," was the response, "and by the living God they have gone through two inches of solid timber, and buried themselves in the logs."

"Well, would that kill a man?"

"Kill a man! It would kill the devil. Let me try it."

His experiments at first were rather awkward; but he was a willing scholar, and in the course of that day and the next he became so great a proficient that it would have been as he expressed it, "dangerous for anything bigger than a snow bird to show itself before the sights."

His lessons did not end here. He was next taught the art of firing from horseback. This was continued until he was able to send a bullet through a tin cup at full speed."

"You need nothing now but a little more practice," said

his instructor; "when I have taught you the broadsword exercise we will be prepared for any emergency."

"I don't mind learning," he replied, "but I can't see what use a fellow can have for any thing more than a rifle, a five-shooter, and a bowie."

"So you thought a few days ago about the pistol. A bowie knife in your hand would be a poor weapon against a good sabre in mine."

"I found out a good while since that a knife in my hand was a poor weapon against you any way; but everybody ain't you; and if there is any other living thing that can git clear of Tom Simpson's knife, I'd like to see it."

"And so would I. Still there may be occasions when the broadsword would serve a better purpose."

Under a preceptor who never had his equal Simpson's progress was rapid and satisfactory. Before a month went by he lost much of the awe with which he had heretofore regarded his companion. He saw that the wonderful dexterity, so incomprehensible at first, was the result of long, and careful training, and began to understand the extraordinary development of which the physical man is capable when diet and exercise are regulated by sound judgment and unremitting watchfulness.

Providing themselves with pack-mules for the transportation of articles of absolute necessity, and engaging two of the settlers to assist them in the erection of their fortification, they set out early in September for their contemplated residence on the lonely waters of the San Saba. A few desperate conflicts with the wild Indians in that vicinity; the terrible rapidity and accuracy with which Colt's revolvers carried death into the ranks of the naked savages; the size, speed, and bottom of their horses, soon caused them to be regarded with superstitious dread, and the roving bands continually wandering over that uninhabited region, would diverge far from the direct path to avoid the palisaded cabin of the white hunters.

"It is best to have no intercourse with them," said Lile to his companion; "neither to sell them any thing or purchase from them. In addition to affording a chance for treachery, any familiarity would lessen their terrors, and teach them we are as vulnerable as other men. The mere fact that we will not trade with, and cheat them, from being a cause of wonder, has become a cause of reverence. The white man's wants have hitherto appeared to them insatiable, and they have unfortunately not been accustomed in their dealings to scrupulous honesty and fairness. They naturally conclude that those who want nothing, are either of a different race, or that they are supplied by some supernatural agency. Already they avoid our dwelling; in another year they will abandon the hunting grounds we frequent, and the paths we travel."

As he predicted, so it turned out. Alone in the wilderness, with thousands of armed foemen around them, they were as safe, and as free from molestation as if girded by the bayonets of an army. Not only so, the women and children along the border slept the sounder from the outpost they had established. In their annual visits to Austin they had become familiar with all the daring spirits continually flocking to the West. To these they were often enabled to impart information that served to defeat a meditated incursion, and not unfrequently the dread of their interference had sent a predatory party to the right about which would otherwise have inflicted much suffering on the inhabitants. It is not the purpose of this history to trace out the adventures that checkered their existence. Unconsciously they were fitting themselves to become participants in events whose coming was as yet hidden in the womb of the future. Silently but anxiously the eye of the great republic was resting on its infant daughter. The petty brawls of the politicians went on unchecked and unheeded, because as yet no actual necessity existed for gathering the young thing beneath its parent wing. The panther will watch its young at play with half closed lids and seeming indifference. It may tumble from a limb, or be rudely bitten by its mate, and come limping to her side, and she heeds it not. But let what she fears as a real danger approach—in an instant all the deadly energy of the animal is aroused; with a fierce bound she springs between it and the threatened attack, and greets the intruder with the sharp tusk, and the sharper claw. In like manner the American nation had watched the struggles and difficulties of Texas. Small statesmen wearied the public ear with harangues on the subject of liberty generally, and Texan annexation particularly, but a drunken shout at a cross roads meeting, was about the most active demonstration that rewarded their noisy patriotism. Secure in their own immutable resolves the people slumbered, or appeared to slumber, while the demagogues grew hoarse with bawling. The time had not yet come. No actual danger was impending. Years rolled on, and Texas had demonstrated her ability to repel any invasion Mexico might project; but troubles of another kind had overtaken her. The debts of her revolutionary struggle, and those that had since accumulated, were pressing like an incubus upon her prosperity. The salaries of her public officers were paid in a currency depreciated to one-fifth of its nominal value. Her soldiers were altogether unpaid, and her seamen not much better provided for. In pursuance of an unscrupulous policy never changed, and always selfish, England was preparing to take advantage of her embarrassment, and reduce her people to a state not far removed from vassalage. Then it was that the sleeping republic waked up. With the bound of the panther she sprung between her offspring and the impending danger. A bold man then stood at the helm of state. A bold, a true, and a sagacious one, though libelled by pensioned presses, and maligned by mercenary declaimers. The throbbings of the great heart of the nation met a kindred throb in his own, and John Tyler signed the treaty of annexation. The thousand insects who had been buzzing about annexation for years, without exciting the most mercurial pulse, hugged to their little bosoms the delusive phantasy, that they had aided in swelling the deep flood that now swept over the land; and creeping things to this day exult in the belief, that their arguments, their eloquence, and their sagacity overwhelmed the matchless orator, and the incorruptible patriot who unfortunately for himself and his country, breasted a current no human strength could stem. Such things, never understood, and never can, that Henry Clay was defeated solely and entirely because, with the uncalculating fondness of a mother for its spoiled and favorite child, the United States were too deeply attached to Texas to estimate correctly its danger, or listen to the reasoning that told them they were alarmed too much. On such occasions, the mother will throw off for the moment the authority of the husband who has loved and cherished her in sickness and in health; and a people will discard in like manner the statesman whose counsels have been to them as a pillar of cloud by day, and of fire by night. Neither are to be blamed; and the historian who records the diversity, if true to his high mission, will refuse to color it on the one side or on the other, save by a falling tear.

To the cabin of the hunters, soon afterwards, came tidings of war on a grand scale. War for their native and adopted countries. The day's hunt was over, and seated on a bear skin by the blazing fire, they were busy with their own thoughts. Lile was the first to speak.

"What say you, Tom? Ten years have gone since we stepped to the side of Milam, on the plain before San Antonio; but these sinews," he continued, extending an arm on which the muscles rose in cords as large as a cable rope, "are as strong as then, and as capable of rendering effective service beneath the starred and striped banner, as under the single star."

"I have been thinking over it all, captain;" replied Simpson, who still adhered, with unchanging pertinacity to the title he had bestowed upon his companion on the banks of the Mississippi. "And just now I saw, as plain as I see you, the wounded boys lying on their bloody blankets in the Mission church. I heard again their feeble voices bidding us take care of ourselves; and felt once more the soft cold cheeks that my lips pressed on the death couch. When that passed off, another picture took its place. It was the cold-blooded, cowardly massacre of Fannin and his men. I can walk blindfolded to the very spot where they fell on the plain of Labahia. I know the exact color of the bark on the two trees where you and I were hid. The whole scene is before me—the unsuspecting victims—the levelled muskets—the smoke curling slowly, and sullenly away, as if it wanted to hide the deed from heaven. The infernal shout as the murderers rushed up to finish their hellish work—the dying groans, and then the dead silence that prevailed about the butchered and mangled mass, it's all present to me now, and I don't feel the easier for having thought of it so little of late."

"They were dark and bloody deeds, certainly, but there was also a bloody atonement. It is not vengeance for the past, but security and liberty for the future, that impels me to take part in the war that will soon be carried to the heart of Mexico."

"It is nothing to me what reasons the President and Congress may give for declaring war. They know more about it than I do, and I am willing to go whenever and wherever a good rifle and a strong arm are needed; but I am not at all sorry that, in serving my country, I shall also have a chance to pay a bloody debt, with bloody interest."

"Will you never get through paying that debt, Tom?"

"Never! Never!" was the reply, in a tone so fixed, and so determined, that his friend knew it was useless to press him further. He thought a moment before he continued.

"We will go together, at all events; no matter what may be our motives."

"Of course we will *go* together, and *stay* together, until one or the other is under the ground. As for our motives, I take it, the only difference will be, that every time I send a bullet through a *Greaser*, I shall think of the Mission and of Goliad, while you may only remember that tyranny has one tool less."

The war had not yet been declared, but every man on the border knew it must come; and Lile and Simpson speedily prepared to abandon their solitary fortress in the wilderness, for the canvass streets, and regular duties of an armed encampment. It was not without sorrowing hearts they turned their footsteps for the last time from the rude logs that had sheltered them so well. That humble cabin was the only home they knew, and they went forth from its portal with a conviction that, in the wide world before them, there was not another roof-tree which would not be viewed with indifference, or recal some memory that was painful.

Before entering upon the stirring scenes of the Mexican

war, we must return to one who has stood out too prominently on these pages, to be unceremoniously dismissed. Pauline Winter sought Monsieur Evadne. That gentleman chose to be in profound ignorance of the movements of his principal. With the never failing politeness of a Frenchman, he feelingly regretted his utter inability to furnish the information she sought, and whether she believed or doubted him, she was compelled to put on the semblance of content. His parting bow was made with his hand on his heart, accompanied with an assurance, that he would ransack the world to gratify a lady of such exquisite loveliness.

"It is no great matter," she said, with as much composure as she could command. "I borrowed a miniature from him for the purpose of having it copied. In the hurry of his departure he has forgotten the original, and I wished to return it to him."

"If madame would be so good as to trust it in my keeping, I do not doubt but that I shall have an opportunity of returning it to the owner."

"Pardon me; I believe I will retain it. I know he values it highly. As you know not where he is, I may as readily be able to restore it as yourself."

"The correctness of madame's judgment is inquestionable; but he has business with me, and must write soon."

"In that case, call on me, and I will hand you the packet. Good morning."

The lady disappeared before the Frenchman had recovered from the low bow which acknowledged her adieu.

The man of business, with all his shrewdness, had been outwitted by the shrewder tactics of the woman in love. He had never seen a miniature in the possession of Bernard Lile, except an extraordinary likeness of Zerah, which was worn habitually in his bosom. Mrs. Winter had also caught a glimpse of that miniature on a former occasion and it suggested her present artifice.

Turning from the banker's door, she sought the studio of an artist, and directed him to paint a miniature of herself, with as little delay as was compatible with perfect execution. Some days later, when it was completed to her satisfaction, she sat down and wrote.

"I know not in what light you will regard the step I have taken, for a wild fire is running through my veins, that mocks at connected thought. That I loved you, you knew, and that you fled from me, as you thought, in mercy, I will not question. But, Bernard Lile, there was no mercy in the dark tortures that desertion has inflicted. Better to be an outcast, shunned by those who would now go into ecstacies at a passing notice, and reviled by those who are now fawning around me with sickening adulation. Better to bear the world's sneers, the stings of poverty, and the loss of self-respect, for an age beyond that of the Psalmist, than endure for a single hour the gnawing agony of a heart that has given away its all, and met with no return. Will you answer, that I have written my own doom, and must abide it. That you shunned me from the first—that I am bound to another by ties—hateful ties—which the laws of man have foolishly undertaken to declare everlasting, and which ought to have preserved me from a danger that came not without warning, and remained not uninvited. All this, and more, I have told myself. In the silent watches of the night I have reasoned and struggled, until a thick mist gathered about my faculties, and I could see nothing through its gloomy drapery. Yet the heart beat on. Love still informed and animated its every pulse. The wrong and the folly that invited his coming were forgotten, but his *presence* was acknowledged, cherished, clung to; and even the delirious madness shed from his fiery wing, was dearer than the cold joys the calm and the passionless have miscalled raptures. As you ought to know, and do know, love is not a matter of taste and judgment, like the purchase of a carriage, or the fitting up a new establishment. It comes without reason, remains against reason, dreads no barriers, and shrinks from the presence of no restraints. Upon you has been lavished the whole wealth of my affection. To you it pleads for toleration, if it may not hope for a warmer return. Come back, and take me with you to the world's limit, if you choose. Speak to me gently and kindly—let me pillow my head upon your bosom, and feel that resting place is secured to it, and I will ask for nothing more. I do not promise to make you happy, but I beg, entreat, implore you to render me so.

"I never professed any attachment to Mr. Winter. He sought it not. He was satisfied with formal observances, and duties; and I lived on ignorant of passion, and contented, until I met you. The burning wishes that have struggled and rioted in my bosom since then, I cannot describe, and your wildest fancies would be inadequate to paint. Come to me if there is pity for human suffering in your nature. I am pleading now not for love, but for mercy. Say not that I am lost if you come. I know it, but there is bliss in the degradation. What care I for the world's opinion? You are the world to me.

"In the package which contains this, you will find my miniature. Keep it, and then I shall be assured that some day my summons will be heeded. Farewell."

The miniature and the letter were carefully sealed up, directed to Bernard Lile, and put away to await the call of Monsieur Evadne.

It was not very long before the Frenchman came to say that he was about sending a messenger with letters and papers to Mr. Lile, and that he should be very happy to accommodate madame at the same time. The package was delivered to him without special instructions, and with apparent indifference. A year went by. A year of agonized suspense. One day a sealed paper was laid upon the table before her. She opened it, and her own miniature fell from her palsied hand. The note accompanying it was brief and decisive.

"My heart is dead to every emotion of love. I should bring you misery and disgrace, instead of joy, by again intruding myself upon your presence. Forget one who is far too unworthy to have excited such a passion in your bosom. In the whirl of society it will be easy to efface the unpleasant remembrance—much easier than it will be for me to obtain self-forgiveness for the uneasiness I have unintentionally caused you. I must not take such an occasion as this to obtrude advice upon you, but you are fitted for higher and holier things than the narrow walks of fashion allow, and it would gladden my exile to know that you were fulfilling your appropriate mission. With the fervent wishes of a lone and blighted man, for your welfare and happiness, I must bid you a final adieu."

"My mission," she murmured, "God knows what it may be."

Mrs. Winter's heart did not break. Hearts do sometimes break in this world, and sometimes they do worse—rot inch by inch, and drop piecemeal into the tomb. But there is a worse fate still, and a far more common one; when with the affections, the virtues also die out—when passion has swept over the breast, like fire over the prairie, burning together the green thing and the dry—the parched stem, and the springing blade. The moral life droops and withers—the animal exists. In the place of a host of affections and sympathies, a fierce thirst, more unappeasable than that of Tantalus, comes and seats itself within, driving us on forever to some new madness, or some foul crime. Such was the fate of Pauline Winter. The hopeless love she had cherished did not kill her, nor die itself: it only forced her to seek new channels of enjoyment—new and more powerful excitements. She had cast a priceless gem upon the waters; it could not be lured back, and she went in search of it amid the troubled depths of a guilty ocean. Before another twelvemonth was told by the tongue of time, she eloped with a libertine, and became a stained and blackened outcast.

Here let the curtain drop. All instruction is not healthful, and that philanthropy is of questionable usefulness which reveals the minute points of a guilty life to the young, with the expectation of turning their footsteps from the pitfall.

CHAPTER XII.

"Not his the heart the Phrygian victor bore;
Not his the brand that gleamed on Granic's shore;
Not his the race all conquering Julius ran;
Not his the star that led the Corsican.
His country called him—called in wild despair.
The warrior came and all his soul was there."

At the instance of Major Donaldson, the American Charge to Texas, Gen. Taylor had been ordered by the President to concentrate a small army at Corpus Christi, for the protection of the frontier, while Commodore Stockton, under similar instructions assembled a considerable fleet in the Gulf. The rude treatment of the American envoy in Mexico, determined the President to occupy the disputed territory between the Nueces and the Rio Grande, and on the 8th of March, 1846, the advance column of the army of Gen. Taylor commenced its march for the latter river. They proceeded without encountering an enemy to the Arroyo Colorado, within thirty miles of Metamoras, where they met a Mexican force, who drew off without offering battle. On the 28th of March, the American army encamped within cannon range of Metamoras, and began a field work which was subsequently named Fort Brown, in honor of the gallant officer who lost his life in its defence. The Mexicans with equal industry erected batteries on the opposite side of the river. But as yet no blow had been struck—no thunder was audible—no lightning played upon the dark cloud that obscured the horizon. Not long afterwards a company of dragoons, who had been sent up the river to reconnoitre, were surrounded by the Mexicans, and the whole taken prisoners. It was the first time they had ever encountered American regulars, and the result was hailed as a happy augury of the coming struggle. Like most auguries except those of a firm heart, and strong arm, it proved to be wofully fallacious. Walker's camp was next surprised, and his company scattered, slain or taken captive. Thus auspiciously for Mexico opened the bloody drama whose closing scenes were played in the heart of her empire. From that time to the treaty of Guadaloupe Hidalgo not another success gladdened their arms. Not a field was fought of which the invaders did not remain the victors. Not a fortress was invested that was not taken. And but a single company of American troops ever grounded their arms in presence of an enemy. For campaigns of such magnitude and such uninterrupted success, the world's history will be searched in vain. On the 8th of May, 1846, the war began in earnest. The two armies encountered each other at Palo Alto. The Mexicans under Arista were six thousand strong. The Americans under Taylor numbered twenty-three hundred, all told. The battle lasted five hours, when Arista drew off, and Taylor camped his victorious army on the hotly contested field. Arista halted at Resaca de la Palma, a strong position protected by a deep ravine, skirted by dense thickets. At four o'clock, on the 9th, Gen. Taylor came up with the enemy. The Mexicans are said to have fought bravely and well, but their columns were at length broken by successive charges, and the whole army fled in the wildest disorder, leaving their artillery, munitions, baggage, camp equipage, everything in the hands of the victors.

Intelligence of these events were borne to the interior, and Lile and Simpson hurried their preparations for joining the invading army. When they reached Metamoras they found that Gen. Taylor had left that city, and was concentrating his army at Camargo, one hundred and eighty miles above, near the junction of the San Juan and Rio Grande, with a view of advancing on Monterey, the capital of New Leon, at that time occupied by Gen. Ampudia with about seven thousand regular and three thousand irregular troops.

An American whose ill fortune has made him for any number of days, a sojourner in the city of Metamoras, can have no difficulty in tracing the origin of the term "greaser," originally applied by the old Texans to the Mexican Rancheros, and subsequently extended to the whole nation. Narrow, muddy, filthy streets, swarming with men, women and children as filthy—enlivened by an eternal chorus of little dogs without hair, except about the muzzles, and the tips of their tails—houses without floors, built of mud and straw, and inhabited by fleas, and other vermin, in the proportion of fifty to the square inch—disgusting sewers—rotting offal, and a hot, sickly atmosphere, make up an assembly of discomforts compared with which the purgatory of an orthodox Catholic is rather an agreeable kind of place. The people look greasy, their clothes are greasy, their dogs are greasy, their houses are greasy—everywhere grease and filth hold divided dominion, and the singular appropriateness of the name bestowed by the western settlers, soon caused it to be universally adopted by the American army.

Lile and Simpson were standing on the upper deck of one of the many steamers sent out by the United States government to transport troops and munitions to Camargo. The deck-hands were lounging idly about the lower deck; some of them sleeping, or trying to sleep in the hot sun—others drawing figures on the rough planks, and others again holding a kind of broken conversation upon disconnected subjects.

"There's a Greaser, I know," said Simpson, pointing to one of the hands, "and he's not here for any good."

"I do not think I have ever seen him before," was the reply. "What do you know about him?"

"He lived awhile at Seguin's Ranche, and the boys ran him away on suspicion of being a spy for the robbers who used to trouble us then. Afterwards he was employed by Kinney; then Cameron took him as a guide when he went to Mier, where he was murdered; and if this fellow didn't have a hand in it, he was damnably slandered."

"May you not be mistaken? I am sure I have never seen this man at Corpus Christi."

"You might not have noticed him, but he was there. I never mistake the ear marks of a Greaser. I'll swear to him on a stack of Bibles."

"We must watch him then; but I do not see what harm he can do here; unless it is to pilfer something from the steamer."

"He was born a thief, and I reckon counts the *stealage* as the best part of his wages. But he has done worse things than steal. He would murder his brother for a *peso*, and betray any thing but his priest for half the money."

The captain had now come on board, and just as the sun went down, the cable was slipped, and the steamer backed out into the stream. A number of convalescing soldiers were lying about the vessel, who had recently been discharged from the hospitals. The strong and the healthy were for the most part sent up by land as they arrived, as guards for the wagon trains Gen. Taylor was collecting preparatory to his advance into the interior. Moving carelessly among these, addressing a question to one, or a light remark to another, Simpson gradually made his way to the front part of the boat, where the firemen were engaged in their duties. By the blazing light of the fires he scrutinized anew the features of the Mexican who had attracted his attention while standing on the upper deck. The examination satisfied him, and placing his hand lightly on the fellow's shoulder, he said slowly,

"When did you see Cameron last, Jose?"

The man started, with visible surprise and alarm, but in a moment a dull, heavy expression settled on his countenance, and he answered,

"*No entende Americana.*"

"The devil you don't! I could find a way to make you, but it aint worth while now."

And Simpson walked away to seek Lile, and assure him there could be no possible doubt of the identity of the individual in question. Later in the night, when all on board were buried in sleep, except the officers and men on duty, Tom Simpson was standing on the lower deck, now watching the ripples made by the paddles on the muddy surface of the Rio Grande, now casting an eye on the dreary and desolate scenery presented along that singular river. From Metamoras to Camargo not a solitary *tree* grows upon its margin. Bleak wastes, interspersed with patches of *chaparal,* everywhere meet the eye. At intervals they glided by whole acres of ground which presented the exact appearance of an old peach orchard, whose withered and sapless trees were rotting in solitary loneliness slowly away. No white-walled cottages; no cultivated fields; no ornamented grounds relieved the sameness of the prospect, or gave evidence that civilized man exercised dominion over the blasted soil. It was the home of a people whose substance had been wrung from them by the tyrant and the priest, and whose energies had been withered by the baleful conviction that any provision for the morrow would only serve to pamper their oppressors. Occupied by the reflections suggested by the hour and the scene, Tom Simpson paid no attention to a crouching form stealthily approaching the spot where he stood. With a sudden spring the Mexican was upon him, endeavoring with all his force to push the sturdy backwoodsman into the rushing flood. Fortunately he was standing immediately by one of the pillars that supported the upper deck, and as he reeled forward, clutching the air without an object, his hand caught the friendly support. But for this his life and adventures would have been brought to a sudden termination. With a mighty effort he drew himself back from the foaming waters, and dealing the Mexican a blow that stretched him upon the deck, he sprang upon him with a deep growl, between anger and satisfaction. Deliberately, but skilfully and securely, he bound his now trembling and pleading captive; addressing him during the operation in a tone that gave no encouragement to hopes of merciful treatment.

"You didn't understand English awhile ago, and by G—d there are some English words I don't understand now. Mercy, eh! Mercy for a sneaking scoundrel, who tried to make catfish meat of Tom Simpson. Well, I'm going to be merciful. I'm going to drop you into this ugly, dirty, crooked creek, that you call a *grand river*, *behind* the wheels. You tried to push me in *before* 'em, where a few thumps from them iron paddles would have interfered with a fellow's swimming most infernally."

By this time the noise had attracted a dozen or more of the soldiers and "hands," to the place. Simpson answered their interrogatories, without desisting a moment from his occupation. Various modes of punishment were suggested.

"Never mind, boys," was the rejoinder. "It's all settled."

Lifting the Mexican, as easily as if he had been an

infant, he bore him back to the stern of the boat. Depositing his burden, and drawing his bowie knife, he again addressed him.

"Now, my beauty, before I let you go, I intend to put a mark on you. A smooth crop of the right ear, and a swallow fork in the left; that was my old father's mark in Tennessee, and I have put it on many a cub bear since, just to keep up the family fashion."

"You don't mean to mark him that way?" asked one of the soldiers.

"If I don't may the Lord take a liking to me," was the reply, and the sharp knife slipped through the upper section of the ear, cutting it smooth and square. Amid the yells and contortions of the suffering wretch, the left ear was doubled up between the thumb and forefinger, when a single cut of the knife transformed it into that particular shape known among hog breeders as a swallow fork.

The ligatures that fastened hand and foot were removed, and seizing the howling miscreant in his sinewy hands, he pitched him far out in the stream. He disappeared for a space under the rapid current, but, by the clear light of the moon, they soon saw him rise above the waves, and strike out for the bank.

"He'll make it easy," said Simpson. "This d——d branch aint wide enough to drown a puppy, let alone a Greaser, who is as much used to muddy water as a tadpole."

The soldiers gathered in a group to make their comments on the scene they had just witnessed, and Simpson ascended to the pilot-house.

"What are you doing up," asked the pilot, "at this time of night, Tom?"

"It's been a long time since the captain and me both went to sleep at once. It's his turn to sleep first to-night."

"There's no use of standing guard on board of the boat."

"May be not, but we don't like to break through a good habit, and besides there's no telling what might happen."

Then suddenly changing the subject of conversation, he asked in turn,

"What do you know of this river, Jim?"

"Not much. None of us do."

"Do you stop anywhere near here?"

"Yes. We have to 'wood' about five miles above."

"What sort of a place is it?"

"It's an ugly chaparal thicket.

"No chance to go by without stopping?"

"None at all. Wood is not piled up here, every mile, like it is on the Mississippi. What do you want to know for?"

Simpson then related all that had occurred below; the pilot's situation and duties having kept him in ignorance of the whole affair. He added what he had known of the Mexican before, and expressed his opinion, that some treachery was afoot. The pilot listened attentively, and when the story was ended, he said,

"Go below, Tom, and call up Captain H———. Tell him I want to see him directly."

When the captain of the boat came above, he was made acquainted with the events of the night, and with Simpson's suspicions.

"We *must* stop to wood," he said. "The probability is that we can do so without interruption. They must have agreed on a signal, and as Jose is not here to give it, they will not be apt to venture on a serious attack. The worst we have to apprehend is, that they may fire from the bushes, and kill some of our men."

The sergeant in charge of the soldiers was called up, and directed to post his men as well as he could behind the boxes and hogsheads, ready for instant action. By the time these arrangements were completed, the boat neared the woodyard. Slowly and cautiously they approached the shore, and as nothing appeared to increase their suspicions, the captain began to think he had been needlessly alarmed.

Lile had been awakened, and together with Simpson, was standing in the shadow of the pilot-house.

"Look out there, Tom," he said. "Do you not see something glittering above the bushes, about forty yards from the bank?"

"Plain enough. I have been trying for two minutes to make out what it was."

"It is the steel head of a Mexican lance."

"I have killed many a buck," said Simpson, "when I could see nothing but the tips of his horns above the bushes, but that lance is too steady to be held in a man's hand. It must be fastened in the ground."

"Nevertheless, the owner may be seated by it. At any rate, there is nothing to be lost but a charge of powder and lead."

He raised his rifle as he ceased speaking, and its sharp report was followed by the sudden disappearance of the lance. Then came a hurried volley of escopetas, and a rushing noise like that of men retreating precipitately through the thorny chaparal.

"There they go," exclaimed Simpson. "The sneaking, thieving, murdering cowards. There's enough of them to eat up this boat, and everything that's on it, and they are running from a single rifle shot, like a herd of frightened cattle."

"There is some excuse for it this time, Tom. They no

doubt supposed, from the absence of any answering signal, that the boat was filled with soldiers. You must remember, they did not know that you had sent Jose on an exploring expedition to the bottom of the Rio Grande."

"I wish I had. But you might as well try to drown an alligator. He was safe ashore in ten minutes after I pitched him in, all the better for his ducking; as the cold water would stop the bleeding from his ears, and save him a doctor's bill"

"Do you ever expect to meet him again, that you were so particular in marking him?"

"Never *but once*," was the ominous reply, "if an ounce of lead, or eight inches of bright steel will be enough to stop his tramping."

At Camargo, Bernard Lile found Robert Wilson. Their meeting was cordial and sincerely friendly, though saddened by memories painful to both. Neither made any allusion to Zerah, but each *felt* she was uppermost in the thoughts of the other. In reply to his inquiries, Lile was informed, that his friend, following the advice of Monsieur Evadne, had resigned his commission in the army, and engaged in business in the North West. Success had attended his efforts, and the Mexican war found him in prosperous circumstances. Abandoning his peaceful pursuits, like thousands of others, he volunteered his services, and came out to the Rio Grande with the rank of captain.

"Thanks to your kindness," he continued, "I am rich enough to serve my country without embarrassing myself, for although all I possess would be regarded as a poor pittance by a New York capitalist, it is wealth where I live, and more than suffices for a man of simple tastes, and unostentatious habits."

"All wealth," answered Lile, "is comparative. He who has the means to supply his wants, whether it be one dollar, or a thousand, is rich: and he, whose wants outrun his means, is poor, though he may count his hordes by the million."

Their intercourse was constant and confidential. They had a common bond, mentioned by neither, but remembered by both. On the 20th of August, when Gen. Worth, with the advanced division, began his march for Monterey, Wilson proposed to Lile that he should take up his quarters in his tent, and make his home in the regiment of which his company formed a part.

"No," answered Lile. "In the last ten years I have acquired a good deal of Tom Simpson's wild love for freedom. He and I will remain together, and it would not suit the discipline of your regiment to have us roving about among you, doing duty when and where we pleased. We expect no pay from the government—draw no rations, and fight always as the Kentuckian did at New Orleans, 'on our own hook.' The camp of the Rangers is the only place where we would be endured. We have, moreover, many friends and acquaintances there who would not be willing to part with us lightly. But I shall be near you whenever a battle is fought."

They parted thus, and did not meet again until the American army had begun to draw its folds around the capital of New Leon.

On the 20th September, Gen. Worth turned the hill of the Bishop's palace, and took up a position in rear of the city, on the Saltillo road. On the 21st, May's dragoons and the Texan cavalry were dispatched to his assistance. The enemy had collected a strong force upon a fortified height, and the daring general, unmatched for chivalry in an army where chivalry was the rule, and the want of it the exception, at once determined on carrying it by the bayonet. A round shot struck the head of the column, before it had deployed into line and ploughed through it. Without losing the step that dauntless soldiery closed the horrid gap, and pressed on in the pathway of death. At the same time the light troops of Texas swarmed up from another side. Here no regular order was attempted. Every man was his own officer. Bushes, trees, rocks, everything that afforded the slightest shelter was promptly occupied, and from behind each one a deadly messenger was sent into the Mexican lines. Better soldiers than ever fought under the banner of Ampudia would have quailed at the fierce assault. From one quarter the disciplined column was hurled with irresistible strength against the leagured works. From another the unequalled marksmen of the south-west poured an incessant shower of lead upon the defenders. The sharp crack of the rifle, the duller roar of the musket, and the thrilling clang of the clashing bayonet met upon the bloody height, and annihilated the struggling garrison as easily as the boa constrictor crushes the quivering life of the mountain kid. The bivouac of Worth's division on the night of the 21st, was a hill-side soaked with gore, and strewed with the dead bodies of a conquered enemy. With the dawn on the 22d, another scene of the fearful tragedy was enacted. The height above the Bishop's palace was now the point of attack. Covered with strong works of earth and stone, bristling with cannon, and filled with a picked soldiery more than double the number of the assailants, the last stronghold that defended the rear of Monterey, the beautiful, reared itself in proud defiance across the march of the invaders. Through smoke and flame, the ringing cannon shot, and the crashing steel, the warriors of the States clambered up the stony height. Bernard Lile and Tom Simpson had early thrown aside their rifles: each with the deadly revolver in his hand, and a long bowie knife in his belt, they leaped from crag to crag, or swung themselves upwards by the roots and bushes on the mountain side. A little lower down Gillespie and his men struggled up the ascent. They reached the top to be greeted by a withering fire of grape and musketry which scattered death in all directions from its angry wing. The gallant Gillespie reeled forward with a death wound in his breast—in a vain effort to steady himself the point of his sword was driven deep into the ground. Again he staggered—the good blade snapped in twain, and he fell upon it a lifeless corpse. A wild cry of vengeance rose from the Ranger ranks. A hundred hands grasped the stone parapet, a hundred stalwart forms were swung above it. Another fatal volley swept away one-third of the assailants, but the survivors dropped among the defenders —the battle was over—it was butchery now—the terrible revolver heaped the camp with mounds of dead, and when the flag of Mexico sunk to the earth the fierce victors gazed with a feeling almost of awe upon the wide havoc themselves had made.

At once Gen. Worth turned the batteries of the Bishop's hill against the city they were erected to defend, and the plunging shot bursting through the roofs of the houses, and carrying dismay and death among the citizens, was the first notice conveyed to Ampudia that his stronghold was in the hands of his enemy.

On the 23d the indefatigable Worth stormed the suburbs of the city, driving the enemy before him and compelling him to concentrate his forces in the citadel, and the plaza. Never was there a general better fitted to be the leader of the impetuous troops who flocked beneath his standard. Prompt as he was fearless, one blow incessantly followed another. Where he fought, no pause, no rest, no breathing time was allowed. The shout that hailed one great success was scarcely hushed before the echoes were again awakened by the sterner shout that answered a new order to rush upon another of the enemy's defences. The Mexicans appalled by the startling rapidity of his movements shivered with nervous dread as the living tide rolled upon them, and the victory was won before a drop of blood fattened the soil.

In front of the city, under the immediate eye of Gen. Taylor, daring deeds were enacted, and laurel crowns abundantly gathered by the republican soldiers. But Gen. Butler had been driven back wounded and bleeding from an assault he led in person, and Col. Garland advancing against a strong redoubt was met by murderous discharges of artillery, which compelled him to retire. The brigade of Quitman alone effected a lodgment, and not until the Bishop's Hill was captured by Worth, did the Mexicans abandon their outworks in front. On the night of the 23d, Gen. Ampudia sent propositions for a capitulation. On the 24th, the terms were agreed to, and on the 25th, the city of Monterey was occupied by the American troops.

On the bank of the San Juan, where it winds nearest to the mountain range of the Sierra Madre, a few nights after the events just recorded, five or six burning fires streaked the limpid waters with long lines of reddish light. Around each of these was gathered a group of old frontier men, to whom the discipline of a regular army was intolerable, and whose notions of wild independence were shocked even by the lighter restraints of the Ranger camp. Here no tents were pitched, no baggage wagons were collected, no regular guard posted, or relieved. They were accustomed in the colder climate of Texas to repose in the open air, and here beneath the soft sky of New Leon, a sense of suffocation would have oppressed them if confined within the canvass walls of a tent. Their baggage consisted of a blanket, an extra pair of pantaloons, socks, and a shirt. Their camp equipage was a tin cup. Wherever they halted, a limb from the nearest bush served the purpose of a spit; or if none were to be found, the ramrods of their rifles were put in requisition. A few grains of coffee, mashed into a powder with the handles of their Bowie knives, were put into the cup and drunk without straining, from the same vessel in which it was boiled. Upon any alarm or any sudden call, they were prepared in two minutes to march, to retreat, or to fight. Never detailing any one for the duties of a sentry, and arranging all things by agreement among themselves, they yet kept better watch, marked more accurately every unusual sound, and were earlier apprised of impending danger than any troops in the army. Refusing to have their names inscribed on the muster-roll, they received no pay, and for the most part subsisted themselves. In battle they were almost always with the Rangers. Wherever the bullets were flying thickest they were sure to be found. Wherever the dead were piled the highest there they had charged. Invariably discarding the rifle as they neared an enemy, and resorting to the revolver, it was terrible to witness the wide havoc which always marked the spot where they fought.

"What are we to do now, John Glanton?" said a large, broad-shouldered man, cramming a huge piece of beef into his capacious mouth. "Old Zack has patched up an eight weeks' peace, and d—m me if I know what to be at while it lasts."

The youth he addressed had not seen more than twenty-two summers. His cheek was smooth and almost beardless; his frame slender and light. There was a peculiar glossiness about the long, raven hair that hung around his neck, and but for the firm lip, and the flashing eye, he might have been mistaken for a woman in disguise. But that slight frame was knit of twisted steel, and the white hand that brushed back his flowing hair had shed more blood than would have furnished its owner a crimson bath.

"Suck your paws," he said, laughing, "like an old he bear in winter. As for me, I hear that Mustang Gray is ordered to Camargo, and I shall *vamos* with him. I hear, too, that some of the boys are to be quartered in Mier. Wouldn't you like to go there, and cheer up some of the widows you had a hand in making when Fisher and the rest of you run your heads into that sweet trap in '42?"

"And what kept you out of it, boy, as you was," was the quick retort, "but the devil's luck, that always follows an imp like you? As for the widows," he continued, "they oughtn't to think hard of me for ridding them of a d—d trifling lot of husbands."

"And I'll swear they won't. I'll bet my revolver against a quart of *muscal* that you may go to a *fandango* and dance with every widow in the house, without hearing a word about the pretty little red puddles you made in the streets."

"I shan't try it, John; for if they didn't think about it I should. I should be thinking too of the d—n—d rusty chains they hammered around my legs, and kept them there until they gnawed into the bone. That job of work aint paid for yet, and I think I will settle up square with the men before I begin to make love to the Senoritas."

"There is exactly where we differ. I'm thinking of the girls all the time, and curse me if I haven't killed half a dozen Greasers for no other reason in the world than because I thought it would delight the black-eyed, orange-cheeked damsels to get rid of the infernal brutes."

"You killed 'em more because you was a born devil, John, than anything else," replied the volunteer, lying down upon his blanket with the air of a man who intended to put an end to the conversation.

"What are you going to do, Tom?" asked Glanton, placing his hand on Simpson's knee, who was seated on the ground by his side.

"I can't tell. The captain and me haven't talked it over yet."

"Where is he?"

"In Monterey, with Captain Wilson, who has got a bullet through his ribs, that is likely to be serious."

"Tom," said Glanton, thoughtfully, "you are the only man in this country that knows anything about Bernard Lile."

"Why he was in Texas, and fought by the side of your father, before you was big enough to shoot a rifle without a rest."

"Yes, I know that, and I have heard my father tell tales of what he did in the Revolution, until I couldn't sleep the whole night for thinking of them. But nobody knows anything about him before that."

"You had better ask him."

"Ask him! I would as soon think of asking old Zach Taylor to give me his gray horse. Ask him! I think you say. No sir-ree. But, Tom," he continued, in a coaxing tone, "just give me a hint, and there's no telling what I'll do for you."

"I don't know anything to tell you, John, and wouldn't do it if I did, unless he said so."

"Well," said Glanton, rising, walking behind Simpson, and putting his hands on his shoulders, "if you wont tell me anything, I'll tell you something."

He stooped, as if to whisper in his ear, and catching the member in his teeth, bit it sharply. With a hasty exclamation, the hunter turned to grasp his tormentor, but the active youth had bounded beyond his reach, and with a loud laugh disappeared in the darkness.

"Plague take the boy," muttered Simpson, rubbing the smarting member, "he's brought the blood."

Very soon a dead silence reigned around the lonely camp-fires, the burning brands were dropping slowly to ashes, and a deep sleep had fallen on the rough, hardy and fearless volunteers. It was long after midnight when John Glanton came in, and touching one of the sleepers with his foot, said,

"Come, Jim. It's your time now."

The man rose—stirred the fire so as to see that the caps on his revolver were all right, and walked off. Glanton quietly stretched himself upon the blanket from which the other had just risen. This was all the ceremony of relieving guard in that free encampment. They had no countersign, and wanted none. The sentry let any one pass out who chose to go, and any one he knew, and did not suspect of mischief, was in like manner permitted to enter. They stood guard *only* to prevent the approach of outward danger. Every thing else was left to the individual's unrestrained inclinations. In an army, such a system would be destruction; with them it was safe as agreeable.

In a small house, close to the plaza, in the City of Monterey, Bernard Lile was seated by the side of his wounded friend. He was too familiar with gunshot wounds to doubt that this one was fatal. With kind and gentle words, he smoothed back the matted hair from the brow of Robert Wilson, and held the cooling draught to his fevered lips; but his attentions were bestowed only to relieve the present sufferings of the patient, without a gleam of hope that they might result in ultimate recovery. Captain Wilson was himself fully aware of his approaching end, and spoke of it with the calm firmness of a patriot soldier, who knows that his duty has been discharged, and feels that a life given to his country is never lost. It blooms again, beyond the grave, in a land where winter never comes, and suffering is unknown. Hanging around the throne of sapphire and gold, a rich garland awaits the coming of him who has died for his country, and when the Eternal Hand has dropped it on his brow, Justice hands the record of his life to Mercy, and turns away until all that is black, and all that is sinful, is erased.

It was near daylight—the strong man leaned his elbow upon the couch of the dying. From his deep and regular breathing, he believed he slept soundly, but very soon a weak voice inquired,

"What time is it now?"

"Nearly five o'clock," was the answer. "Do you feel easy?"

"Too easy. The pain is gone, and death is coming. Put away the curtain from the window, that I may see the first rays of the rising sun. Before its setting, these eyes will be shrouded with eternal darkness."

Lile did as he was directed; when the wounded man again called him to his side.

"Sit down. There is one thing which has been pressing upon me for days, and I must mention it before I go. Your wife died believing me churlish, and it may be ungrateful. I would not have you live on in the same belief."

"Do not distress yourself," answered Lile, "by dwelling on so sad a subject. She knew all, and did you justice."

"All! are you sure of it?"

"As sure of it, as I am of my own existence." And he drew from his bosom the letter he had received from Zerah in Texas, and read it slowly and plainly.

Robert Wilson raised himself slightly, and listened with

eager attention. When it was concluded, he fell back upon his pillow, and murmured, faintly,

"Bless her! She was an angel, who strayed away from heaven for a little while to gladden the earth with her presence. I shall see her soon."

He never moved again. Without a sigh, without a gasp, without a shiver, the spirit passed away, and the hand of his friend rested on a pallid corpse.

When Simpson came into the city that day, according to his custom, he was met at the door by Lile.

"It is all over, Tom. He is gone like most of those I have loved on earth. Yourself and one other remain. Who can say how soon those links may also be shattered?"

"It will be a sorrowful day, captain, when you and I part. But there is no telling when it may happen. We've both got a habit of gitting in the way of bullets, and one or the other is like enough to be picked off whenever a battle is fought."

They entered the house, and the backwoodsman gazed long in silence upon the cold clay before them. His voice was choked and husky, when he spoke.

"He was a *good one,* or I'm no judge of a soldier. He's gone to heaven, I reckon."

"I hope so."

"Don't you believe, captain, that a man who is killed in his country's battles *always* goes there?"

"I believe, Tom, that such a death is a meet atonement for many an error, but I pretend not to understand the purposes of the Almighty. His justice and his mercy are inscrutable, and he is wisest who questions not, and murmurs not at his decrees."

CHAPTER XIII.

"See! how calm he looks, and stately,
Like a warrior on his shield,
Waiting till the flush of morning
Breaks along the battle field.
See!—Oh! never more my comrades,
Shall we see that falcon eye
Redden with its inward lightning
As the hour of fight drew nigh."

In obedience to the injunctions of Robert Wilson, Bernard Lile had enclosed the body in a double coffin, and prepared to carry it to his native village for interment. The sad duty was in some degree lightened by the reflection that it gave him an opportunity of meeting John Abbott, and enjoying a brief intercourse with that true and faithful friend. Perhaps also he anticipated a melancholy pleasure in visiting the grave of Zerah, after an absence of years, and kneeling on the sod which became holy ground the day her remains were deposited beneath it. An eight weeks' truce had been agreed on by the hostile commanders, and no active operations were anticipated within the time his absence would necessarily consume. Tom Simpson rode a few miles with the escort which conveyed the bodies of Robert Wilson and many another gallant soldier, back to the land they had loved so truly, and served so faithfully. In that funeral train there were, beyond doubt, corpses of men whose lives had not been altogether free from reproach. But whatever vices may have rioted in their bosoms they had made all the atonement this world can demand, and whatever censure may have attached to them while living, was lost in the admiration excited by the manly devotion to liberty, and the unmistakable love of country which sealed its sincerity with blood. The rough backwoodsman, as he rode by the side of Lile, gave expression to feelings that had a place in the bosoms of ninety-nine in every hundred composing the American army.

"It will be a solemn day when these poor fellows are landed at New Orleans, but a proud one. Their sweethearts will all be crying, but if they are the right grit, and I know our gals are, they wouldn't swap off these dead bodies for the best men who stayed at home when Old Zack crossed the Rio Grande."

"There are thousands upon thousands there, Tom, who would have come as cheerfully, and fought as bravely as these, but the opportunity was denied them."

"They were in bad luck then. I would rather have died at Monterey, than to have been kept at home nursing babies, when *men* were playing the game of life and death with lead and steel."

His companion made no reply at the moment. When he again spoke his thoughts had traveled to a different subject.

"What do you purpose to do while I am gone?"

"I haven't settled on it yet. There's Jack Hays, Ben McCulloch, and old Lamar, to choose between, and a fellow can't go wrong, no matter which he takes."

"They are true soldiers, all of them. True and tried; and what is better still, kind and upright men. I shall come back as soon as I can."

Months rolled away, and Bernard Lile did not return. On the 12th of November, the division of Gen. Worth was again pushed forward, and in a few days thereafter that indomitable officer took possession of Saltillo. In December he was joined by a column under Gen. Wool, and soon afterwards Gen. Taylor himself hurried to that point to meet an attack threatened by Santa Anna with overwhelming numbers. The operations of General Scott had made it necessary for him to withdraw nearly the entire regular force from the command of Gen. Taylor, and Santa Anna who hoped to win an easy victory over the undisciplined volunteers who remained, moved from San Louis Potosi with an army of twenty-two thousand men admirably equipped, and abundantly supplied with all the munitions of war. A daring reconnoissance made by Ben McCulloch apprised Gen. Taylor of the approach of his enemy. On the 20th of February, Lieutenant-Colonel May was despatched to the Hacienda of Hecliondo, and Major McCulloch again sent to Encarnacion. On the 21st Gen. Taylor fell back to Buena Vista. On the 22d, the army of Santa Anna came in sight, and soon after midday the battle began between a force of twenty thousand disciplined troops, and less than one fourth that number of volunteers, most of whom now for the first time looked upon a stricken field. Throughout that day and the next the murderous conflict raged, but at last the stubborn heroism of the republican soldiery triumphed over the desperate odds; under cover of the darkness Santa Anna retreated, leaving the ensanguined plain thickly strewed with his dead and dying—his army completely disorganised—his own laurels forever withered. A death blow was struck at the energies of Mexico, soon to be followed by others as fatal from another quarter, until even Castilian pride was humbled, and the haughty descendants of the early conquerors were crushed beneath a heel as heavy, if not as pitiless, as that which blotted the Aztec name from the map of nations.

On the 9th of March, the army of Gen. Scott landed at Sacrificios, and on the 27th of the same month the city of Vera Cruz, and the famed castle of San Juan De Ulloa, were surrendered to his arms after a regular investment of only fifteen days.

The movements of Santa Anna in the mean time had exhibited an almost incredible amount of daring energy. Defeated at Buena Vista on the 23d of February, he had returned to the city of Mexico, a distance of more than seven hundred miles,—quelled a serious insurrection, collected another army of eighteen thousand men, and advanced to the heights of Cerro Gordo, which command the national road between Vera Cruz and Jalapa. All this had been accomplished before the middle of April, and here in this seemingly impregnable position, strong by nature and rendered doubly strong by art, he awaited the coming of Scott. Every defence that science sould suggest had been added, and the Mexican general was so well satisfied that he was heard to exclaim, "If the Americans can storm this position, they can storm hell itself."

.On the 17th of April, Gen. Scott completed his arrangement, and issued his final orders. The battle began at daylight on the 18th, and before two o'clock every battery had been carried, Santa Anna was a fugitive, his army was annihilated, and forty-three pieces of brass ordnance, together with all his munitions were in the hands of Scott.

Still, Bernard Lile had not revisited the land where these stirring scenes were enacted, and Tom Simpson, who had borne his part in all that had transpired on the line of the Rio Grande, began to feel uneasy at the absence of his friend.

At length he received a letter, and when he had glanced at the signature, eagerly perused its contents.

"I regret that I could not be with you at Buena Vista. It was a glorious field and will be embalmed forever in the hearts of the American people. Many things I could not foresee have detained me, and besides I wished to make a final disposition of everything I possess, for I have a presentiment that my race is nearly run. All is arranged, and I shall set out in a short time for Vera Cruz. Meet me there. It is along that line the war must be henceforth waged, and I am sure you feel as I do that the place best suited to us is that where the hardest blows are given and received.

"Bernard Lile."

A column of volunteers, under Gen. Lane, were about descending the Rio Grande for the purpose of reinforcing Gen. Scott. Uniting himself with these Tom Simpson embarked at Brasos Santiago, and in the month of August, 1847, leaped from a surf-boat to the shore at Vera Cruz. He was greeted by Lile who had waited his coming, and the next day it was arranged that, as Col. Hays was still behind with the Rangers, they should attach themselves to Walker's company of mounted rifles, and accompany Gen. Lane on his march to the interior. Many causes conspired to hasten the movements of Lane. The deadly *vomito* was raging throughout the *tierra caliente*, and impelled him to seek safety from its attacks among the mountain ranges. Gen. Scott's communications with the coast had been entirely cut off, and the most painful uncertainty as to the fate of his gallant army existed. Joe Lane was not a man to remain idle at such a time. As a partisan officer he had no superior, and it was doubtful if he had any equal in the American army. Always in motion; always on the alert; shrouding his own plans with impenetrable secresy, and divining, with scarcely ever failing certainty, those of his enemy, he spread terror and dismay in all directions. At one time the head of his column, at sun-down, would be directed eastward towards some garrisoned town or fortified place, and the Mexican scouts would ride off at full speed to give warning of the threatened attack. The next morning he would pounce upon an encampment, and cut up a guerilla troop resting in security twenty-five or thirty miles off in an opposite direction. Sometimes he would abandon a place, carrying with him his sick, wounded, baggage, munitions, and every thing which indicated an intention to move entirely off. At night he would return with a picked body of men, and destroy a company or more of guerillas who had been tempted to occupy his old quarters after his departure. The armies of Napoleon melted away before the system of guerilla war adopted in Old Spain. In Mexico, Gen. Lane turned their own tactics against themselves. Padre Jarauta was beaten with his own weapons. Every day the number of his lancers lessened. He was more than once surprised himself, and narrowly escaped the clutches of his indefatigable foeman.

At Jalapa Gen. Lane at length received information that put an end to the system of warfare he had thus far pursued so successfully, and with such beneficial results. The battles of Molino del Rey, Chepultepec, and the Garitas, had followed those of Contreras and Cherubusco. The city of Mexico was in the possession of Gen. Scott, but still his position was critical in the extreme. When that wonderful commander descended from Ayotla into the valley of Mexico, his field reports showed an effective force of only ten thousand eight hundred men. With that little army he had fought five bloody battles, and with its shattered remains now occupied a city of more than two hundred thousand hostile inhabitants. Every moment the hero and his veterans were in danger of being overwhelmed by numbers no human strength and courage could resist, and without waiting for orders in a case so plain Gen. Lane at once took up the line of march for Mexico.

CHAPTER XIV

"All was prepared—the fire, the sword, the men
 To wield them in their terrible array.
The army, like a lion from his den,
 March'd forth with nerve and sinews bent to slay—
A human hydra, issuing from its fen
 To breathe destruction on its winding way."

THE sun of an October morning was stealing over the hills, bathing in its rays, rock and tree, and tower, and temple. Not the pale sun of our northern clime, cold, misty, and cheerless; but the bright sun of the tropics, bursting from its ocean bed, in all the gorgeous beauty of that enchanted land. Upon a fair city, on the vast "table land" of Mexico, that sun was shedding its earliest light. Not yet had the day's toil begun. Not yet had the busy hum of life roused the luxurious sons and daughters of the far South from their slumbers in the balmy air. The stillness and the silence of *rest* was about it. Even as the messengers, in the vision of Zechariah, who came to the angel of the Lord, that stood among the myrtle trees, and said, "We have passed to and fro through the earth, and behold! all the earth sitteth still, and is at rest." Even so, hour by hour, through the night, the sentries on the ramparts of Huamantla had proclaimed, "all is well."

Morning came—such a morning as the first that broke over the garden "eastward in Eden." Even the rude soldiery of the guard, shook off the lethargy of the night watch, to feast their souls upon its glorious beauty. Never in his untold wanderings had the day-king burst upon a lovelier scene. The high peaks of the Cordilleras, wrapt in the snowy mantles, borrowed from nature centuries ago, and gleaming in the mellow sunlight, with that unspeakable lustre that almost wins us to adoration—the wide plain, teeming with fruits, and adorned with flowers—the great city, built by the conquerors; rich in all the works of art, glowing with all the gems of earth, and proudly claiming to be the fairest child of the brilliant chivalry of a by gone age—the deep blue sky, added to the fragrance of the early morning, together made a Paradise in reality, far brighter than any creation of a poet's fancy.

All now is loveliness and peace; but it is the deceitful lull of the air, when the tempest is gathering its fearful array for the battle of the elements. Not alone from mountain top, from spire, and minaret, flash back the morning's beams. There, away to the south-east, glitters a long line of terrible beauty. In the far distance, it seems, as it winds through fields of cactus, like a pathway of molten silver. Now it catches the glance of the soldier upon yon tower, and for him the loveliness of the morning has faded, for to him it speaks of a sterner metal. It is the glancing of the sunbeam on musket, and bayonet, and sabre, and, beneath that line of glowing light, the dreaded warriors of "the States" are moving on the doomed city, with firm and rapid tread.

Rouse thee, fair denizen of that lovely city, and yet lovelier land, thy dream of peace is at an end! The splendid panorama, now spread out before thee, will soon be swept away to make room for a bloodier landscape, and the eye that has opened from slumber, on a scene which might tempt angels from the skies, will close upon a picture painted by the fiends of hell.

At a considerable distance from the great national highway, and of no absolute importance as a military post, the City of Huamantla had been passed unmolested by the invaders. There it lay in its beauty, and its pride; unmarked by fire or sword, and unconscious of the desolation which was approaching. In the months, of August and September preceding, the decisive battles of the valley had placed General Scott in possession of the City of Mexico; but his army, at all times much too weak for the mighty undertaking entrusted to his management, had been sadly weakened, and cut to pieces on the bloody and unequal fields over which he had won his victorious way. He was a conqueror in the capitol of his enemy; but a conqueror whose mightiest energies had been taxed to the uttermost, and to whom rest and repose were as necessary as grateful. Taking prompt advantage of the crippled condition of the Americans, the great chief of the Mexican nation, with a tireless energy, and a military skill rarely surpassed, rapidly collected the remnants of his beaten armies, and precipitated himself upon Puebla, a post that had been for some time beleaguered by an irregular Mexican force, and the maintenance of which was of the last importance to the American commander, since through that alone his communications with the sea coast could be kept open. For more than thirty days the roar of battle resounded through its streets. The little garrison, under Colonel Childs, was daily wasting away. Disease struck down the strong man, whom the cannot shot had spared; and hunger gnawed away the strength no fatigue could overcome. Still they fought on; with the iron nerve, and the unyielding obstinacy of the Anglo-Saxon race, they repelled assault after assault, calmly bidding defiance to danger and death from without, and sternly quelling the ceaseless cravings of hunger and thirst within. Every soldier was aware of the immensity of the stake depending upon his courage and endurance. All looked forward to the probability of a bloody grave, but none ever dreamed of a surrender. That post might become the burial place of a band of heroes, who were worthy to have stood side by side with Leonidas in the pass of Thermopylæ, but never until then could an enemy's flag wave above its defences. Suddenly there was a cessation of active operations on the part of the beseigers. The iron hail of the past thirty days was succeeded by a comparative calm. Occasionally only, a heavy gun belched forth its volumes of smoke and flame, as it dispatched a winged messenger on an errand of destruction; while long intervals marked the rattling volleys of musketry, and escopetas. The stubborn resistance of the garrison had accomplished its end. Time was everything, and time had been gained. They knew not how near at hand was the assistance they had longed for—they only knew that their orders were to maintain the post at every hazard; and, if no assistance ever came, they were thankful for the privilege of writing another glorious chapter in the history of the great republic. Not so with the Mexican leader. Every step of General Lane's progress had been reported to him. Day by day he had calculated the lessening distance, and day by day his assaults upon the *Cuartel* had been more determined. Often superintending in person the direction of the guns, he watched with intense anxiety the effect of every shot, and the result of every assault; still, as each night closed in, he had the mortification of finding that he was as far as ever from the accomplishment of his object, and that his greatest efforts had only succeeded in spreading an additional feast for the vultures, already so fully gorged, that they refused to banquet on anything but the eyes of the slain. The reports of his scouts now advised him, that he had delayed to the last moment of safety. Instead of the assailant, he was about to become the assailed with that indomitable garrison on one side, and a fresh army, in high spirits, and burning to rival the almost incredible deeds of their brethren in *the valley*, on the other. In this crisis he resorted to one of those masterly manœuvres that distinguished the whole of his operations. He was an enemy, and a bitter one, but let us do him justice. No man ever lived who accomplished more with feebler means. No campaigns were ever better planned. It is doubtful if the impartial critic will be able to detect hereafter a single serious error. It is true, he failed signally in all his undertakings, but those failures flowed from no want of military skill, courage, or energy, on his part. They were the results, rather, of circumstances beneath whose weight Napoleon would have been crushed. In this, almost the very last of his military operations, he vindicated his right to the title of a great commander. Withdrawing all his disposable forces from the siege of Puebla, he moved silently and secretly to encounter the "Marion of the war." The soldiers of the northern republic had won a terrible fame in the bloody campaigns of Mexico, and not daring to trust his own men in an open encounter with an enemy by whom they had been so often beaten, he left only a small body upon the high road, with instructions to fall back as the Americans advanced. With the main body he moved himself in the direction of Huamantla, intending, when Gen. Lane had passed that point, to make a decisive attack the succeeding night upon his rear—the body in front having orders to assail him at the same time from the direction of Puebla.

Riding at the head of the column, as was his wont, about mid-day Gen. Lane ordered his bugler to sound the usual signal for an army on the march to halt, and rest. Throwing his bridle reign to an orderly, he took refuge, with a portion of his staff, under the thick shade of a spreading tree, to partake of such refreshment as the time allowed.

A piece of cold beef, a hard biscuit, and an onion from a haversack, with a supply of Mexican *aguardiente*, from an India-rubber canteen, constituted the homely fare of the republican general. While thus occupied, Lile and Simpson rode up. Nodding familiarly to his old favorites, the general invited them to get down, and join in his repast.

"This *aguardiente*," he added, "is not the best liquor in the world; but it will do to wash down dry beef and sea-biscuit, when no better is to be had."

Thanking him for the courtesy, but touching very lightly the proffered liquid, Lile continued,—

"We have come, general, to ask a favor."

"Ah! Well that is something which does not happen often. What is it?"

"With your permission, we propose to take one of Dominguez's spies, and ride on as far as Amazoque, for the purpose of learning something more reliable of Santa Anna's movements."

A shade came over the weather beaten visage of the general, and he thought deeply before he replied.

"It won't do, Lile. I can't afford to send the two best men in my army on such a desperate errand. Mexican light troops are swarming over the whole country; your guide, too, would betray you for a single *peso*."

A slight smile played, for an instant, on the haughty lip of the daring soldier.

"Pardon me, general, but you over estimate the danger. Simpson and I are better armed, and better mounted, than any *caballeros* in Mexico; and ten to one is an odds we have faced before now, without any great apprehensions."

"Besides, general," broke in the Ranger, "there is no danger in the world from 'the Greaser.' I can trust him any where."

"Don't you think, Tom," asked Gen. Lane, "that a man who *has* betrayed his country, would betray any thing?"

"Undoubtedly that's my opinion, *provided* he didn't have a fore-knowledge that he would be started on the road to *kingdom come* in five minutes after he did it. But this fellow, Antonio, knowed me on the Rio Grande, and he's got a suspicion in his head, that if he tried to play me any tricks, his kin would have to scrape up all the *tlacos* they could get together, for the *Padre* to pray him out of purgatory."

"I do not like this," said the general, again addressing Lile, "the risk is very great; but I need reliable information sadly, and should not be excusable as a soldier for rejecting your offer. Go, sir; God knows I have not shunned danger myself, when our country demanded it, and I will not baulk your wish to serve her."

Lile bowed his thanks; but Simpson was not content so to part with the officer to whom he was attached so much.

"Good-bye, general; the captain will bring you all the news, and if there is any thing to eat between here and Amazoque, or in the town either, you'll have a better dinner to-morrow than you are eating to-day."

As they rode away they were joined by the Mexican, who had halted a little way off when they approached the general, and the three men were soon lost to view in the winding of the road. They had not ridden far when Lile inquired of the guide how long they could travel the main road with safety.

"Not a league, senor," was the reply. "Padre Jarauta is at El Pinar, and his lanceros never sleep."

"Well, take the lead. Choose the safest paths, but push on rapidly."

This injunction, however, was much easier to give than to obey. The cross country it was necessary for them to pass over, was often filled with a tangled undergrowth of thorns, and their progress was still further delayed by the stone fences running in all directions through the country. At nightfall they were still four or five leagues from their destination. A heavy bank of clouds, that had long been gathering in the west, now spread rapidly over the horizon, and broad sheets of lurid lightning, growing brighter and brighter at each successive flash, portended that a tropical storm was at hand.

"We're in bad luck, captain," said Simpson, as they leaped their horses over a low wall of loose stone; "not that I care a straw for the rain, or the wind, or the darkness either, if we only knowed the land-marks about these 'diggins;' but Antonio has been figuring that string of beads about his neck for a full quarter of an hour, and I don't believe he will know his right hand from his left in a quarter more. The devil only knows where he'll carry us, and then, if he takes us wrong, I shall have to blow his brains out upon an oncertainty."

"There must be a Hacienda close by," rejoined his com panion, "and we will stop there until the storm is over. Antonio," he continued, calling to the Mexican who was still in advance, "do you know any Hacienda near at hand where we could obtain shelter from the storm?"

"*Si, señor.*"

"Take us there; and mark me, speak English when you address either of us. Remember, that we are deserters from the American army, and do not understand a word of Spanish."

The guide, whose spirits had vastly improved at the prospect of escaping the coming tempest, soon brought them to the heavy gate of a country house, surrounded by a high wall, crenelled and loop-holed, for defence against the robber bands who infest that misgoverned land. At the loud summons of the guide, torches and lanterns began to flash through the enclosure, and the quick hurrying of feet, in different directions, spoke rather of the watchfulness of a beseiged garrison, than the calm security of the inmates of a peaceful country house. After a long parley, and a thousand protestations from Antonio, that they were "friends," "great friends," the massy gate swung lazily back on its iron hinges, and our party, passing underneath the arch, found themselves in a square court, planted with flowers, and laid off in tiny walks, with a cool, clear fountain bubbling up in the centre.

In the same enclosure, separated only by a narrow gravel walk, the stables, the poultry house, and the pig-stye, presenting a wide and disgusting contrast, to these evidences of a refined and cultivated taste. In nearly every house in Mexico, may be witnessed the same admixture of filth, and cleanliness; of order, and disorder; of the beautiful, and the disgusting. It is the struggle of intellect and refinement, against governmental misrule and priestly superstition. In such a land the same house, of necessity, contains the biped, and the quadruped: for there alone is there any assurance of safety for either; but the fountain played by the pig-stye, and the flowers blooming around the dung hill, have each a voice to proclaim how high in the scale of civilization the people might attain under happier auspices.

By the time the clanking sound of the closing gate had died away, the rain came pouring down in torents, and the winds howled fiercely around the solid walls of the Hacienda. Leaving Antonio to tell what story he pleased to the owner of the mansion, our two friends proceeded directly to the stable with the horses. Like true soldiers, their first care was for the noble animals, whose strength and speed might at any moment be taxed to the utmost. Not until their glossy hides were cleared of every speck of dirt, did Lile and Simpson enter that part of the building designed for the exclusive habitation of man. In the meantime Antonio had learned that there were none but servants about the establishment, under the control of a superintendent; the owner of the country house having joined the army of Santa Anna, in Puebla, with most of the *peons* on his estate. He had also, succeeded in impressing upon the superintendent a very exalted opinion of the liberality of his fellow travelers, as was sufficiently attested, by the pains he had taken to prepare a supper after the most fastidious Mexican taste. Scarcely had the substantial repast been concluded, when a bugle note mingled with the low mutterings of the thunder without. The superintendent rushed from the room, and Antonio's yellow complexion was instantly changed to a livid white.

"What does this mean?" sternly demanded Lile.

"They are lanceros of the body guard, Señor, and I shall be shot in less than an hour as a traitor."

"Quick; to the gate, and see how many there are. We'll save you, unless there is more than one troop upon us.

When the Mexican departed upon his errand, Simpson quietly drew his revolver—set it upon the half cock, and with his thumb and forefinger, turned the cylinder twice round, to see that it worked smoothly; then loosening his bowie knife in the sheath, he seated himself again at the table, and pouring out a glass of *pulque*, drank it off with as little concern as if he had been in the heart of the American camp. His business, as he understood it, was simply to execute whatever plan his comrade devised; and he had no idea of troubling his head with useless conjectures, before his orders were received. Lile walked to the door, to which Antonio now returned in breathless haste, to announce that the party outside consisted of one *teniente* and eight *soldados*.

"No more? Then you are safe enough, and need not trouble your patron saint with any prayers for the present; but mind that you do exactly as I direct you. Keep out of their sight, and when the lancers are quartered for the night, go to the stables and saddle our horses. Yours is a sorry brute, and I advise you to exchange him for the best one in their troop."

"Si, Señor," interposed the Mexican, to whom this appropriation of another's property, appeared the most equitable thing imaginable.

"When you hear me sing 'La Ponchada,'" continued Lile, "lead the horses at once to the gate. You know the words?

'Ya no se llaman negros
Los hijos de Arragon;
Se llaman defensores
De Isabel de Bourbon.'"

"I know the song well, Señor, and shall not forget."

"Now begone. I will manage every thing else."

Returning to the table he seated himself by the side of Simpson, and said, in a low tone,

"You heard that there is but nine of them."

"Yes; and unless I am worse mistaken than the fellow that burnt his shirt, that's just nine more than will ever ride out of this caboose with whole skins."

"It may come to that; but we must try and take the lieutenant alive to Gen. Lane. It will be worth double the lives of his whole regiment."

"Just as you please, captain, only let me know what's to do, and I'm thar."

The lancers had now effected an entrance into the court yard. The troopers made their way to the stables with the horses. The officer, preceded by the temporary host, took shelter from the inclemency of the night without delay. At the door he stopped, and asked, sharply,

"Who have we here?"

"Two American deserters, Señor, on their way to join his excellency, the President."

"Ah!" said he, lifting the scarlet bonnet from his head, and shaking the rain drops from its lofty plumes. "I shall have the pleasure then of introducing them to his excellency myself."

He was a young man, who had apparently seen some service. Like most of his countrymen there was a good deal of the coxcomb about him, but his manner was bold and soldierly, though a little tinged with suspicion, as he addressed our two friends in excellent English.

"I am told, Señors, that you seek his excellency Gen. Santa Anna. I am myself bound for his head-quarters. If it is agreeable to you we will ride in company."

Lile readily expressed his assent to the arrangement, together with his gratification at having accidentally fallen in with so excellent an officer.

Numerous questions were now propounded as to the strength of Gen. Lane's army? What proportion of troops were regulars, and what volunteers? What was the number and size of his guns? What was his cavalry force? Where he had encamped for the several preceding days, and where he had now probably halted? From the manner the answers were received, Lile judged correctly, that the lieutenant was already perfectly acquainted with Gen. Lane's movements, and that his questions were put more for the purpose of detecting any inconsistency in the statements of the reputed deserters, than that of acquiring additional information. Accordingly his answers were all plain, brief, and strictly true; but the Spanish blood is by nature suspicious, and the lieutenant was far from being satisfied that all was exactly right. His non-commissioned officer had reported to him for orders, and been instructed by him to wait. Apparently satisfied, he rose from his seat, and went out to the apartment occupied by his men. In obedience to a sign from Lile, Simpson followed him with noiseless steps. He returned quickly, and said with a shrug,—

"Humph! He's taking as much pains to catch us as the boy took to catch the rattle-snake. He has ordered the sergeant to post one sentry at this door, and one at the gate; and to be ready to march at four o'clock."

The entrance of the officer put an end to further remarks, and soon afterwards they were aware that a sentry was posted at the door. Without paying any attention to this unusual precaution, Lile commenced a conversation with the Mexican, and gradually drew him on to listen to many a feat of chivalry, and many a tale of love in other lands. Discarding the harsher dialect of the Saxon, he employed the soft, musical tongue of Grenada, to tell how he had stood by moonlight in the shadows of the Alhambra, and listened to the story of the Cid, of Pelayo, of Bobadilla, and the long line of heroes who had rendered Spain's history, for a hundred years, the wonder of the world. Mingled with these, were descriptions of the fair hands that had braided their pennons for the battle-field; of the bright eyes that welcomed their return; and the sweet lips that repaid a thousand fold the wounds of war. Eagerly, as the young always do such things, the lieutenant drank in his words. His suspicions had fled; and when the first sentry was relieved, he was listening with wrapt attention to the rich, full voice of Lile, as he sang with melting tenderness, that sweetest of Spanish songs,

"Cuando me llaman bonita,
El corazon me palpita."

This was the moment for which Lile had waited. He knew that it would be two hours before the sentries were again visited, and during that time every thing about the Hacienda would be buried in profound repose. Pretending to be much engaged with the lieutenant, he reached his hand to the pitcher of water, and purposely spilled the whole of its contents. With an ejaculation as to his own carelessness, he handed the pitcher to Simpson, and bade him refill it from the fountain in the court. Simpson advanced to the threshold, but there he was promptly halted by the sentinel. The officer, without turning his head, sharply ordered the soldier to "let him pass." Simpson stepped out, pulling the door after him. The sentry turned away with a muttered *caramba.* The next instant the heavy stone pitcher was swung aloft—it descended with a dull, crashing sound, and the sentry sank into eternal sleep upon his post. Almost at the same moment, Lile had seized the lieutenant with one giant hand, and pressing the other on his mouth, sternly whispered,—

"Attempt to move, or utter a syllable, and you are a dead man."

By the time Simpson had moved the dead soldier from the door-way, the Mexican officer was securely bound and gagged. But the Ranger paused not to see what success had attended his companion. With the stealthy step of a cat he entered the gloomy arch of the gateway. When he reappeared his arm was crimsoned to the elbow with blood. Entering the room, and cautiously closing the door, he said,—

"All is ready except another horse, and that we must have. If I go to the stable, that coward Antonio will either hide himself, or make some cursed blunder that will betray us."

"That is easily remedied," answered Lile, "I will give the signal, and carry this young gentleman to the gate. When Antonio comes, I will keep on the outside until you join us."

Extinguishing the light, he sang the first stanza of "La Ponchada," and lifting the Mexican in his arms carried him quickly to the gate. Antonio soon came out, and before they had fastened the officer securely on the horse the guide had selected for himself, Simpson also appeared, leading another. The storm had cleared way, and the stars shone clear and bright in the heavens. Lile noticed Simpson tying something to his saddle-bow as he mounted, and inquired what it was.

"Nothing but a cotton bag," was the reply, "containing two chickens and a goose. I promised the general he should have a good dinner to-morrow, and I don't like to break my word; especially to as clever a fellow as he is."

Under the guidance of Antonio, the party made directly for the National road. Rapidly they pressed on—not from fear of pursuit, but in order to reach the American encampment before the army was put in motion. Simpson, who was leading the captive's horse, took advantage of the first smooth piece of ground to offer him all the consolation his situation admitted of.

"Make yourself easy, lieutenant, 'Old Lane' is as clever a fellow as ever trod shoe leather, and though I don't know what he wants with you, I'm dead sure he'll treat you *according to Gunter.* A fellow that's tied and gagged, must feel mighty uncomfortable, I know, but you aint the first one that ever was fixed that way, when no great harm was meant to him. The old general has got a soft heart in that rough carcase of his, and its seldom he's hard on any thing but a thief or a coward."

The consolatory harangue of the Ranger was cut short by a sharp challenge, "who goes there," followed by the rattling of a musket brought suddenly from a *shoulder* to a *ready*.

"Friends, with a prisoner."

"Stand friends. Advance one friend, and give the countersign."

Lile explained that they had been out upon a scouting expedition, by direction of the general, and were not in possession of the countersign.

"Stand where you are. Officer of the guard; number five."

The words ran along the line until they were caught up, and repeated by the sentry at the guard tent. The steady tramp of marching men followed, and very soon, Lile and his party, were admitted within the lines, and furnished with a guide to the general's quarters.

It was hardly one in the morning, but the general was already astir; examining with his adjutant general, a map spread upon a mess chest in his tent. Lile entered with his prisoner. A half hour passed. The form of the adjutant general emerged from the canvass screen. A few brief orders were given. Aids hurried in different directions. A bugle sounded the *reveille*. Drum and fife, and brass band, answered the signal. Light after light glimmered over the plain. The human hive was roused, and woe be to those upon whom its anger fell.

Gen. Lane had learned all the plans of his enemy, and with the prompt decision of his character, he put his army in motion; abandoned the road to Puebla, and marched directly upon Huamantla. Wholly unconscious of this unexpected movement of his active and vigilant foe, Santa Anna was approaching the same point from another direction.

The morning of the 9th of October came, and the startled citizens looked out upon a field glittering with the burnished arms of a gallant host, in their war array. Ignorant of the near approach of their countrymen under Santa Anna, and deeming resistance hopeless, white flags were immediately displayed from the house tops, and the steeples of the churches. The gallant Walker, who commanded the advance, at once entered the city with his small band of "mounted rifles."

"I thought," said the rifleman, turning to Lile, who rode by his side, "that we should be certain to have a battle here that would do to talk about in the States, but the cowardly dogs don't mean to give us any chance for glory to-day."

"We may have our mettle tried sooner than you expect," replied his companion, pulling the thick buckskin gauntlet from his right hand, and for the first time drawing his sabre. "I do not like the signs. There are too many heads above the parapets of the houses. The women have all left the windows, and yonder is a strong body of horse hastily forming on the Plaza. Keep your men well together, and move slowly."

So saying he reined up, and with his unsheathed sword, beckoned Simpson, who was considerably in the rear, to come up.

"Keep near to Walker, Tom. He will need our help directly. These 'rifles' are new recruits, and know nothing about the old Ranger mode of fighting; while Walker understands no other. He will be killed unless—"

The remainder of the sentence was lost amid the rattling of musketry, and the infuriated cries which ran along the whole length of the street.

"Close up men," shouted Walker, "and charge."

They did charge but it was upon their own destruction. Shielded by the houses, the Mexicans poured volley after volley, into their lessening ranks; while from the parapets above, huge masses of stone were incessantly thundered upon their devoted heads. In a few seconds the dauntless captain rode almost alone. A hand was laid upon his bridle, and the calm voice of Lile, calmest ever amid the roar of battle, sounded in his ear.

"Are you mad? your men are nearly all dead. You must back with me, if you would live to avenge this treachery."

With a bitter malediction the infuriated officer permitted his horse's head to be turned towards the gate. Some distance down the street, a little squad of the rifles had formed in something like regular order, and were contending with desperate courage against overwhelming odds. Placing himself at the head of these, Walker again gave the order to charge. The words were yet on his lips when a musket ball struck him on the breast. The reins deserted his hand, and he reeled like a drunken man in the saddle. With a wild shout, a body of horsemen rushed from a cross street, and threw themselves upon the shattered ranks of the Americans. The lance of the leading file struck the dying captain in the face, and hurled him from his steed. Lile reached his side too late to save, but time enough to avenge him. Through bonnet and skull, down to where the neck and shoulder join, bit the forceful steel. Not for an instant did he pause where the luckless lancer fell. Right through the bloody press he cleft his dreadful way. The friend whose blanket he had shared by the camp-fire —whose last *tortilla* he had divided at the mess table, had been butchered before his eyes, and all the fiend was roused within him. Right and left flashed that crimson sabre. Right and left heads, and arms, and men, and steeds were falling around him. Appalled at the wide havoc of a single arm, the boldest lancers turned and fled. Loud and clear rang his voice above the din.

"Retreat," he shouted to the rifles, who still desperately maintained their ground. "Cut your way through the foot. Simpson and I will keep back the lancers until the gate is gained."

The Mexican cavalry, who had drawn off a short distance, were reformed, and again thundered to the charge. Simpson was now by the side of Lile. They waited not to receive the shock, but striking their spurs deep in their horses' flanks, with the rush of an avalanche met the advancing tide. The light small horses of Mexico went down like wisps of straw, before the battle chargers of the States. Again the lancers broke and fled, and two men were the victors over a hundred.

"Let us be off, Tom," said Lile, "the few rifles who are left, have passed the gate, and we have sent enough ghosts to join Walker on his dreary journey."

"By the Lord," rejoined Simpson," if they travel the same road he does, they will have to fight every inch of the way to the other world."

At the gate they found a young rifleman sitting with his back against the wall, and his pistol in his hand. To an inquiry as to what he was doing there, he answered,

"My horse is dead. My leg is broke, and I can't get any further. Tell the general to say to my mother, when he gets home, that I died fighting to the last, as my grandfather did at Lundy's lane."

"Gallant boy!" exclaimed Lile, "I hope you will live many a year to tell this day's story yourself."

Leaning forward, he seized the wounded soldier with his sinewy hand, and lifted him to the saddle-bow, as easily as if he had been an infant. Touching his steed with the spur, he flew across the plain to where the American army was drawn up in battle array. He now learned, that soon after the advance guard had entered Huamantla, Santa

Anna had appeared in sight, and the sudden hope inspired by this circumstance, had caused the treacherous assault in the city.

As they lighted from their jaded steeds, he noticed that Simpson walked with difficulty, and the color had entirely deserted his cheek.

"Are you hurt, Tom?" he inquired, anxiously.

"Yes, sorter. I've got a bullet through my left arm, and a tolerable deep furrow in my side; ploughed there by one of them cursed poking sticks, no Christian people would use. But I reckon the fellow that did it got full pay, for it's my opinion, I cut his backbone clear in two as he went by, after jobbing me with that d——d long iron-headed stick."

When General Santa Anna drew out into the plain before Huamantla, he found himself suddenly confronted by the American forces. Confessedly unable to cope with his enemy on an equal field, he labored under the additional disadvantage of being forced into a battle, under circumstances amounting to a complete surprise. In such a contest victory could not be a moment doubtful. He was quickly beaten at all points, and forced to take refuge in the mountains. Now came the hour of retribution for the treacherous city. The sacred emblem of peace had been stained with blood, and the usages of all wars gave up the offenders as a "prey to the spoiler." It is fearful to see a soldiery fevered with victory, turned loose to pillage and to slay. Then, and then only, the red demon of war is clothed in all his horrors. Vengeance, lust, hate, and rapine, walk abroad unrestrained, and the air is tortured with a mingled discord of horrible sounds, that might shame the builders of Babel into silence. The dull grating noise of the sharp steel, as it bites through skull and brain—the vengeful shout of the slayer—the despairing shriek of the agonized victim—the clatter of muskets and pick-axes—the crash of falling doors and windows—the ringing shot, and the muttered curse, are fit accompaniments to deeds the furies might look upon and envy.

All day, through that fair city, the work went on. All day the fierce license of the soldiery was unrestrained, and yell and groan, and prayer, and curse—the death-shot—the shriek of the virgin, and the wail of the infant rose mingling up to heaven. The sun went down; and now, the wild notes of a solitary bugle pealed shrill and clear upon the air. Then from each regiment, battalion, and corps, the hoarse drum sent forth its summons. The blood-hounds were called off from their prey. The lawless passions of the hour before were stilled at the stern mandates of an iron discipline. The feast of death was at an end. The last mellow tints of the golden sunset melted from the sky; star after star came forth, and it was night in Huamantla. A night of strange and fearful contrasts; of beauty, and of desolation. Without the walls, thousands of homeless wretches—old men, women, and children, were shivering in the night air, while near at hand, a horde of hungry wolves were feasting on the dead bodies of the slain. The savage growls of the ferocious animals mingled horribly with the low moans of the wounded. At intervals a sharp cry of agony would rise above all other sounds, as a ravenous beast fastened his fangs upon some unfortunate being, in whom the vital spark was not yet entirely extinct. Within the walls, whole streets were literally McAdamized with fragments of broken glass, china, and gilded porcelain. The costliest furniture, shivered to pieces, was scattered every where around; and groups of soldiers were cooking their suppers, or washing off the stains of carnage by the light of fires fed with mahogany and rosewood, which had adorned palaces that morning. Here and there a smouldering mass of ashes, a blackened wall, or a smoking rafter, marked where a stately mansion once stood, and a happy family gathered about the hearth-stone. In other quarters, the red glare of the still burning houses, revealed, with horrid distinctness, the mangled bodies of the dead; and shed a sickening light upon the dark pools of blood that dotted the ground. Occasionally a faithful dog would crawl out from his hiding place, and, smelling around the carcase of his dead master, send up a long and mournful howl; but beyond this no living thing was moving in Huamantla, save the fierce soldiers who had made it a desert.

So passed the first hours of the night. Again that solitary bugle sounds its piercing signal, and from each separate command, the beat of the "tattoo" proclaims that it is the hour of silence, and of rest. Strange power of discipline! There was not one coward in all that host. Not one, who, under the eyes of his comrades, would not have moved on certain destruction with an unfaltering step. Not one who would have obeyed the order of a monarch on his throne. Not one who had not that day done deeds, at the bare recital of which the blood runs cold. Yet there was a spell in the mandates of that stirring music, that bent every feeling to instant obedience. Its last notes had scarcely died away, before every sound was hushed, and every soldier had thrown himself upon the soft couch the day's plunder had procured. With his hands dyed red with blood—among the homes he had desolated—in the very midst of the ruins he had wrought; he laid himself down to dream of his own peaceful home. He who had that day made widows and orphans by the score, murmured a blessing upon his own wife, and little ones, far away in his native land; and his last waking thoughts were of the joy and gladness his return would impart.

Slumber spread its mantle over the conquerors. The armed tread of the sentry, ringing on the stone pavement, or crashing sharply, as it crushed to atoms some costly article of luxury, alone broke the stillness of the night. And now from garret and cellar, and secret hiding place, stole forth the frightened citizens, who had escaped the day's violence, vainly hoping, under cover of the darkness, to escape beyond the walls, and join their countrymen in the mountains. Along the dark alleys; close in the shadows of the houses; over the dead bodies of their kindred; through puddles of blood, slowly, and painfully they crawled along. At each opening, the clear starlight revealed the form of a sentry on his post, and the startled fugitives shrank back, to try another, and another avenue, and be again, and again disappointed. Poor fools! you cannot pass that argus line, nor would it profit you to do so. You would only escape from the company of the dead, who feel not; to that of the living, whose own woes leave no room for sympathy with yours. Be still, and you are safe. No one will harm you now. The fever in the blood of the victors has subsided, and the most pitiless of that host would share with you the contents of his haversack, or cover you with his blanket.

With the first light of the morning, the American general was on his march. Stretched in an ambulance, upon the softest couch the plundered city could supply, lay the giant form of the veteran Ranger. Reining his fiery courser back to the slow pace of the mule team, Lile was riding thoughtfully by his side.

"Captain," said the Ranger, putting aside the curtain of the rude conveyance, "you say poor Walker was decently put away."

"Yes, Tom, all was done that a soldier could do."

"That's some comfort. But I wish all the ashes of that

d——d town, mixed up with all the blood spilt in it, had been piled over him for a tombstone."

"The monument would have been a high one, Tom, for everything in Huamantla, that would burn, is ashes now; and never in the old world, or the new, have I seen a bloodier spot than that within those walls."

"I reckon so; and I'm glad of it. But I'm glad too I had no hand in it."

"You are right, my friend. Blood shed in any but our country's battles, or our own just defence, is a dark thing to think of. You will sleep the sounder hereafter for striking no blow after resistance ceased. The punishment of treachery is needful, but the office of executioner is a thing to be avoided if possible."

"Was any of the wimen folks hurt?"

"I do not know. There are bad men in every army, and a bad man, turned loose on such a day as yesterday, will do anything."

"By God, if I had seen a fellow lay his hand upon a gal, except in kindness, I would have mashed his skull, if he had been the general's own brother."

"So would I, Tom; but it might have happened without my seeing it."

The thoughts of the Ranger now took another direction. The wild melee, in which his comrade had put forth all his terrible strength, was again before him. There was a fierce exultation in his voice, as he said,

"That charge you made when Walker fell, was a thing to be proud of. I wouldn't have missed seeing it for a thousand. Them fellows must have thought hell had busted loose; and I reckon they wasn't fur wrong either. That first one you struck, set his horse five seconds after his head tumbled on his shoulders; and the side of his face that fell next to me, looked like he hadn't made up his mind whether he was killed or not. I have had a hand in a good many fights in my time, and ought to know something about them; and I am keen to swear there's no ten men in Jack Hays's regiment could do what you did."

"Pshaw, you did as much yourself."

"No I didn't. I never saw the day I was able. What's more, if it hadn't been for you, I should have been sleeping with Walker, instead of riding along here on the softest bed I ever laid upon. I wish to God you would tell me where you were brought up: and why it is that no living thing can hurt you."

"I may tell you all about myself some day; but the story is too long and too sad to be repeated here. Now rest. You have talked enough for a wounded man."

As he spoke, the bridle rein was slackened—the impatient animal cleared the ambulance at a bound, and the Ranger was left to his own reflections.

CHAPTER XV

"The city is taken—only part by part—
And death is drunk with gore; there's not a street
Where fights not to the last some desperate heart,
For those for whom it soon shall cease to beat.
Here war forgot his own destructive art
In more destroying nature."

The Mexican army, beaten before Huamantla, was too much disorganized to be again reassembled. It was scattered to the four winds of heaven. A considerable detachment having taken refuge in Atlisco, General Lane resolved, if possible, to surprise it, or failing in that, at least to capture the munitions and supplies there collected. It was near sunset when, after a long and fatiguing march, his column appeared in sight of the town. The hurried ringing of bells, and other notes of preparation, indicated that a desperate resistance was contemplated. Ignorant of the nature of the defences, and willing moreover to give his wearied army the repose they so much needed, the American general determined to delay the assault until the following day. Disposing his little force in such a manner as to command the approaches by the main roads, the men were ordered to lie down upon their arms, and await the reappearance of daylight. In the meantime the citizens were in a state of the most dreadful apprehension. Believing from the disposition of the American army, and the known character of its commander, that a night assault was intended, sleep fled from their eyelids, and hurrying feet and moaning cries gave token of the wild disorder within. The garrison exhibited a weakness almost as abject. Afraid even to trust a patrolling party beyond the walls, they resorted to the expedient of throwing out fire-balls at brief intervals to light up the space around them, and enable them to detect an approaching foe. The invaders did not fail to notice these evidences of unmanly fear, and augured rightly that the morrow's work would be a light one. Major Lally, a giant New Englander, as much distinguished for unfailing good-humor, as for dauntless courage, turned to a brother officer, with a broad grin upon his countenance—

"It is my opinion that old Lane is violating the constitution of our country."

"How so?"

"He is inflicting cruel punishment upon the soldados in yonder town, and I think Gen. Scott ought to court-martial him for frightening the poor devils so unmercifully."

"What the devil would you have him do, major?" was the laughing rejoinder. "Do you want him to march in and quiet their fears by cutting their throats by the light of burning houses?"

The brow of the gallant soldier darkened.

"No," he said, "there was enough of that done at Huamantla. Vile and treacherous as they are, and richly as they deserved it, I hope never to see another sight like that."

"It is not the first time they have deserved it, major. For twelve long years they have broken treaties, murdered prisoners, robbed and burned defenceless houses, and I am glad they have learned at last that mercy may be overtaxed.

"I guess you are right. I do not mean to question it; but I do not want to have blood shed in that way upon my hands. I would rather let Padre Jarauta practice at me forty days more with his escopets."

You might do that without any great risk, unless the

doctor slanders you. He swears that the bullet which struck you at the National Bridge, was mashed as flat as a pan-cake, and that it made no more impression on your jaw-bone than if it had been shot against an iron column."

"I'll make an impression on his with my knuckles," replied the major, with a good-humored smile, "if he continues to repeat that story. By the Lord, I did not eat a pound of meat for a week, or drink a drop of whiskey for double that time. I would like to see him put upon such rations, if he thinks it is a thing to be laughed at."

"He would rather charge the heaviest battery at Atlisco by himself to-morrow. By the way," he continued, "speaking of Padre Jarauta, what message was that you received from him at Jalapa?"

"I sent him word, by an officer who had come in with a flag, that, after shooting at me forty days in succession, I thought I was entitled to a good dinner at his hands. He sent me in a lamb and a turkey, with an apology for the bad marksmanship of his men; saying, they were new recruits, but he was drilling them daily, and hoped, that by the time I started for Perote, they would be able to hit a man of my size with tolerable certainty."

With a light laugh his companion walked away, and the major stretched his huge form upon the ground, and slept until the signal bugle once more waked the slumbering host to conquest and to glory.

A little more than half a mile from the walls of Atlisco there was a deserted Hacienda, to which was atttached a small chapel with an enclosed grave-yard. Within this yard two companies of horse had taken up their temporary quarters. It was night when they entered, and picketing their horses as well as the darkness allowed, they dropped down to sleep among the silent graves. When morning came, Bernard Lile found that he had been reposing on a tomb-stone, which bore the inscription,—

"*El sepulchro de mi madre.*"

With a feeling of bitter contempt, the soldier ran his eye over the letters. "My mother's grave," he muttered. "Shame upon the coward wretch who had feeling enough to rear this monument, but lacked the nerve to defend it. The hand which traced these words was in all probability trembling behind that town's defences, while the slab its owner ought to have died to protect from insult, was the couch of a foreign foe. Great God will such a people long be permitted to hold dominion over the fairest portion of the globe? Will the eagles now perched upon its hill tops, or screaming over its valleys, again wing their flight to the northward of the Rio Grande? Will party strife at home, or a weak fear of senseless censures from abroad, recal the immortal army which has planted the standard of the republic upon the regal hill of Chepultepec, and flung its glorious folds to the breeze from the halls of the murdered Montezumas? A high mission will be unfulfilled if one foot of the Aztec empire is restored to the despot and his slaves. A great work will have to be commenced anew; but it *will be* commenced, and it *will be* completed. This land was not made to be the home of those who will not defend the spot where reposes a mother's remains."

The Mexicans had kept up the amusement of throwing out fire balls upon the plain until near midnight; by that time the little courage they possessed had completely oozed out. First, one or two at a time, then larger groups, slunk off along the narrow sheep paths, and made their way into the country. At daybreak not a soldier remained in the town. Without firing a gun, Gen. Lane marched in, and took possession of the public property they were too much terrified to destroy.

Affairs had by this time assumed such a shape in the valley of Mexico as to remove all immediate necessity for additional troops, and Gen. Scott ordered Gen. Lane to assume the governorship of the department of Puebla, and establish his head-quarters in that city of mobs and pronunciamentos. The repose thus granted enabled Lile to devote his whole time to Tom Simpson, whose wounds turned out to be much more grievous than he anticipated. A strong constitution aided by care, and skilful treatment brought him back from the brink of the grave. He began to recover, and Lile was enabled to calculate almost the exact time when the stout backwoodsman would be able to ride by his side through the ranks of war. In the meantime Col. Hays had landed at Vera Cruz with his Rangers, and was making his way up to the new field of adventure before him. The Mexican government had been removed to Queretaro, and the American Commander-in-chief was industriously engaged in organizing and drilling the new recruits sent out by the States, preparatory to following the steps of the flying congress. The rich mining regions were as yet untouched, and a full harvest of glory was still anticipated by the hardy soldiers of the republic. They knew not that petty intrigues were at work in Washington to darken the laurels the hero had gathered, and deprive his country of nearly all the fruits of his hard won victories.

In the month of November Col. Hays came up with his Rangers, and after a series of brilliant services, which it does not fall within the scope of this history to record, was ordered to the city of Mexico. With them went Lile and Simpson. That regiment was the home to which they had been accustomed—the men with whom they were familiar, and to whom they were bound by the strongest ties. Moreover it was there alone they were annoyed by no disagreeable regulations, and fettered by no troublesome requirements.

Three leagues from the city of Mexico, a high hill rises out of the lake Tezcuco—the great causeway through the lake touches its base—around this hill the Mexicans had drawn three tiers of works, and filled them with cannon. The strength of the position had induced Gen. Scott to go south about, and approach the city from the side of Chepultepec. It was now in the possession of the Americans, and the formidable batteries had all been removed. At this place the rangers halted for the night. John Glanton was standing on the causeway examining with the curiosity of a first comer the hill, the lake, the great city, and the towering mountains around. A heavy hand was laid upon his shoulder, and Tom Simpson said, in a voice which boded mischief.

"Do you remember, John, taking a regular wolf snap at my ear on the bank of the San Juan, at Monterey?"

"Can't say I recollect anything of the kind," answered Glanton, laughing, and trying at the same time to jerk away from the grasp that held him.

"I'll see if I can't refresh your memory."

Stooping with a quick motion he seized him by the leg of the pantaloons, and raising him in his sinewy arms pitched him out into the lake.

Practical jokes were too common in that rude camp, and Glanton knew the stout hunter too well to exhibit the least ill-temper, he struggled out of the lake, and scrambled up the causeway, swearing it was a "d—d careless trick."

"Why the devil," he said "didn't you give me notice, so that I could have pulled off my revolver, and bowie knife. This water is as salt as the Gulf of Mexico, and I shall have two hours hard work to keep my *documents* from spoiling with rust.'

"It took my ear more than two hours to get well, Johnny, but if you have got anything fit to eat for supper in your mess I will go with you, and help you clean up."

Scenes like these were of almost daily occurrence, and instead of serving as a pretext for the fierce brawls that not unfrequently disturbed other regiments, they bound the individuals closer together and made that wild camp a model of brotherly kindness. For one Ranger to possess a days rations, or a canteen of *aguardiente*, while another was destitute, was something they never learned to comprehend. From the Colonel down, everything, except their horses, revolvers, and knives were common property. These alone were sacred from any but the owner's touch. The lonely frontier, where these soldiers were made, is now thickly peopled by inhabitants as dissimilar from the first settlers as it is possible to imagine. Ten years in the history of any other nation passes unmarked and unnoted. Ten years in America works out mighty results. This day twenty years ago, (March 19th,) the roar of battle swept over the prairie between the San Antonio and the Coleto, and there were none to listen to the booming cannon, as it sent death through the devoted ranks of the patriot band under Fannin, save the wild deer, and the wild horse which fattened among the flowery meadows the footsteps of man seldom pressed. To-day a city casts its shadows upon the turbid waters of the Rio Grande two hundred miles to the westward, and all between, the springing crops, and the grazing herds proclaim that the old Ranger's occupation is gone. Not now is heard the gathering song,

'Mount, mount and away,
O' the green prairies wide,
The sword is our sceptre,
The fleet steed is our pride.'

A new race has come to take the place of the old. Are they better? No. Are they more useful? No. Have they added to the nation's strength, or the nation's real wealth? No. Let dreaming moralists, or sickly sentimentalists preach as they may, the strong arm, the bold heart, the life in the open air, the generosity that was never overtaxed, and the friendship that never grew weary, are poorly exchanged for the Dutch traffickers in tallow and cheese, who have settled in the old homes of the free rovers of the prairie.

An army of twenty thousand men was now assembled in the City of Mexico. The license of men unfettered by any restraints except those of military discipline, made the splendid capital anything but a pattern of morality. At the *Sociedad*, and at the *Bella Union*, there assembled nightly a throng, who, in the absence of the feverish excitement of the battle-field, eagerly trod the no less fiery mazes of pleasure. In one suite of apartments the gambler established his head-quarters. Billiards, roulette, faro, monte, and other games, held out their tempting baits, and hooked their victims. In another, all the delicacies that could gratify the female palate were exhibited. In another were to be found the stronger stimulants, better suited to the taste of the Northern soldiery. In still another a regimental band sent forth its music; but the stirring notes of the *charge* have died away, and it is the soft *waltz* that now floats upon the air. The brilliant uniforms of the officers are glittering in mingled radiance with the flashing jewels that decorate the brows, and arms, and necks of the dark eyed Senoritas. Voices, which have been heard above the cannon's roar, are softened to a lover's pleading; and arms that had shattered ranks of steel, now gently encircled tapering waists, whose lines of perfect symmetry wooed the fond caress. Around the cool fountains of the Alameda, where the struggling moonlight makes its way in scattered patches to the earth, loving couples have stolen away to bowers, which even the bright eyes of the stars cannot penetrate, and there drink from luscious lips a nectar sweeter than the dew of Hermon, or the dew that descended upon the mountains of Zion.

In these light scenes, it is needless to say that Bernard Lile did not mingle. To him the fountain of pleasure was as bitter as the waters of Marah, and he turned from it in sad and severe reproof. Other employments better suited to his taste were at hand.

The seventeenth of February, eighteen hundred and forty-eight, was a stirring day in the City of Mexico. For sometime rumors had been afloat that the general-in-chief was about sending an expedition upon some secret service, the nature of which none knew, but the character of the officer to whom the command was assigned, gave assurance of new dangers to be encountered, and new honors to be won. In a large army, a report of the kind never fails to excite the liveliest emotions. Situated as the American forces then were, these emotions acquired a degree of intensity seldom equalled. The hardy veterans, who had waded through fire and blood to the capital of Mexico, wearied with a "dull repose," were burning for new opportunities to gather the laurels of war; while their less fortunate countrymen, who had been denied participation in the great battles of the preceding campaign, were hurrying from the Sociedad to Paoli's, and from Paoli's to Laurent's, vainly endeavoring to ascertain if at last there was "a chance" for them.

On the morning of the 17th, it was made known that the detachment was to consist of the Rangers, under Colonel Hays, part of the third dragoons, and one company of mounted rifles, under Major Polk, and a few officers from different corps, who had obtained leave to join the expedition as volunteers. There is less of selfishness in the character of the American soldier than in that of any other living thing. Those who expected to be detailed for the service, and were disappointed, naturally gave vent to their feelings in a few deep and bitter curses; but the next impulse was to hurry up and congratulate their more fortunate fellow-soldiers. In giving and receiving these congratulations, together with the cordial interchange of friendly sentiments, the time passed gaily enough until the hour of parting arrived. Then came clustering memories of hardships and perils encountered together, of kind words spoken, and of good deeds performed through all the changeful drama of a soldiers' life. Hands, joined it might be for the last time, lingered in each other's clasp. Bold hearts felt an inward sinking, and cheeks were blanched that had never paled at the cannon's flash, as injunction after injunction was laid upon those who remained, to send this or that article to a mother, or a sister, or a wife, if the chances of battle should cut off its owner, and his body be left to moulder beneath a foreign soil.

The parting cup was pledged and many a fervent "God bless you," mingled with the bugle notes that sounded the "advance." The gallant troops filed into the street leading to the "great causeway," through the *Garita* of El Pinon, and were soon lost to view. For the purpose of deceiving the Mexican spies, or at least of leaving them in total uncertainty as to his intended route, Gen. Lane moved steadily along the road to Vera Cruz as far as the Hacienda of San Felipe. Returning upon his footsteps during the night he made a dash to the right, hoping by forced marches to surprise the town of Tulancingo, at which place Paredes, Almonte, and Padre Jarauta were then understood to be arranging some plan of operations against the American forces. Early on the morning of the 22d he entered the town without resistance, the enemy having by some means obtained information of his approach, and hurriedly evacuated the place. The bed in which Paredes had slept was still warm, but the bird had flown. Allowing a brief rest, to recruit his men and horses, the indefatigable partizan was in the saddle on the night of the 23d moving with his accustomed celerity on Zicaultiplan, a town to the northward of Tulancingo, whither Padre Jarauta with his force of lancers had retired. A night march over a broken and mountainous country is decidedly the most distasteful duty in a soldier's career. The light laugh and the free jest, or the gay notes of a joyous song, which rob the day of a portion of its fatigues, are all wanting now. Every thing catches from the night its sombre hues; and the muttered imprecation, as a clumsy horse tumbles to his knees, or a hanging branch scratches unexpectedly across the face, is almost the only sound that breaks the stern silence of the riders. Darkly through that wild region toiled on the warriors of the States: now clambering the rough sides of a lofty mountain: now skirting the edge of a dark chasm, where one misstep would plunge horse and rider into an abyss of unknown depth: now recoiling from the brink of a deep *baranca* which the darkness had hidden from view, and painfully searching for a crossing place among stones, brush, and thorny cactus: now sliding down a sharp descent, and anon moving at a quick trot along a level space, the curses of the troopers, and the snorting of the frightened horses, giving place to the jingling noise of the steel scabbards striking against spur and stirrup. In the midst of such impediments and discomforts slowly wore away the night. At day-break the general seized upon a mountain Hacienda, and placing strict guard over every inmate of the establishment to prevent them from spreading a report of his movements, gave the order for rest and refreshment. With the night the toilsome march was resumed, over a country even more wild and rugged than that they had already crossed with so much labor and peril, but obstacles to men like them are only incentives to greater exertion, and when the light streaks of dawn began to appear in the east, on the morning of 25th, they were in full view of the town. It had never entered the head of Jarauta that so small a force would venture so far into the interior over roads impracticable for artillery. His lancers were for the most part unarmed, and watering their horses in the little stream near the town when Gen. Lane came in sight. The alarm soon spread, and preparations were rapidly made to receive the adventurous Americans. Entering at a gallop at the head of his command the general was saluted by a heavy fire from a *cuartel* on the right, which proclaimed that the famous guerilla chief, though surprised and taken at advantage, was determined to dispute the ground with his usual desperate courage. Detaching a company of Rangers to engage and destroy this outpost, the general passed on, side by side with the daring Hays, into the heart of the town. From the house-tops, from the doors and windows on each side of the street a storm of bullets was poured upon them. Returning the fire of the Mexicans only by an occasional shot when some eager assailant incautiously exposed his person, the Americans pushed forward with unabated rapidity for the main plaza. Here they were encountered by a body of lancers under Jarauta in person; but as well might a feeble barrier of sand be expected to stay the current of the mighty Mississippi. On went the Rangers, neither sword nor lance in the right hand, but in lieu thereof the terrible revolver, ready poised for its bloody work. A little nearer, and without a word of command; without a signal, save the example of their leader, they poured in their deadly fire, and, with a wild shout, burst with irresistible fury on the Mexican ranks. Down went horse and rider—down went lance and guidon. Like a tempest the men of the States swept over them, and the gay uniforms of the lancers, their red bonnets and gaudy plumes carpeted the stone pavements of the plaza. For the success of this charge Col. Hays had relied on the bone and muscle of his horses even more than the dauntless intrepidity of his men. The enemy once broken and scattered, the battle became a succession of single combats in which man after man went down before the fire of the revolvers with appalling rapidity. Not a single lancer was unharmed. Jarauta himself was twice wounded, and finally, after doing all that courage and conduct could effect, made his escape almost by a miracle.

In the meantime Major Polk was not idle. Dismounting his rifles he entrusted to them the duty of storming a *cuartel* where a party of the enemy were quartered, and charging himself with the remainder of his command along the street beyond the plaza, encountered and cut to pieces a body of the enemy in that direction. Here the sharp sabre did its silent work, and the track of the dragoons could be distinctly traced by the mangled bodies that lined the way. At one place a lancer, cloven through bonnet and skull, cumbered the street—close by him was stretched a comrade with his head nearly severed from his body, and the blood gushing in dark torrents from the veins and artery through which the keen blade had glided. A little further on, a horse cut down by a sabre stroke was gasping his life away, while his master was groaning in concert from a ghastly wound passing through from breast to back. Along the whole street the fierce horsemen had left bloody tokens of their presence.

In still another quarter of the town a little squad consisting of Truett, Chevallie, Lile, Simpson, and four or five others, were slowly driving before them a Mexican force of more than ten times their number. These were old Rangers of the prairie and mountain, to whom a deadly conflict was an everyday occurrence, and whose perfect coolness enabled them to take advantage of every post, stone, and door-facing. Armed with revolvers they had a fearful advantage in the narrow street, over the escopetas of the foe, and fearfully did they use it. Thirty-one Mexicans killed or wounded attested the fatal accuracy and efficiency of their weapons. Pressing the enemy into a yard surrounded by a high stone wall, and entering with them, with the daring confidence of men who had tried each other in a thousand scenes of carnage, steadily and coolly they gathered in the harvest of death. The enclosure proved to be the stable yard of a *Posada* in which were piled up large stacks of straw for the use of the muleteers of that mountain region. Both parties sought to avail themselves of the protection these stacks afforded, and the consequence was that the combustible material was soon ignited by the flashes of the fire arms. Rapidly the flames were communicated to the thatched roofs of the adjoining buildings. The most dreaded of the elements had come to the aid of man in his work of destruction, and vast volumes of flame leaping over alleys and streets, rolled on from house to house. Women and children lost their terror of the Americans before this new and remorseless enemy, and throwing open their doors and windows rushed wildly into the streets. The mother with her babe clasped to her breast; the young girl with her long hair floating over neck and shoulders; the little child bare headed, and its feet dabbled in blood, it might be that of a father—with shrieks, and tears, and prayers for mercy, fled before the devouring element. Silently the stern warriors to whom death was a plaything, gave way before the distracted throng. Silently they let the helpless human tide pass on to seek shelter in the neighboring haciendas. All felt that any offer of protection, or any effort at consolation would be a mockery; but many a heart unused to pity swelled to the very throat, and many a bloody hand instinctively put away the weapons of war as the piteous crowd swept by.

The business of the day was over—Jarauta's band were dead or captive, and Zicaultiplan fast crumbling into ashes. Collecting his scattered troops in the main plaza, around which the stone buildings with their tiled roofs were impervious to fire, Gen. Lane made his dispositions for a day of repose. The town burned on—heavy masses of smoke hung in dark clouds above—the dying and the dead were around; but amid all the soldier threw his tired limbs upon his bed of blankets, and slumber, sweeter than an infant's in its cradle, chased away all memory of the carnage and the strife—all thought of the living wretches whose homes were ashes.

CHAPTER XVI.

"They laid him in the earth, and on his breast,
Besides the wound that sent his soul to rest,
They found the scattered dints of many a scar,
Which were not planted there in recent war,
Where'er had pass'd his summer years of life,
It seems they vanish'd in a land of strife;
But all unknown his glory or his guilt,
These only told that somewhere blood was spilt."

On the peak of a high mountain, about seventy miles to the northward of the city of Mexico, four men were seated around a table in a Hacienda, on which were placed a roasted turkey a platter of *tortillas*, and a stone pitcher of *pulque*. The four consisted of Bernard Lile, Tom Simpson, John Glanton, and a lieutenant of volunteers who had accompanied Gen. Lane's expedition as an *amateur*. The general himself had pushed on with Hay's Rangers and Polk's Dragoons to Pachuca, where Col. Withers was quartered with a regiment of infantry, a field battery, and two companies of the 3d dragoons.

"Guajolote, I think you said this place was named," said Glanton, helping himself to the wing of the turkey.

"*Hacienda del Guajolote*," replied the lieutenant.

"Well, by God," rejoined the Ranger, "there never was a place more appropriately named. Turkey is the only meat to be had about the premises, and the infernal Greaser says that is all we can get in the morning."

"You are getting dainty, John," put in Simpson; "I've seen the time when you would have thanked God for such a meal as this."

"Very likely you have, Tom; and very likely you will again. But I know a greater variety is to be had here, and I'll be d—n—d if I don't have it in the morning, or I'll put your mark on this fellow's ears."

"There must be no violence, John," quietly remarked Bernard Lile; "at least while you are with me. Gen. Lane is already seriously vexed at the accidental burning of Zicaultiplan. The Mexicans will charge him with burning it designedly, and we must not do any thing to give color to the accusation."

The supper was concluded without further conversation, when the party adjourned to the stables to make a final inspection of their horses before retiring for the night. No armed parties of Mexicans had been heard of in that vicinity since the capture of Zicaultiplan, and it was believed that no roving band would dare to show itself so near the American forces. It was therefore more from habit than any belief of its necessity that a sentry was posted over the horses, while the other three returned to the Hacienda, and threw themselves upon the couches which had been prepared for them by the sullen and moody host. The room they occupied appeared to have but one entrance, which opened upon the square court inside, immediately fronting the stables, but about midnight Bernard Lile was startled by a gleam of light from the opposite side of the room; raising himself upon his elbow, he observed a concealed door slowly opening in the wall, and directly afterwards a young girl of sixteen or seventeen summers, stepped into the room; she walked lightly by the bed, and discovering that he was awake, whispered, "It is not good to sleep more, señor;" then extinguishing the light, passed out into the yard.

A very few minutes sufficed to rouse John Glanton and the lieutenant, and to call in Tom Simpson, who was on guard at the stables. None of them doubted that danger of some sort was impending, but the nature of that danger was a question of more difficult solution. Their first care was to examine the door by which the girl had entered. They found this to consist of a strong wooden frame, filled with iron nails, driven into the wood, and painted so as to resemble exactly the adjacent wall. With difficulty they discovered the spring by which it closed, and opening it looked out upon a sharp precipice on the face of the mountain, accessible only by a very narrow and difficult foot-path.

"That will do," said Lile, after completing his examination of the premises; "Tom, do you and Lieut. ——— take post at the outer gate—see that it is securely barred and fastened, and that no one opens it from the inside. John Glanton and I will make good this pass against more men than can be assembled in these mountains on a few hours' notice."

The lights were extinguished. Each one took the post assigned him, and awaited with the patient watchfulness of the cat the coming of the foe.

The moon was shining brightly overhead, but the thick foliage of the mountain-side covered the earth with its shadows, and the glimpses our watchers were enabled to catch of the little pathway, were dim and indistinct. Presently there was a noise as of feet clambering over loose stones, and then, where a little patch of moonlight fell unobstructed through the trees, the flash of arms was distinctly visible. The party appeared to be about ten in number, but Lile judged correctly, that there was a supporting party in the rear. When the advance had ascended to the summit of the mountain, the leader paused and seemed to hesitate. The secret door was wide open, a circumstance upon which he had not calculated, and which excited rather unpleasant suspicions. The dead silence which reigned within quieted his apprehensions, and after a brief consultation with his men, they again advanced. They were now within five feet of the door when two revolvers, in quick succession, hurled as many victims to the ground. Two more followed, and the remainder of the Mexicans, without firing a shot, rolled, rather than fled, down the mountain. Once under cover of the trees, they commenced a harmless fire upon the doorway. Their friends from below also joined them, and the balls came pattering thick and heavy through the narrow entrance. Lile and Glanton did not attempt to return the fire, but husbanded all their energies for the assault which they supposed would soon be made.

At the first sound of firearms, Simpson and the lieutenant had drawn themselves deep in the shadow of the arched gateway. Directly hurrying steps were heard approaching from the inside, and their host, rushing to the gate, began with eager hands to unfasten the heavy bars. A grasp of iron was laid upon his shoulder—he was drawn suddenly back, and before he had time to utter more than a single exclamation, the bowie knife of the hunter was buried in his heart.

"Now," said Simpson, "one of us is enough to keep this post, I'll go in to help the captain and Glanton."

Soon afterwards the firing from below ceased, and it became evident that the enemy were preparing for a "rush." Leaving the pathway, they climbed up the mountain, and collected in knots on each side of the door, where they were completely sheltered from the fire of the defenders. At a preconcerted signal, they rushed into the narrow entrance with levelled lances, and a wild yell, that would have struck terror into hearts less bold and self-reliant than those opposed to them. At the first step they were greeted by a deadly fire of revolvers, and then the heavy sabre of Lile, and the knives of Simpson and Glanton were applied with murderous fury. In less than two minutes the dark passage was piled with ten ghastly corpses, and their surviving comrades were flying in terror from the bloody scene.

"They are gone this time," said Life, after a moment's pause, "and will return no more. Strike a light, John, and let us see what has been done."

His voice was calm and unruffled as if nothing extraordinary had occurred, and neither of his comrades suspected that he had received a scratch, much less that he had a death wound in his bosom.

When the lights were brought, the dead bodies thrown outside, and the secret panel closed, he sat down upon a couch, and said,

"Bring me a basin of water, and tear a bandage from one of these sheets. There is an ounce ball in my bosom, which must prove fatal, but I do not want to die here. We must do what we can to save my strength for the journey to the city."

The wound was washed—it bled but little, and there was a dark blue ring around the ragged edges, which, to their experienced eyes, spoke too surely of approaching death. When the bandage was securely fastened, Tom Simpson turned away—the big tears were rolling down his cheek, and his voice was choked and husky, as he exclaimed,

"Oh! God, this is horrible."

"Not so, Tom," was Lile's reply. "You and I have inflicted a hundred such wounds in our day, and we knew long ago that fate might well have in store something of the sort for us."

John Glanton spoke not, but there was a deadly, snaky glare in his eye, and none who knew him could have doubted that he was revolving some scheme of wild and fearful vengeance.

The premises were now searched, and a light cart with a couple of mules procured to transport the wounded man to the City of Mexico. This was filled with straw and clothing from the hacienda, and soon after sunrise the melancholy party took up the line of march for the head-quarters of the American army. John Glanton had remained a little behind. At the first bench of the mountain they paused to await his coming. A heavy smoke was now rising from the hacienda.

"What have you done, John," asked Lile of Glanton, as he rode up.

"Set fire to the d——d den of cut-throats in four places," was the fierce reply, "and pitched the dead body of the owner on the flames. It is well the Peons had fled, or I should have piled them on alive."

"I am sorry for it. It will do me no good, and you will remember it hereafter with sorrow."

"Not I," answered the reckless Ranger. "And besides, if I had gone home and told my father that I had left one rafter on that infernal hacienda, he would have disowned his son."

Proceeding along the bench of the mountain, their attention was soon attracted by one of those natural phenomena, which the dwellers on the plains never witness.

Around them the sun was shining brightly, and the heavens above were unmarked by a single cloud. Far beneath them, midway between the valley and the mountain top, the tempest had gathered its army of clouds, and the pall of night was over the land. Upon its dark surface, the lightning was tracing lines of terrible beauty, and the loud artillery of heaven rolled upward from the vast and gloomy depth. With wonder and awe they halted to gaze upon the wild sublimity of the scene. After awhile the lightning played less fiercely upon the gloomy curtain —the thick darkness began to disappear—slowly and sullenly, cloud after cloud detached itself from the blackened mass—one by one they melted away, and lake, and field, and hamlet, and city, lay stretched out before them, glowing and glittering in the glad light of the glorious sun of the tropics.

"There, Tom," said Lile, slowly and thoughtfully, "is a type of the life now drawing to its close. For many years there was a curtain before my vision, which shut out all things bright and beautiful, and was checquered only by images as fearful as the pathway of the forked lightning. I remember when I sought in vain to penetrate the future, and catch but a single ray of hope. The tempest and the night were there, and all beyond was darkness and sorrow. But, thank God, he sent an angel to bring sunlight to an overshadowed heart, and now, when about to stand face to face with my Maker, I can join in the rejoicing song. 'Lo! the winter is past, and the rain is over and gone. The flowers appear on the earth; the time of the singing of birds is come, and the voice of the turtle is heard in our land.'"

Simpson had ridden by the side of Lile, sad, silent, and dejected. The certainty of the speedy death of his friend, had bowed that iron man even to the dust, and he answered his cheering words only with sobs and tears. Glanton and the Lieutenant were also silent and moody. Neither replied to the observations of their wounded comrade, but descended slowly and mournfully into the valley of Mexico.

For miles the country gave evidence of careful cultivation. White haciendas every where dotted its surface. Plantations of *magua*, spread out on either hand, and hedges of cactus added a wild and singular beauty to the scene. The country was unscathed by war, and long lines of pack mules, loaded with grain and other provisions for the market in Mexico, thronged the roads. But as the party approached the head of Lake Tezcuco, a wide change was manifest. A white salty coating crusted the earth. Dreary marshes, through which struggled up a tough russet colored grass, wearied the eye. Not a living thing was moving on the wide expanse, and over all the hot sun poured down his fierce and fiery rays.

> "Far as the eye could reach, no tree was seen;
> Earth clad in russet, scorned the lively green.
> No birds except as birds of passage flew;
> No bee was heard to hum, no dove to coo;
> No streams as amber smooth, as amber clear,
> Were seen to glide or heard to warble here."

The gloom and melancholy around accorded well with the feelings in the hearts of the travelers, save that one on whom the shadow of death even then was resting. From time to time, he addressed cheering words to his comrades —suppressed every utterance of pain, and spoke in a tone of hope and confidence they had never heard him indulge before.

At night, when they had stopped to rest in a lonely hacienda, he called Simpson to the side of his couch, and said,

"My strength is going, Tom, faster than I thought, and I had better tell you now what I wish done when I am gone. Carry my body to the village of ——, in New Hampshire; search out one John Abbott, and tell him that is all that remains of Bernard Lile. He will know what to do. You know where my papers are, take them with you. There is a will among them, dividing my property between John Abbott and yourself. Read all you had written there together, and when the perusal is ended, commit all but the will to the flames. If you wish to know anything more of the early history of the friend you have served so faithfully, ask him, he will tell you. And now, my friend, grieve not for me; my task on earth is fulfilled, and it is fitting I should die thus. For many a year I have not known so happy an hour as this. There is an angel waiting for me above, and that glad meeting will repay me a thousand fold for all the trials, and sorrows of this life below."

Simpson promised all that he was asked, but the sobs that shook his sturdy frame, told how little he was able to comply with the hard injunction not to mourn over the doom of a friend he had loved so long and so well.

The next morning, Lile was much weaker, but very cheerful. He was placed in the cart, and on the road, conversed, at intervals, with his companions in his usual unimpassioned voice. He had been silent for some minutes, when, as they approached the little town of Gaudalupe Hidalgo, Simpson addressed him a question. There was no answer—riding up to the side of the cart, he laid his hand upon his breast—almost instantly a cry of agony rent the air, and the hunter fell from his horse, as if a rifle ball had passed through his brain. Glanton rushed to the aid of Simpson, and the Lieutenant approached the cart; Bernard Lile was a corpse. Calmly, peacefully, as an infant in its slumbers, his spirit had passed away.

"He is gone," said the Lieutenant, as Glanton, after assisting to recover Simpson, also approached.

"Yes!" said the Ranger, looking mournfully upon the dead body, "the best soldier the world ever saw, or ever will again, has left our camp forever."

Here, reader, we must let the curtain drop. There are those still living to whom all that follows would be distasteful. The after fate of the actors in the wild scenes we have painted, is not necessary to develope whatever instruction is to be drawn from the pages of this history, and you must pardon us for not gratifying a curiosity which would certainly bring sorrow to others, and no probable benefit to you.

THE END.

www.ingramcontent.com/pod-product-compliance
Lightning Source LLC
LaVergne TN
LVHW010225110826
845151LV00004B/1189
* 9 7 8 1 4 2 5 5 2 5 8 4 2 *